The
Katz
Solution

HUGH A. FLOWERS

Cover Design – C.A. Simonson

Paperback-Press
an imprint of A & S Publishing
A & S Holmes, Inc.

ISBN-13: 978-1-945669-41-5

ACKNOWLEDGMENTS

Thanks to Paperback-Press and Sharon Kizziah-Holmes for publishing my books. You go above and beyond.

To Springfield Writers Guild, thank you for helping me rename the Katz. What a great group of writers and critique partners.

EARTH
APRIL 2021

PROLOGUE

The armada of fifteen spaceships approached the beautiful blue and white water-world without fear of reprisal. They took station 5,000 miles above the planet, positioning themselves to always have their ships backlit by the planets larger than normal moon. Anyone looking at the moon could see the ships, the largest being over four miles long.

The ships held station for twenty-four hours before communicating with the planet. During this time they observed with interest what the planet's response was to their sudden appearance. Taking notice of the different languages and sensor readings of the planets defenses, their admiral determined whom to contact first.

EARTH
AUGUST 2021

CHAPTER 1

Commander Eric Bloodworth was finishing his morning coffee while reading the local newspaper about the latest information on the arrival of alien space ships, when his phone buzzed. Vice Admiral Randall's yeoman informed him to report to his office at 09:30 hours. Disconnecting, Eric started to wonder if it had something to do with his recent promotion to captain of the new Heavy Missile Cruiser, U.S.S. George W. Bush. It was due for sea trials next month.

Eric's selection to this position was unusual because of his age. At thirty-eight he would join only a select few who achieved this position prior to reaching the usual benchmark of forty years of age. He grimaced as he recalled what he sacrificed for his career. His marriage, soon after graduating from Annapolis, lasted only three years because of his frequent tours of sea duty. His subsequent romances seldom lasted longer than his next sea duty. Shaking off those thoughts he started dressing for his appointment with the admiral.

The admiral's yeoman pointed at a seating area when he arrived, saying "The admiral is running fifteen minutes late."

Commander Bloodworth took a seat noting that there were three others ahead of him and he knew two of them. "Hey Boyd, do you know what's up?"

The commander he addressed, answered, "Hell no! I was

getting ready to report for my new command and now I'm here. You don't know either?"

The other two commanders looked up and muttered together, "Oh shit!"

Eric looked at the others in surprise. "You all have new commands pending?"

Seeing them nod, he settled back into his chair in dismay wondering what was happening. Twenty minutes later the yeoman said, "Commanders; you may go in now."

The four commanders came to attention before Vice Admiral Randall, saying together, "Sir, reporting as ordered."

* * *

Vice Admiral Randall sat at his desk and inspected what the Navy Selection Board considered the best they had to offer for this task. Commander Bloodworth was thought their best tactician and consistently got the best results from his crews. The other three commanders closely followed his scores. The possible problem was how they were going to take his news.

"Gentlemen, take a seat in the area behind you and I'll tell you a story you'll find hard to believe."

They all sat, each sitting forward anxiously in their chairs, and waited for the admiral to begin. Vice Admiral Randall stood before them and smiled, "Commanders, this is going to take some time, so relax and make yourself comfortable. Do you want coffee before we begin?"

At their refusal, he began. "As you know, about four months ago an alien space fleet arrived here. What the general populace doesn't know is they want our help against a common enemy.

"Since Earth is not space capable they offered to bring us up to their level of technology in space weapons. They have the ability to train our crews to operate their ships in less than ninety days by inputting the information directly into our brains. We agreed and the first ship's crew was ready in sixty days. They crewed a warship they called a Cruiser with 2,850 personnel, plus 900 marines. The ship itself is about the size of ten of our aircraft carriers."

Bloodworth held up his hand.

"Yes, Commander Bloodworth."

"Sir, is the U.S. the only one crewing these ships?"

"No, every country is sending volunteers. By learning a new common language called universal, which the aliens also use, solved the language barrier. The first crew is from the U.S., France, England, China, and Russia. The first ship's captain is a Russian man and the Executive Officer is a French woman. The aliens call themselves Katz and closely resemble humans; two arms, two legs, torso, one head, and two eyes located forward, but with better peripheral vision. Differences are their skin color; males are light brown while the females are off-white, almost a cream color. The males are slightly larger than the female, but the females are the dominant gender and cover all the senior grades in their military."

The admiral took a drink of water before continuing. "The Katz first discovered Earth about 100 years ago during World War I. They thought us too aggressive and moved on, but when they encountered the Xones, who closely resemble reptiles, they had second thoughts. The Katz has lost several critical battles and need our help to defeat the common enemy. The Xones ravage all captured worlds and kill their populations."

Commander Bloodworth interrupted, "Sir, what are your plans for the four of us?"

"You four will compete with the other countries' volunteers for command of a ship. You are the best we have, so do us proud. You basically will be gamed in tactics against the other countries' representatives; winners will get command, and losers will become Executive Officers. There are six ships available for command and eight countries contending."

* * *

A few months later Captain Eric Bloodworth was in a shuttle departing from Earth's first space port located near Phoenix, Arizona. He had spent a week with his parents not knowing when or if he would return. He grew up in a small city in southwest Missouri and wanted his parents to know what he had achieved.

While his parents held hands he explained what he had been doing to prepare himself for this mission. "The learning machine was amazing. I was given a sedative and while I dozed I was taught a new language and how all objects interact in space. My new ship weapon systems were taught as to its abilities and limitations, and I learned the abilities and limitations of my ship."

Eric's thoughts returned to the present as he watched the monitor as the shuttle approached his new command. Since his ship would never enter atmosphere it didn't need to be streamlined; yet it needed to be functional for weapons deployment, sensor arrangement to cover 360 degrees around the ship, and thruster placement that would be balanced for the shape of the ship. A space ship could not maneuver like a sea ship. A rudder would be of no use in space. It's thrust and other planetary bodies determine where the ship is headed. His new ship had the appearance of a big white fat cigar that was about a mile long and a quarter-mile high, and to him it was the most beautiful ship he had ever seen. A ship's bay door opened as his shuttle approached and closed when it settled into position.

The loss of ship atmosphere was minimal when they entered the shuttle bay because of a force field that allowed a shuttle to enter. A Marine Honor Guard quickly assembled outside the shuttle and when its hatch opened, he heard pipes playing outside welcoming him aboard. At his first step, Captain Bloodworth was startled at how normal the ship's artificial gravity felt, then he blinked away the moisture in his eyes as he approached his Executive Officer, Commander Hanna N. Lundberg from Germany. The Space Force adopted their own uniform similar to the English and American Navy, the two largest wet Navies of the World. Their ranks were arrived at by a coin toss between the English and American, with the United States winning.

The Earth Flag was a virtual copy of the old United Nations Flag that Captain Bloodworth now saluted and asked permission to board from Commander Lundberg. She granted permission and after shaking hands they left the shuttle bay together. Eric followed her to the Bridge, where the marine guard yelled, "Captain on Deck!"

Everyone stood at attention until he ordered, "At ease. Continue your duties."

When the crew returned to their stations he walked around the Bridge making sure he knew what every station was doing. He addressed the acting captain, "Lieutenant, what is our degree of separation from our closest parked ship?"

"Sir, SOP calls for at least 500 miles separation. We are currently 615 miles from our closest ship."

Taking a last look around the Bridge, he said, "XO, show me my office and let's get to know each other."

"Sir, it's this way," she said and he followed close behind her until they reached there nearby destination. Eric took a seat behind a small desk, which held a computer station. He asked her to take a seat while he studied her for a few moments. "How long have you been aboard?"

"Sir, five days. A very busy five days."

"How many of our key personnel are still missing?"

"You are the last senior member to arrive. As of one hour ago we were still missing another 276 crew personnel and 215 marines."

"Very well, we need to meet with the department heads and the marine commander. Is there a room large enough to accommodate everyone?"

"Yes, sir, there is a conference room that was designed for two hundred people. For ship-wide conferences with all personnel, you can reach them through monitors throughout the ship."

"XO, I want to start readiness exercises ASAP. Do you think we are capable with what crew we now have?"

"Uncertain. After consultation with the DH's we'll be in a better position to find out."

"Very well, schedule the meeting with the DH's for 07:00 hours. Wait, I need to adjust my time with ship time. What time is it?"

The XO smiled. "Sir, it is now 22:30 hours. Do you still want the meeting so early?"

"No, let's make it 09:00 hours instead. I still need to find my own cabin and make it right, assuming my luggage has arrived."

"Sir, your luggage arrived six hours ago and your steward has already taken care of it."

"Steward? I have a steward?"

"Yes, sir. The Katz insisted that each captain had a male steward."

"Crap! What if the captain was female?"

"Especially if the captain was female. Remember, they are a female dominated society."

He frowned as he recalled that fact. "XO, what are your personal thoughts about this bias?"

"Did you know that most of the XO positions are filled with females?"

"What! How many?"

"So far we have crewed seven ships, six have female XOs with male captains. One ship with a female captain has a male XO."

When he looked at her with a surprised expression, the XO slowly smiled. "I think this is going to make for an unusual state of affairs."

"XO, don't say *affairs*. This may become a sticky-wicky situation. How about the rest of the crew? What's the gender allocation?"

XO Lundberg quickly approached his desk and input his requested information into the computer and they both looked at the resulting data with wide eyes. "Crap! This can't be right!" He whispered in exasperation. "Seven of ten department heads are women and sixty percent of the ship's crew are women!"

XO Lundberg pointed at another revelation. "Forty percent of the marines are women and they are commanded by Major Alice Mae Prescott."

Captain Bloodworth stared at the information for several seconds hoping he had read the information incorrectly. "What department heads are men?"

They both read the resulting information – Environmental Systems, Maintenance, and Food Service. He looked at the systems named and thought a moment before speaking. "Environmental Systems was the only system normally dominated by men. What other ship systems would women not normally be expected to excel?"

XO Lundberg cleared her throat before replying. "Let's not take that tact. We need to know if all our DH's are qualified for their jobs. I recommend asking headquarters for documentation of qualifications for all our DH's. However, we should ask their reasoning for the women marines we are getting."

Captain Bloodworth nodded his head in agreement. "You're right. Send a comm to headquarters under my name requesting this information."

He stood and motioned toward the office's seating area. "Let's sit and exchange some personal information."

The XO followed him and they sat facing each other. He asked, "Apparently you didn't qualify for one of the commands?"

"No, but I must have finished high because my XO position was on this ship whose captain had the highest score."

Captain Bloodworth's eyebrows arched in surprise at her response. "I hadn't heard how I had placed, only that I had gotten a ship. What was your military experience?"

"I was in the German Army at a similar rank and was tasked to fight terrorism within my country. Sir, what is your experience?"

"I was in the Navy eighteen years after getting my commission, serving on several ships, including most recently as captain of a Light Cruiser. I was to serve as captain on a Heavy Missile Cruiser when I got pulled into this. I'm divorced without any children and currently have no girlfriends."

She shook her head slightly. "I can understand the relationship problems. I've never married and relationships while in the military are difficult. Any other questions?"

"Not now. Let's meet before the conference, say 08:30 hours here to go over a few things before we meet with the DH's. Now, if you can direct me to my quarters I'll try to get some rest."

The XO smiled. "Very well, I'll take you there. It's not far."

When they reached the captain's stateroom, XO Lundberg pressed the admittance button, which was soon answered by the captain's steward. He bowed slightly and responded, "Captain Bloodworth I am your steward, Yue He, and I have been tasked to serve you. My room is in your quarters and you have only to ask if you require my services."

Yue He then stepped back and allowed them to enter. Eric looked around his quarters marveling at its spaciousness, when Yue asked, "Sir, may I take your jacket while you explore?"

Eric turned to his XO uncertainly. "I'm a little overwhelmed by this treatment. Do you rate a steward as well?"

She smiled at his discomfort. "No Sir. Only the captain gets a steward. Do you have any more tasks for me before I send for the requested files?"

"No, XO, thank you for your patience. I'll see you in the

morning."

She came to attention clicking her heels while giving her head a small bow before turning and leaving the stateroom, the door closing on its own. Eric turned to his steward, who retrieved his jacket and followed him as he explored his quarters. He noted the storage unit that contained the emergency suit used if the ship should lose its atmosphere. Later, after checking out his quarters, he asked Yue, "Does the room have any stored weapons?"

"Yes, sir. Here, I will show you how the weapons can be retrieved." He went to the bed and touched a button that caused a shelf to slide out from under the bed. Inside were two rifles and three pistols.

"Yue, what kind of projectiles do these guns fire?"

"The rifles fire laser beams, while the pistols fire flechets only harmful to unarmored individuals."

"Thank you, Yue. Please wake me at 07:15 hours. If possible I'd like a breakfast of fruit, eggs over medium, sausage, and English muffin ready at 08:00 hours."

"Very good Sir. Have a peaceful sleep."

CHAPTER 2

Eric, surprising had a restful sleep. His day started on time and after finishing breakfast he walked to his office and made some computer inquiries while awaiting his XO's arrival.

At exactly 08:30 hours there was a knock on his door. He checked the time and smiled before saying, "Enter!"

When his XO entered, he greeted her with a smile. "Commander, I hope I didn't cause you to lose any sleep with my requests?"

"No Sir, I picked up the requested information on my way here. Do you want me to go over them with you?"

After fifteen minutes, he looked over at his XO. "Commander, so far the Department Heads all seem well qualified with both education and experience outside ship duties. I hope the education machines did their jobs."

She nodded her head in agreement. "Yes, we all have to see how we react to real experiences now. We should gain some feeling about this after we interview the DHs."

He responded, "Yes, and I'm anxious to meet Major Alice Prescott. I hope she's a typical hard-ass marine commander. Bring the files and let's check out the meeting room before the DHs arrive."

Commander Lundberg opened the conference room door for her captain and followed him inside to find the room full. She shouted,

"Captain on deck!" Everyone stood at attention as Captain Bloodworth and his XO walked crisply to the speaker platform. He stood looking at the group for a moment before saying, "At Ease!"

Nineteen men and women stood before him, all but three were women. He smiled at the group before saying, "Welcome to your new home for the foreseeable future. It's a beautiful ship, presently without a name. That's going to change today. Before we get into that, look around at your fellow DHs. Is this an unusual sight?"

The women began to smile at the obvious gender superiority before turning their eyes back toward their captain for an explanation. He smiled at them and said, "Ladies and gentlemen our hosts have a gender bias, much as we humans do. It makes us rethink how we operate, so everyone of you will have to prove you are up to the task of your jobs, including myself. We all have excellent test scores, but can we do the job? Tomorrow, beginning at the first shift change we will start readiness exercises; the first simulation will be leaving this solar system, eventually after we become comfortable with operating the ship, we will test our battle readiness. We were told we have the knowledge to do our jobs. Let's find out if that's true. Any questions?"

Captain Bloodworth fielded questions for the next half-hour about the exercises before he called a halt. "People, our ship has to have a name the crew can get behind, a name associated with our Planet Earth. Perhaps a battle name associated with past conflicts, such as Wasp or Hornet. Think about it, talk to your sections. I want each DH to submit at least three names by 15:00 hours today. I'll name my choice by 18:00 hours. Commander Hanna N. Lundberg is my Executive Officer. So far every ship has a female XO, except for the one ship with a female captain. Women, if you want this experiment to succeed you need to make sure you support your own people. Bring your problems to the XO and she will make sure they get resolved. Those problems too big for her, I'll take care of. I don't think you want me to take care of any problems, so don't overwhelm her. Handle the problem yourself first. Remember, how you operate your section is how I will judge you. Any questions before we adjourn? No, okay the XO and I will stay behind for a while for any private questions. Major Prescott, I want to see you in my office after this is over."

Thirty minutes later Major Prescott followed Captain

Bloodworth and Commander Lundberg to the captain's office were he asked the two women if they would like a beverage of their choice before starting? Major Prescott said, "I'd like a stiff drink, but a cup of strong coffee will do."

After everyone had their drink of choice in hand, they sat for a few moments looking at each other. Captain Bloodworth asked the major, "Did you receive any briefing or instructions when you were given command of your detachment?"

"No Sir! It was as much a surprise to me as it appears to be for you."

"Have you had a chance to determine if your women have been trained for combat?"

"All my men have received proper training, but about half the women were trained for noncombat jobs."

"How many exactly?"

"178 women. I've checked with my sergeants and we should send 150 of these woman back home."

"Should we ask for men or can properly trained woman do the job?"

"My marines, if properly trained, can handle ship security whether they are male or female."

"Major, what if they are tasked with repealing boarders or taking control of a captured enemy ship?"

The Major's face turned white. "Shit! If we're going to do that I'll need specially trained troops."

"That's what I think we'll need too! Do we have any in your detachment that can do this?"

"I'll have to check with my sergeants and get back with you later today. Captain, I know I don't have the training for that either."

"Major, it's best to know your own limitations. I'll await your numbers on what we have that meet our needs."

After the major left, Captain Bloodworth looked at Commander Lundberg and shook his head in disgust. "Well, I hope this is as bad as we find in our manpower. As soon as we get her numbers I'll have to contact headquarters for replacements. If we are first, maybe we'll get what we need."

* * *

A week later the readiness exercises of the (United Earth Ship) UES Thunder were starting to show improvements to a point Captain Bloodworth thought they could start battle exercises. Major Roger Blevins replaced Major Prescott as the new marine commander. He brought with him 700 seasoned male marines and more were expected as they become available. None of the original women marines remained; however, fifty male marines of the original detachment had the needed experience. Major Blevins was using an empty shuttle hanger bay for training purposes.

All the DHs seemed to have a handle on supervising their sections, but weapons had not yet been tested. UES Thunder had both missiles and lasers for defense and offense purposes. The lasers were used mostly for short-range defense against enemy missiles, but can be used as an offense weapon if an enemy ship entered their range. Lasers were effective up to 5,000 miles, whereas missiles powered flight could reach 100,000 miles and were programed to self-destruct at one million miles. While in powered flight the missiles had limited trajectory ability.

The ship had armor plating which gave it limited protection against both types of attack, but once struck that area could fail if struck again, so the defense strategy is to spin the ship or turn that side away from the battle. The Katz report that the enemy ships' weapons are similar to our own. So far the Xones have attacked only if they had the superior numbers. The Katz hesitate to initiate any battles, which has resulted in a losing strategy.

Captain Bloodworth consulted with the DH of weapons, Lt. Commander Alice Beeker, as to her training schedule. She reported, "My team of laser gunners have done well in computer simulations against incoming enemy missiles. However, the ships supply of defensive missiles is small and in a prolonged battle would be exhausted after three salvoes of ten from each side. Lasers alone don't give the ship adequate protection."

"How many more do we need?"

"We need double what we now have and if the battle is not won after the sixth salvo we should withdraw."

"Lt. Commander Beeker, how many offensive salvoes does the ship carry?"

"Six salvoes of ten missiles from each side, but if we carry three more salvoes of defensive missiles we lose one tube of offensive weapons."

"So we would be dry of both defensive and offensive missiles after six salvoes from each side?"

"Yes, sir!"

"Crap! That means the commander of the fleet needs to keep some ships back to offer cover for the fleet if it withdraws. Write me a memo to make those changes and I'll ask the Katz for additional defensive missiles. Well-done Lt. Commander, you get a gold star for this recommendation."

When Captain Bloodworth got back to his office he composed a message to all Earth Ships informing them on the shortcomings of the missile defenses and his solution. He then proposed a meeting of all the ship captains to discuss common problems discovered. He commed XO Lundberg and asked her to report to his office. When she arrived he handed her a copy of the messages he was planning on sending. "XO please read these messages and make any comments you feel needs to be made."

She took the printout over to the seating area and began to read. After reading and rereading the messages she frowned at him. "This is crazy! No wonder they are getting the shit kicked out of them. Add that you would be happy to host such a meeting at UES Thunder at 10:30 hours tomorrow and to bring their XO's."

Captain Bloodworth nodded his head in agreement, made the adjustment and forwarded it to Communications for transmission. He turned to Lundberg and asked, "Anything else the DHs found unusual enough to report?"

"Nothing like weapons. I wonder why the Katz didn't fix that problem?"

"Maybe they'd cut and run before they fought that long."

Commander Lundberg shook her head in wonder. "No wonder they came to us for help in this war."

"I still need to send a request to the Katz for another allotment of short range missiles before the other ships beat me to it." He quickly composed the message and forwarded it for transmission.

CHAPTER 3

He looked at the time – 12:50 hours. "Commander have you had lunch yet?"

"No. I was hoping to catch you free and have a working lunch. Are you ready now?"

He smiled as he replied, "Great, let's go now. I want to keep tabs on what they have been serving the crew, so let's try the crew's main dining room."

"I think they call it the mess hall," she said with a smile.

When they entered the eating area someone yelled, "Captain on deck!"

He and Commander Lundberg walked to the head of the line where he turned and addressed his crew. "As you were! I'm eating with the crew today to make sure you are getting as good food as the officers. I'm going to put a complaint box next to the exit, so make use of it. Put your list of favorite foods down as well, who knows maybe you'll get it more often."

When the two officers began serving themselves at the line the volume of conversations immediately picked up. They took their food trays to a table in the corner of the mess hall. Those sitting nearby soon left and no one else ventured to sit close to them.

He compared his tray to hers and raised his eyebrow. She smiled at him uncertainly. "What's wrong?"

"All you got was rabbit food – there's no protein."

"I'll have you know I like steak as well as you, but generally my mid-day meal is green. I have to watch my weight, so I eat like this in addition to daily exercise."

He nodded his head. "Yeah, but I probably exercise more to burn what I eat. I've been running with the marines each day at 05:00 hours. They keep me moving along."

She replied with wide eyes, "Do you think they'll let me do that too?"

"The marine women do it, so why not you?"

"I didn't know they brought women with this new detachment. How many are there?"

"Not many – only twenty-five, but they look hard as nails. If you run with them it's going to be hard to keep up."

She gave him a little smile. "We'll see about that. What do you want to put on the agenda for tomorrow's conference with our fleet leaders?"

"Their thoughts on somehow carrying a resupply of both long and short range missiles. We shouldn't have to return to base every time we have a skirmish with the enemy. I need to ask Lt. Commander Beeker to join tomorrow's conference to expand on what she's learned about our missiles shortcomings."

"Yes, I've talked to her as well and I was impressed with her depth of knowledge. She also runs her department with a stern hand. They jump when she asks them for anything."

He nodded his head in consideration, and then said, "After lunch let's ask her opinion on some of what we've been considering and get her input."

After disposing of their trash and stacking their trays they started heading toward the weapons section. Commander Lundberg touched the captain's arm. "I think we should contact Beeker before barging into her section."

"Good idea," he said as he retrieved a small comm device from his pocket. After making his call he turned to Lundberg. "She's in storage area 12b. Do you know where that is?"

"May I use your device?" She said as she held out her hand. Taking the device she asked, "Show me where SA 12b is located?"

On the screen of the device an outline of the ship appeared with a blinking arrow noting where the room was located, then a short description on how to get there. Handing the device back to him she said, "Note the overhead light blinking ahead of us, you just follow it."

"Cripes! Sometimes I think I need a seeing-eye dog." Fifteen minutes later they were at their destination and found Beeker with two other crewmen. "Lt. Commander Beeker, I've found you. What's happening here?"

"Scoping out possible storage areas for missiles. Can I help you sir?"

"It appears that you are ahead of me on this matter of missiles. What have you come up with?"

"This is the third place I've looked and they all appear accessible to reloading the missile tubes."

"Great! How long do you think it would take to move any missiles from here to their tubes?"

"Depends on whether we load port or starboard tubes. Either position can be reached from here, but the closest are the starboard tubes, which would take about twenty minutes, thirty minutes for the port tubes. However, if there's ship damage its anyone's guess."

He considered her answer and then asked, "Have you considered emptying out any closer rooms?"

"Yes, sir, these are the largest rooms with the access we need. I'm still looking however."

"Great! I'm glad we have you on the job. Tomorrow at 10:30 hours I'm hosting a meeting with the heads of all the other Earth ships. I want you there to answer any technical questions relating to weapons, especially with regards to our problems with missiles. The meeting is going to be held in the conference room the DHs met in previously. Have you found any other major problems?"

"No sir, nothing major. I hope to find large outside rooms with access to both sides of the ship. Hanger bays would work if we have enough otherwise."

He looked at her a few moments before pulling out his comm device and asking it for locations of all hanger bays. Lundberg and Beeker both copied his action with their units until Captain Bloodworth said, "There are three hanger bays on each side of the ship. Which ones would be the closest to the tubes?"

Lt. Commander Beeker held up her device and pointed at the lower left hanger bays. "These would be perfect if we can use them; however, I'll need to check the hallways from there to the tubes."

Captain Bloodworth asked, "Assuming everything works, how many missiles of each type can they hold?"

She answered, "I estimate each bay could hold ninety long range and sixty short range missiles. But that is variable depending on what the ship's needs are. We could store additional missiles in other storerooms, but they would be harder to access."

"Lt. Commander, please conduct a survey of available storage areas with estimated total missile capacity. Check with environmental and food service for their storage needs for a six month cruise. That will probably reduce the number of available storage rooms."

"Yes, sir. I'll get that information to you later today."

"In any case please contact me tomorrow at 08:00 hours for possible additional information."

The Captain and his XO made their way back to his office where he sat at his desk and started making notations, while she took a chair and thought. After a few minutes he looked up and said, "The ship has ten offensive and ten defensive tubes on each broad side. If we spun the ship after the first offensive salvo and released another salvo we could have twenty missiles heading toward an enemy in two waves or 140 from all seven ships. Instead of spreading these against all the enemy ships, we could target only one or two ships and overwhelm their defenses. We also need to plan our defenses to protect our own ships from enemy missiles. I was thinking that from an initial horizontal firing position when the missiles are first released, we would then shift our positions to three horizontal with two above and below them with a spread of 500 miles from each other. We could practice until its second nature. What do you think?"

Commander Lundberg stood and asked for seven objects from his desk, then she initially placed them horizontally facing a single larger object, and then she moved the seven objects into his planned defensive pattern. Since she couldn't stack them she did it as a flat depiction. She asked, "How far apart would the fleets be when starting the attack?"

"Ideally, about 300,000 miles, but I would like to try cutting off the missiles' power at about 80,000 miles and when closing to about 8,000 miles, turn the engines back on and adjust their course toward the true target. It would give the enemy less time to kill our missiles and they would be coming in at a faster pace than originally thought."

Lundberg thought through the plan twice more and then said, "I like it. I know someone who can place this plan on graphics, which should make it easier to understand. We'll review it again before we show it at the conference."

Captain Bloodworth nodded his head in agreement. "Well, at least we have the start of an attack strategy. We'll see what the others have to contribute."

* * *

The next morning Captain Bloodworth met the shuttle's as they arrived and when all were present he escorted the group toward the conference room where his XO met him at the door. After a quick discussion he said, "Captains and XOs, we have provided sweets and hot drinks to your left before we begin our meeting."

They mingled together with some reestablishing past friendships and acquaintances before taking their seats at a round table. Captain Bloodworth stood and began speaking, "For those who don't know me, I'm your host - Captain Eric Bloodworth of the UES Thunder. I'm sure you other captains have had the same problems I've encountered after taking command. I've replaced my marine detachment with a force that can defend my ship against boarders and secure an enemy ship that has been incapacitated. In addition, I found that our offensive capability was limited to six offensive missile salvoes per side and only three defensive short-range missile salvoes per side. I immediately corrected the short-range missile problem and have a plan for further increasing both missile inventories. Lt. Commander Beeker is my DH for Weapons. Please step forward and explain what you found."

"The captain and I were trying to find a solution to our ship's short supply of missiles, which would have required us to return to base after every battle. The solution was for us to carry extra missiles. We intend to use Hanger Bays 3 and 6 as additional storage for both long and short-range missiles. I estimate we can carry an additional combined total of 180 long-range and 120 short-range missiles at these locations. This mix total would change if a different ratio of missiles was used."

Captain Bloodworth said, "Thank you Lt. Commander, and please stay close in case there are questions later. In addition to arms we are going to have to develop battle strategy. Those of us with surface water experience will find their former battle strategies ineffective in space. We have equipment limitations that we must work around. Together, my XO and I came up with a strategy that might be effective at least once against an enemy formation. Powered missile flight is limited to 100,000 miles; however, if we want extra space between us in a fight we can launch from further out, say 300,000 miles. But, our missiles would be ballistic once they exceed 100,000 miles. I propose we program the missiles to shut down after say 80,000 miles and when they are within 8,000 miles of the enemy, we turn them back on and reacquire our targets. Our missiles would select the target we want and they would be harder to kill since they've picked up speed. Depending on our targets we might want to concentrate on one or two targets so that we overwhelm their defenses. Please look at the overhead projection for a short demonstration."

Captain Bloodworth continued his talk. "Our defense strategy would be to redeploy our ships after our initial salvoes to better defend against the enemy's missile attack. I propose going from a horizontal firing position to a stacked position of two ships at the top, three ships at the center, and two ships at the bottom. All ships would have a 500-mile separation, and if the ships move at least 5,000 miles away from their original firing position, should ensure that fewer missiles would follow them and would be easier to kill by the concentrated fire power from our ships."

Captain Bloodworth looked at the rapt attention his display was receiving from his audience and smiled to himself, thinking I've certainly gained their attention. One of the captains got to his feet and started clapping his hands, quickly followed by all the others.

The sole female ship captain came around the table and shook his hand. "Captain, I'm Captain Inez Macchi originally from Italy and I'm impressed by your strategy and the way you presented the information. In addition, I wasn't even aware I had a problem with my ship's marine force. May I leave my XO with you for a few days to make sure my ship is brought current?"

"Certainly Captain Macchi. What did you name your ship?"

"She's the UES Surprise."

He smiled as he replied, "I bet there's a story behind that name."

"Captain, if only I could tell you," she said with a smile on her face.

He laughed and seeing his XO nearby motioned her to join them. "Captain Inez Macchi this is my XO, Commander Hanna Lundberg. XO, the captain wants to leave her XO behind after she leaves so that he may bring his ship up to our standards. Captain Macchi, what's your XO's name?"

"Commander Henri Kohis. He's from Germany too. Maybe you have common friends? Oh, I see him over there. Come I'll introduce you."

The three of them approached a tall muscular commander, who must have sensed them because he quickly turned and clicked his heels together as he bowed his head to the captains.

Captain Macchi said, "Henri, this beautiful woman is Commander Hanna Lundberg, this ship's XO. I plan on leaving you behind until you are brought up to speed on what changes we need to make on the Surprise."

"Yes, of course madam. Captain Bloodworth it's a pleasure to meet you after that surprising insightful presentation. I foresee a great adventure in our future under your leadership."

"Thank you commander, but our Squadron's leadership has not yet been determined. But, I appreciate your vote of confidence. If you would excuse me, I've got other hands to shake."

CHAPTER 4

After Captain Bloodworth left, Captain Macchi turned to Commander Lundberg and asked, "Commander, is your captain married?"

"No, and he says he currently has no girlfriends."

"He's not gay is he?"

"Not from the way he looks at attractive women."

"I feel sorry for you commander, such a hunk of man and out of your reach since he's part of your chain of command."

"Well, we all have our crosses to bear."

Hanna turned to Macchi's XO, "Commander, when this party breaks up stick around and we'll see if I have any others to impart wisdom. In the meantime I have to shake some hands too."

* * *

An hour later, they had a lunch break in the officers' mess, where they met other officers of the Thunder. It was a little tight with the extra people, but everyone was happy to meet new people with maybe a fresh approach to common problems. One table was set-aside for only the seven ships' captains.

Once seated, Captain Bloodworth sought out the two captains he knew personally. "Captains Reynolds and Adams, what ships do you now command?"

Reynolds smiled as he replied, "The Charger is my new command."

Captain Adams replied with a smile, "Mine is the Lightning, and she's a real lady."

"Gentlemen, would you others give your name and your ships."

"Captain Vlad Pavlova of the UES Striker."

"Captain Marcus Frank of the UES Crusader."

"Captain Jock Adams of the UES Lightning."

"Well, it appears that the closest that any of our ship names is mine and Captain

Adams, the UES Thunder and UES Lightning. Maybe we'll become a one-two strike team."

That comment brought forth a laugh from the group. Captain Reynolds asked, "Captain Bloodworth, has anyone been named as our commander?"

"Not yet, at least nobody has announced our commander."

Suddenly there was a loud call, "Admiral on Deck!"

There was sudden loud commotion as everyone seated rose to attention. Vice Admiral Randall walked to the Captains Table where he said, "At Ease everyone, except for Captain Bloodworth. Captain Bloodworth, you have continually demonstrated your leadership since becoming captain of the UES Thunder. Being commander of the Thunder Squadron seems only appropriate. Today, you are officially designated as Commodore of the Thunder Fleet. You may now shake the hand of your new leader, and let me be the first."

After Vice Admiral Randall shook Commodore Bloodworth's hand, the other captains stood in line to do the same, followed by the officers of the Thunder. Later, after everyone finished their lunch, the Admiral cornered Bloodworth in a quiet corner.

"I snuck in and watched your strategy conference and was greatly impressed. Just from that display I knew we had made the right decision making you the commander of this unit. Before your Squadron leaves Earth orbit, schedule a meeting at ground headquarters. The Katz want to send an observer with you on this first cruise."

Captain Bloodworth gazed at him in wonder. "You're not kidding me, are you? My strategy would probably scare the shit out of them and they would want to immediately return home."

"There is that possibility, but they won't let us leave without an observer."

"Crap! Well, I guess we can lock him or her up until we get back if the Katz go bat-shit crazy."

"Let us pray that won't happen. Let's get back with the others before they miss us. You've got some time before you're ready to leave in any case."

Captain Bloodworth sought out his XO and found her speaking to three female officers. As he approached she held up her hand to stop an ongoing conversation. She smiled at him and said, "Captain … I'm sorry I meant Commodore Bloodworth, I'd like to introduce the XOs of the Charger, Lightning, and Striker; Commanders Olivia Willoughby, Sara Bazyn, and Annalisa Hansen. They are the last to request further briefing after their captains return to their respective ships."

"Great! I'm glad to have you all aboard. I'm sure that Commander Lundberg will take good care of you. Please excuse me while I consult with my XO for a few minutes."

They walked away from the group and stood close while he quietly said, "The Vice Admiral informed me that shortly before we sail I'm to come down to Earth Headquarters to meet with representatives of the Katz. They want to send a Katz officer with my ship. We need to find out what the officer's needs are for quarters and diet. I don't know if the officer will bring anyone else with them. Try to find out what we need to satisfy her needs; I'm sure the officer is female. They wouldn't send a male for this job."

Commander Lundberg frowned at him and started to curse "sh…"

"I know commander, I had a similar reaction. Let's just grin and bear it, this too will pass. Go on and make your arrangements with the XOs while I talk to the other ship captains."

* * *

Commander Lundberg watched him square his shoulders and head back into the fray. She smiled to herself thinking, *he really is a fantastic hunk of a man and she's going to have to watch herself before she falls in love.*

She joined the three other XOs who gave her a knowing smile. Commander Annalisa Hansen asked, "How is it working with our new commodore? I get a little weak kneed when I'm close to him."

"Come on girls, he's just a man. An almost perfect example, but just a man."

Commander Willoughby smiled as she said, "Sure he is. However, I saw the smile on your face as he left. You just keep telling yourself that, maybe you'll eventually believe it."

* * *

A month later the ships were provisioned and ready for their sailing orders. Commodore Bloodworth was in Space Headquarters located on the outskirts of Phoenix, near Earth's Space Port. The headquarters building was still under construction and was operating out of a converted warehouse. When the commodore arrived he was shown into Vice Admiral Randall's office.

After reporting to the admiral, he was told that the Katz representative wanted a private audience with him. "Admiral, don't let me go cold into this. What's her military rank? What does she look like? Tall, short, ugly, pretty?"

The admiral shook his head at him. "The representative was adamant that they see your first reaction to their appearance. The representative has the equivalent rank of a admiral."

Bloodworth took a deep breath and slowly exhaled trying to calm himself. "Okay, I'm ready. Where do I go?"

The admiral pointed to a door. "Though there. Good luck."

Bloodworth stepped though the door and walked toward an apparent female creature. He came to attention and said, "Madam, Commodore Eric Bloodworth reporting as ordered."

The female was not dressed in what we would call a uniform; she was clothed in multiple layers of a thin silk-like cloth that gave him glimpses of her cream colored body. She wore a metal band around her head that had a single large gold star at its front. She appeared to be his height, slender to a fault without any defined muscles in her arms and legs. She had the same type of hands as a human with five fingers including an opposing thumb. Her breasts were small but well defined. Her head appeared human-like; two eyes were now looking at him with the same intensity as he at her. They were almost twice the size as ours and were oval in shape. The nose and mouth placement were the same as humans. However, both of her ear placements were at the top of her head that gave her a feline appearance, which was unfortunate considering their race name of Katz. Her hair was short and straight, cut shoulder length and had the appearance of human hair. Overall, he would gage her appearance as exotic.

"Commodore, I see you have cataloged our differences as fast as I did yours. My name is Admiral Gamma Killa. Please give me your honest opinion on my appearance."

"Admiral, you put me at a disadvantage. Frankly, you have an exotic appearance to me."

"You are what humans call a warrior, one who is bred to fight?"

He smiled at her assertion. "No, however in our early history I'm told that was possible. Today, we have freedom of choice and I trained to be an officer in our wet Navy. You know, ships that sail our seas."

"Apparently, you are very good at what you do to achieve your rank at such a young age. It took me twice as long to achieve my rank."

"I don't want to cause you any hurt feelings, but you don't appear to be any older than myself."

"You honor me commodore, but let's now talk of your plans to meet our enemy. I believe you have developed strategies to defeat the Xones. I wish to observe how you place these plans into operation. If successful, perhaps we may wish to follow them as well."

"I will be honored to have you join me on my ship, the UES Thunder. Will you be alone?"

"No, I will have an attendant, what you call a steward."

"You may use my cabin doing your stay on the Thunder. It is the best accommodation on my ship. I will find another cabin during your stay with us."

"You honor my person. I use a similar cabin on my ship."

"Do you have a special diet that we should make provisions for?"

"Thank you commodore, that has already been provided for and should have reached your ship by this time. However, I am curious about your food and have brought equipment to test any food that I might want to try."

Bloodworth smiled as he said, "You appear to be an adventurous person admiral."

She gave him a small smile. "Perhaps, but it's nothing compared to your race. I hope to learn much during this cruise."

They were approaching the UES Thunder two hours later and were soon docked. When the hatch opened he heard the familiar pipes welcoming him aboard. When the sound ended he offered his hand to the admiral and they walked together toward the welcoming formation of marines, with Commander Lundberg at its lead. He saluted Earth's flag and asked permission to enter with an honored quest. Lundberg returned his salute and granted permission. He then introduced the admiral to Commander Lundberg and asked, "Has my quarters been prepared for the admiral."

"Yes, Sir, and your possessions have been moved to my cabin along with your steward."

Lundberg led the way until they reached the admiral's new cabin where she and her male steward entered with her luggage. The admiral turned and smiled at the commodore and his XO and said, "Commander Lundberg, please stay and brief me on some matters of importance if your duties permit."

Lundberg looked at Bloodworth, who nodded his head. She then replied, "Certainly, I would be happy to comply with your wishes."

She then entered the cabin and shut the door, turning to face the admiral, who pointed at the seating area where they settled facing one another. Admiral Killa told Lundberg her name and asked, "Are you and the commodore mated?"

Commander Lundberg's face colored in embarrassment. "No Ma'am. Our regulations prohibit any sexual relationship within the same chain of command."

"Yet, you share a cabin?"

"Yes Ma'am, but not at the same period of time. Both of us need quarters close to the Bridge and there were no others that fit that need. It is unusual, but we agreed to try this until we can find another solution."

Admiral Killa smiled at the commander. "You seem flustered. Are you not the second in command of this ship. Yet you defer totally to the commodore, why is that?"

Lundberg slowly smiled at Admiral Killa. "Admiral, what do you really want to know about my relationship with the commodore?"

Admiral Killa looked at her in surprise, and then with consideration. "You are second to this male, but you personally consider yourself his equal. He appears to value your insight and is your friend. In our culture this does not happen often and generally results in a mating bond."

Killa considered Lundberg closely until the commander looked away. "Aha! Even though a relationship is forbidden you feel a strong bond with him. This is interesting. You can work together without a mating bond. We could never do that, this is really interesting."

Killa then asked, "Commander, do you think me unattractive?"

Commander Lundberg's eyes opened wide in surprise. "You are not unattractive, but you are not sexually attractive to me. You do appear rather exotic."

"That's what the commodore told me. Oh well, perhaps we can be friends. Otherwise this is going to be a very long cruise."

Lundberg smiled at Killa. "I think we can be friends. Maybe we can exchange more information about our cultures. Us girls should stick together."

CHAPTER 5

The Thunder Fleet ships refueled by making a close orbit of Jupiter, scooping up reaction mass before approaching their first warp jump. While the jump gate was located near the orbit of Jupiter, it took over a day of travel to reach. In order to position the ship properly to arrive at the next jump point they needed to pass through this gate at two gravities 2g ship speed. The seven ships positioned themselves to follow one another through the gate with the UES Thunder leading.

When everyone was through the gate the Thunder's science officer took a reading on where they now were. Commodore Bloodworth was astonished that they had traveled over 180 light years from Earth and were now further inward on this spiral of the Milky Way Galaxy. Admiral Killa smiled at his wonder. "Commodore, you have to make two more jumps before we are in the territory of the Xones. The next jump gate is near the largest planet in this solar system, and that will take at least three days. I suggest you take readings of this system to ensure that we are alone before proceeding."

Commodore Bloodworth told the science officer, "Make it so."

He then ordered the comm officer to inform the other ships, "Standby while the Flag Ship takes readings for other ships within the system, after which the squadron will proceed to the next jump, about three days travel from here. In the meantime check your ship systems for problems and inform me if there will be a delay before proceeding."

"XO, please check with our DHs for any problems."

"Yes, sir, so far there have been no adverse reports."

"Admiral, XO, let's retire to my office as I have a few thoughts to share."

When they were all seated he asked the admiral, "Madam, how far has the Xones explored this arm of the Galaxy?"

"Not far. They prefer to pillage as they slowly expand their reach. They regroup and resupply after they eliminate any intelligent systems they come upon. They are quite vicious and most systems they've found with intelligent life were not space capable, making them easy targets."

"How many systems like ours have you encountered?"

"Not many, only one other has developed to your level and they were extreme pacifists, which would make them useless in this fight. Your people on the other hand are very aggressive and with the tools we give you are at least a match for them. At least we hope you are."

Bloodworth smiled at her. "I notice that your armaments don't include nuclear weapons. What are your reasons?"

"They are messy in that they leave residual contamination and we haven't needed them?"

"Admiral, I don't believe in leaving anything out of my bag of weapons and have included one missile with a nuclear warhead on each ship, just in case I find a need. If I discover a large tightly packed enemy fleet heading my way, I might send a nuclear missile their way that they won't see coming. Do you think that might get their attention?"

"Killa's eyes opened wide in surprise. "Yes!! That would shake them up. They have never been attacked so viciously before. They would have to regroup and determine whom they now faced. They might even withdraw from further expansion in this direction."

"How will we know if we are facing a enemy ship?"

"They broadcast on a specific wavelength a signal that tells their own kind who they are. Our ships only broadcast as needed, but when encountering a silent ship we broadcast our ships identification and the other ship responds with theirs. We have never had a problem knowing who we were facing."

Bloodworth shook his head and frowned. "I have a feeling that will change after our first encounter with the Xones."

"Commodore, are all your people this willing to go into battle?"

"No, we have pacifists as well, but those of us who have volunteered to enter our country's military believe that when fighting an enemy their can by no hesitation when we are at war. Recently, Earth has not had a planet-wide war since the 1940's, but we have continually updated our weapons in case that changes. Admiral, I think turning our aggressive tendencies against the Xones may have saved our world."

"Our people, the Katz, have decided to risk our future with the human people. Our largest ship is an industrial platform from which you can produce your own ships. By the time we return to Earth, the learning machines will have produced trained workers to staff this platform. In addition, they will train crews to man three heavy lift ships capable of transporting finished and raw materials to the platform. Hopefully, you will add your own designs to your fleet."

Bloodworth was taken aback by Admiral Killa's disclosure, but soon recovered. "Admiral! That is indeed good news. Are there more cruisers now available for human crews?"

"Only three more are earmarked for human use. They were held back because you may need replacements for battle damage."

"Hopefully, that's not going to happen. Commander Lundberg, as soon as we're certain we're alone out here, take your down time. Is my shared steward working out for you? No embarrassing moments?"

"No, Yue He has been a great help. How he keeps our personal stuff separate is beyond me."

Bloodworth grinned in appreciation. "Very well, I see we have the all-clear sign, so I'll see you later."

"Good night sir."

After Commander Lundberg left the Bridge, Admiral Killa commented, "The Commander is very talented. Do you think she's ready for command?"

He smiled at the Admiral. "She's very talented to the point I'd hate to lose her as my XO. But you're right, she's ready for command and if we survive this cruise I'll recommend her for her own ship."

Admiral Killa asked, "I don't understand this chain of command business regarding personal relationships."

He looked at the admiral in surprise for a moment before replying. "Generally, it means a personal relationship cannot exist if one of the parties has command authority over the other."

"That would make it difficult for anyone working within the same department, or in your case, anyone else on this ship. Do I have that right?"

"Almost. Since I'm the Commodore of seven ships, it would preclude a relationship with anyone on those seven ships without a ruling from Headquarters."

"Commodore, I feel sorry for you. You must get very lonely." She said with a frown on her face.

"Command is a lonely place in any case."

"I'm not needed here, so I will take my rest while I can. Goodbye commodore."

"Goodnight admiral."

* * *

Ten days later they were preparing to transit through the last warp point before entering the system inside the Xones influence. Commodore Bloodworth's strategies were finalized, with each ship commander assigned their position according to the numbered plan transmitted to them.

Bloodworth winked at his XO before ordering, "Sound Battle Stations…Send probe through the portal!"

Twenty minutes later the science officer was reviewing the probes message torpedo. "Contact! Twelve contacts stationary above a large planet."

Bloodworth asked, "What's their distance from the gate?"

"Sir, the distance to the planet is about 821,000 miles. That's about a ten hour cruise at 2g's"

Bloodworth considered a moment before saying, "Comm, inform fleet to proceed through gate and cut speed to one-half g's before initiating plan Bravo A at my command. Helm initiate plan when I inform fleet."

Bloodworth waited three minutes before saying, "Comm, send to Fleet - initiate Bravo A."

The fleet immediately started the maneuver they had practiced during their journey here. Once in position, Commodore Bloodworth asked his science officer, "Any change in the disposition of enemy ships?"

While he waited for a reply, he asked Admiral Killa, "Any chance these are not the Xones?"

"No chance. If it were our ships they would have broadcast to us by now."

Science Officer Betty Conner said, "Commodore, the ships have all left station and are now heading in our direction. From sensor data they appear to be approaching at 3g's."

Admiral Killa said, "3g's is about their limit. They want to engage us before we can turn tail and leave."

Bloodworth asked, "Lt. Commander Conner how are the Xones ships grouped?"

"Sir, they initially were strung out in a single line, but now have formed a ball formation where each ship can fire at us."

Bloodworth considered a moment and then asked, "How long before they are 400,000 miles from us?"

"Sir, at their current rate of closure it would take them about four hours."

"Lt. Commander, how long would it take one of our nuke missiles to reach 400,000 miles?"

"Sir, it would reach that point in 2.15 hours."

Bloodworth said, "Get me Lt. Commander Beeker on the comm."

"Beeker here, Sir."

"This is Commodore Bloodworth. In 2.13 hours launch a nuke missile at the center of that formation of enemy ships heading our way. Launch code is 2140 Wilco."

"Aye, aye Sir. SOP requires that I verify launch in two hours."

Bloodworth replied, "Agreed. You will ask for verification of launch in two hours."

Bloodworth said, "Send comm to fleet that I intend to launch nuke toward enemy fleet in two hours. We will observe enemy actions for the next four hours for needed adjustments to our actions."

* * *

Two hours later after receiving verification for launch, Lt. Commander Beeker began a count down. At zero the missile was launched and a clock started as it hurled itself toward the enemy ships.

Twenty minutes later Lt. Commander Conner said, "Launch from enemy! Sir, it appears only a limited response from our single launch. One ship appears to have launched ten birds our way."

Commodore Bloodworth said, "Comm fleet – maneuver plan Alfa One at my command."

Bloodworth said, "Lt. Commander Conner please let me know when the incoming birds have exceeded 100,000 miles from launch."

"Aye sir! Counting down now."

"Sir, the birds are now beyond control from the enemy fleet."

"Thank you, Lt. Commander. Comm send to fleet – Execute Alfa One!"

The Earth fleet immediately repositioned itself 5,000 miles away from its previous course and waited for a response from the opposing fleet.

"Lt. Commander Conner, how long before enemy missiles reach us and how long before our bird reaches 50,000 miles from enemy fleet?"

"Sir, ten minutes and counting down for our bird and twenty minutes for enemy attacking missiles."

"Comm Lt. Commander Beeker."

"Sir, this is Beeker."

"Lt. Commander Beeker, when our bird reaches 50,000 miles from the target fleet, restart its engines and maneuver our bird to enemy fleets center. Its proximity fuse will do the rest."

"Aye Sir, I see the countdown has nine minutes remaining. I will take control of our bird at that time."

The countdown continued until it reached zero, whereupon Lt. Commander Beeker took control over the nuke missile, restarted its engines and guided it toward the enemy fleet's center. Less than ten minutes later the Earth fleet's sensors picked up a huge explosion about 300,000 miles distant, where their sensors showed the enemy fleet to be.

Bloodworth asked, "Lt. Commander Conner, is our ship

experiencing any EMT effects from the blast?"

"Sir, sensors are all working and there has been no adverse reports from within the ship."

"Comm, query all fleet ships, inform flag if any adverse EMT effects."

Commodore Bloodworth now turned his attention toward the enemy fleet's missiles. "Lt. Commander Conner, how close are the incoming missiles?"

"Sir, they are passing us now and we are well out of their path."

"Good! What effect did the nuke blast have on the enemy ships?"

"Sir, I can only identify three ships remaining and there is a large debris field. The remaining ships are no longer under power."

"Comm, send to fleet. Reverse course at 3g's. I intend to inspect the damaged ships for information on our enemy, both physical and equipment. We will stay together as a unit for the time being. Reduce standing to Battle Ready."

Bloodworth felt the ship begin its flip, placing it tail first before beginning its reverse course burn.

Admiral Killa said, "Commodore Bloodworth, you have won a great victory. None of our ships would have dared such a maneuver. You have made it like child's play and this was only your first space battle."

Bloodworth smiled ruefully at the admiral and held out his hand that had a slight tremor. "Not without some misgivings. XO, you have the Bridge. I need a break so that I can take a shower and then get some rest before dealing with the remains of the enemy fleet."

After Commodore Bloodworth left the Bridge all hands followed his departure with newfound respect and awe.

Admiral Killa hissed her pleasure. "What a mate he would make. If only our males were more like him. Commander Lundberg I can see from your expression that you agree with me. It's too bad about your silly regulations about fraternization within the chain of command. Oh well, we'll see about that won't we?"

Commander Lundberg watched the Admiral's departure from the Bridge with trepidation and some hope, in spite of herself. She was thinking, *I wonder what she's up to.*

CHAPTER 6

Eight hours later Commodore Bloodworth relieved his XO from command and asked, "Commander, what's our current status?"

"Sir, we have completed our braking maneuver and will be approaching the blast area in four hours. There has been no change noted from the three enemy ships. Recommend that we slow to 2g's in preparation to matching speed with target."

"Agreed XO. When do you recommend we reverse thrust?"

"Sir, now at 2g's for one hour, then another thrust as needed."

"Very well. Comm, inform fleet to reduce thrust to 2g's at my command."

At his mental count to ten, he said, "Reduce thrust now."

Thunder's helm said, "Sir! Thrust reduced to 2g's."

"Lt. Commander Betty Conner you have the Bridge. The XO and I are going for breakfast. In one hour compute the needed reverse thrust to match course with the debris field and notify the fleet."

"Aye sir, I have the Bridge."

Commander Lundberg followed her commodore off the Bridge and was wondering what he had on his mind. Bloodworth stopped at the admiral's cabin and buzzed for admittance.

Her steward answered the door and Bloodworth asked, "Commodore Bloodworth to see the admiral."

The admiral's voice could be heard emanating from the Head,

"Come in Commodore."

The two entered cautiously, not knowing what to expect. "Admiral, we would like you to join us in the Officers Mess for breakfast. That is if you haven't already eaten?"

The admiral looked at the two officers knowingly. "Do you need a third to avoid personal problems?"

"The commodore's face flushed red. "No, no. I had some questions for you and I enjoy your company."

She said, "I see. Very well I'm going to try your fish. It's on my approved list of Earth's foods."

When Bloodworth turned with his back to the two women, the admiral winked at the commander as they followed him out of the room, causing her to roll her eyes at the admiral.

They entered the Officers Mess and took a table away from the other officers who were dining. After placing their orders Bloodworth asked, "Admiral, has there ever been any direct contact with the enemy before?"

"No, in the few instances where we were the winner of a battle, the Xones blew up their disabled ships. The bodies we recovered were in pieces."

"I'm concerned that the Xones might be carrying a disease harmful to humans and Katz."

"No, we didn't discover anything like that in our tests of the bodies found. However, humans might have a problem with their biology."

"Crap! That means we should limit our exposure to anything we bring back from their ships. Bodies and weapons should go into airtight containers. Let's give our Earth scientists an opportunity to earn their keep. To be extra safe let's put all the Xones material on a single ship in an isolated area."

Commander Lundberg asked, "What if the three enemy ships have active crews. How are we going to handle them?"

Bloodworth shrugged his shoulders. "Until we know if they are biologically safe, I'm inclined to use our lasers on the ships to open them to space. Why risk our marines to some unknown germs."

He looked at the two women. "What are your thoughts?"

Admiral Killa shook her head. "I would recommend you use your lasers; besides the crew will suicide if you attempt to board any of the ships. Why risk your marines?"

Commander Lundberg said, "I agree. In fact we should stay a safe distance from the enemy ship while using our lasers on them."

After their meal, Commander Lundberg went off duty while the admiral and the commodore left for the Bridge. Upon arrival, the commodore relieved Lt. Commander Conner from command and asked, "What's the status of the fleets slow down to achieve parity with the enemy ships?"

"Sir, we have another twenty minutes before the end of the first reverse burn. Before we do anything else we need to determine our closure rate."

"Very well, continue with your duties."

Twenty minutes later the fleet ceased reverse thrust and Conner took readings for their current closure rate. "Sir, the fleet is now closing at a rate where we will need an additional reverse burn of six minutes in one hour to achieve parity with the enemy ships."

"Thank you Lt. Commander. Comm please inform the fleet that in one hour we will make an additional reverse burn of six minutes to achieve parity with the enemy."

"Lt. Commander, do we have any harmful radiation readings yet?"

"Sir, any radiation readings would come from the ship debris. Radiation from the blast would have already dissipated. So far all I'm getting is normal background readings."

Bloodworth frowned as he considered which ship he was going to order to carry away any enemy artifacts. He also had to worry about radiation, in addition to biological hazards. He walked to Conner's workstation and asked, "Lt. Commander, do you have a sheet of paper I can have?"

She handed him a scrap of paper. "Sir, is this sufficient?"

"Yes, I also need a pen or pencil."

She handed him a pen, which he used to make six separate numbers on the paper. He then tore them from the scrap of paper after writing a ship name beside each number. He folded the individual bits of paper until each was only a wad. The bits of paper fit easily into his folded hands as he shook them together and then opened his hands to her surprised face.

"Lt. Commander, pick one."

She tentatively picked out a bit of paper and handed it to him.

He exchanged the other bits for the one she picked. "Please dispose of these," he said as he walked back to his control station.

Bloodworth gently opened the wad of paper until he could read the name, "Striker". *Captain Vlad Pavlova commanded the UES Striker. At least now he had a ship he could designate when it came to carrying contaminated cargo.*

"Comm, I need to talk to Captain Pavlova of UES Striker."

"Commodore Bloodworth, how can I help you?"

"Captain Pavlova I have a dirty job for you. You need to prepare a space on your ship; I would suggest a shuttle bay, to store contaminated cargo from the enemy ships. One large area will be easier to clean up, than several. We don't know if the bodies are a biological hazard, so we must use caution. In addition, they probably all have radiation contamination. Check with your marine commander if his men have received contamination training. Please get back with me on what your plans are."

"Commodore, I acknowledge your instructions and I will get back with you ASAP. Captain Pavlova of UES Striker."

Admiral Killa said, "He appears to be an excellent officer. No complaints when he's been tasked with a difficult job."

"Yes. But it's these officers who will be given difficult assignments and judged when promotions are handed out."

The final slowing reverse burn was made and the fleet moved among the enemy debris field. Their sensors quickly discovered that the three enemy ships, while generally intact were all open to space.

"Comm to all fleet. All ships of fleet take sensor readings of the debris field and especially the generally intact enemy ships. Before proceeding I want all captains and their XO's to shuttle to the UES Thunder for a general conference ASAP."

"Comm the XO to contract me on the Bridge."

"Commander Lundberg."

"We have arrived at the enemy's location and I have ordered a conference here of all ship captains and they're XO's ASAP. I need you to make the conference room ready for their arrival."

"Aye Sir, I'll get right on it."

Bloodworth thought, *Is there anything I've missed? Crap!!*

"Lt. Commander Conner, I want to be immediately notified if there are any new contacts."

"Aye sir. Shuttles have started to be launched from the fleet."

"Very well. Have marine escorts available for their arrival."

Bloodworth reviewed Thunder's scan of the debris field. It now encompassed over 2,000 miles and was still expanding. The enemy fleet initially was in a ball formation of only 600 miles when the nuke exploded in its center. *I wonder what their scanners will make of this battlefield?*

"Comm, connect me with Major Blevins."

"Sir, this is Major Blevins."

"Major, have you or any of your marine detachment received contamination training?"

"Sir, I and two of my sergeants have received such training."

"Very good, all of my captains and their XOs are heading toward the Thunder for a conference with me relating to collection of contaminated bodies and weapons. Please plan on attending in case I have questions for you."

"Yes, sir! Is that CR 1?"

"Yes, better bring a sergeant with you as well."

"Sir, Blevins out."

Bloodworth stood and said, "Lt. Commander Conner you have the Bridge,"

"Aye sir, I now have command. Lt. Worley please assume my duties."

Bloodworth waited until Conner was settled before leaving the Bridge. When he arrived at the conference room he found Commander Lundberg putting the finishing touches on a projection screen.

She smiled at Bloodworth and said, "I have connected our sensor feed to the projector in case you want visuals."

"Very good. I've picked the UES Striker, Captain Vlad Pavlova commanding, to carry our contaminated cargo. The three intact enemy ships were all open to space, so we have no need to fire upon them."

The ship captains and their XOs began to arrive and he moved to greet them, with Commander Lundberg at his side. After the last ship's representatives arrived and he saw his ships marine commander was present, Bloodworth stood behind the stages podium and held his hand up for quiet.

"Our strategy appears to have worked in our first battle against our common enemy. Now we have the opportunity to learn more about him and his weapons. It has been pointed out to me that the bodies of the Xones have the potential to be a biological hazard for humans, although they have not posed such a threat to the Katz. In addition, because of the weapon we used against them they now pose a radiation hazard."

"Captain Pavlova does your marine personnel have contamination training?"

The captain stood saying, "Yes, sir, both my marine commander and several of his personnel."

"Very well. The Striker will be the designated ship to bring Xones Intel back to Earth for study. Each of the other ships will send out one shuttle to find things of interest for the Striker to pick up. Attach a beacon to those items, but try to be selective. The Striker has limited storage capacity for this function. The Striker will send a shuttle to one of the relatively intact Xones ships to pick up no more than five bodies, two of which should be officers based upon their clothing. Videos will be taken of the outside and inside of the ship, including their major armaments. A sample of the various small arms may be returned with the bodies."

"Captain Pavlova, have you considered how you are going to transport these items back to your ship?"

"Yes, sir, we have enough lead-lined body bags and a large lead-lined box for the hand weapons. Unless the others find something unusual, I don't believe we'll need anything else."

"Captains, please heed Captain Pavlova's advice, don't bring him any bodies unless you think you've found someone of high rank. If we do this right we won't be here long."

"Any questions?"

"No, I'll be here if you want to talk to me."

Most of the audience left immediately, but two remained behind. Captain Pavlova and his XO Annalisa Hansen stood aside until they were alone.

Bloodworth shook both of their hands before asking, "You have a question, captain?"

"Just something I was curious about. Why my ship over any of the others?"

Commodore Bloodworth smiled as he shook his head. "I didn't know any of you captains well enough to make an intelligent decision, so I drew your name out by chance. You won or lost by pure luck. Just remember, the crews that demonstrate good performance receive advancement over the others."

Commander Hansen chuckled. "I told you, Vlad. It was just what I would have done."

Captain Pavlova gave Bloodworth a rueful smile. "Commodore, you won't be sorry you selected us."

They both saluted and hurried out of the room together. Commander Lundberg chuckled, "They appear to get along will together."

"Yes, almost as well as we do. Well, commander you better get back to your quarters to rest up before you relieve me in five hours."

She gave him a lopsided smile. "Sir, yes, sir. I am relieved for sack time."

When she reached her cabin, her borrowed steward took her uniform jacket and asked, "Madam would you like a cup of soothing tea?"

She smiled as she thought *I'm going to really miss this treatment when the captain moves out.*

CHAPTER 7

The Earth Battle Fleet moved into orbit above its planet a little over three months later. A month cruise for them was two months for the people of earth. The fleet found that time passed slower while in warp space.

Commodore Bloodworth sent his greetings to Space Headquarters along with news of their victory in a battle with the Xones' fleet. In addition, he sent them recordings and sensor readings of the battle. Three hours later he was ordered to transport his contaminated cargo to an isolated area in the Arizona desert. The shuttle would be decontaminated before its return to space.

After informing Captain Pavlova of his orders, Bloodworth said, "Captain you and your crew have done well and will receive a unit award. Since it's a first, please be patient for its arrival. When the shuttle departs for Earth assignment you should take the opportunity to decontaminate the area where the cargo was stored. Any questions?"

"Commodore, I want to be the first to congratulate you on the success of this mission. Your battle strategies were the key to our success. It's like none I've ever been exposed to in the wet Navy."

"Thank you Vlad. I had to scrap almost everything I'd been taught because in space we work in three dimensions, not two. In addition, our ships' movements are restricted and limited to the realities of space. I just knew I had to do something different than the Katz did with their capabilities and same restrictions."

Bloodworth took a deep breath to settle himself before looking for his XO, who was standing next to the command chair looking at a monitor showing Earth beneath them. "Commander, where do you plan to go on your shore leave?"

She looked at him with a start. "Oh sorry. I was daydreaming. I think I'll go to Hamburg. That's where my mother and two sisters live."

"How do you like the duty now that you have completed your first voyage?"

She turned and looked into his eyes. "It was great! However, I was just following your lead. Your plans worked out perfectly; what happens when they don't? That's my fear; can I adapt?"

He smiled at her earnest expression. "Would you believe that was my first live fire mission? I wasn't entirely certain my plans would work. Didn't you see my after action adrenaline let down?"

"You mean when you showed the admiral your shaking hand? I thought that was bravado."

"Nope. That was my relief that it was over."

"Crap, I just hope I don't wet myself."

"I knew a captain who wore diapers for that very reason."

She grinned at him, and then shook her head. "Thanks, but I know that's just you trying to make me feel better about myself."

"Did it work?"

"Yeah! It really did. What are your plans for shore leave?"

"I'm not sure I'll get any. I'll expect to be grounded until they get everything they can about my battle strategies and what I would recommend for future movements. But if I do, I'd like to go home and visit my family in Springfield, Missouri."

She slowly smiled at him. "Where's that?"

"That's hillbilly country near Branson, Missouri."

"You're pulling my leg."

"No, I'm serious. I'll take you there if we can wrangle leave at the same time."

"You're serious aren't you?"

He looked deeply into her eyes until she blushed and looked away. "Well, that's not likely to happen."

"Comm from Space HQ to the captain."

"Aye, this Captain Bloodworth."

"Captain, you and Commander Lundberg will accompany Admiral Gamma Killa immediately to Space Headquarters to meet with the Governing Body."

"Aye sir. Commodore Bloodworth out."

He ordered, "Lt. Commander Conner to the Bridge ASAP!"

Three minutes later Conner arrived at the Bridge still buttoning her tunic. "Sir, Lt. Commander Conner reporting as ordered."

"Lt. Commander you have the Bridge. Arrange your relief until the XO and I return from Earth. Any questions?"

"No sir. I have the Bridge until relieved." He and the commander hurried to the admiral's quarters, but found that her steward was already moving her luggage. They then went to their shared quarters and found that their steward had already packed their two bags. They each grabbed their hats, ID's, and bags before hurrying to the shuttle bay.

They left their bags with the crewman who was loading the last of the admiral's luggage and then entered the shuttle sitting across the aisle from Admiral Killa. He nodded his head in greeting as he sat. They were in space five minutes later and on the ground in less than an hour.

They exited the shuttle and were immediately driven away in a small convoy of vehicles, their armored vehicle sandwiched between two armed escort vehicles. Commander Lundberg asked, "What the Hell is going on?"

Admiral Killa said, "I think it has to do with me. Some of your people have expressed hatred toward me, or to be more accurate, toward the Katz as a whole."

Commodore Bloodworth grimaced. "I told them that hiding the Katz mission was going to bite them in the ass and here it is."

The convoy soon pulled into a garage entrance and stopped before a bank of elevators. They were hustled into an elevator that surprised everyone when it descended three floors. Armed guards escorted them to a nearby set of doors, which opened into a large room dominated by an oval table now seating twelve people. Vice Admiral Randall sat at its head, who now stood and greeted them. "Admiral Killa, Commodore Bloodworth, and Commander Lundberg we're honored that you have joined us. Please take a seat near me at the head of the table."

"Admiral Killa has brought to our attention a problem their Navy has already acknowledged that we should address. That is, personal relationships between genders on space ships. Long space cruises involving warp travel leaves anyone left behind on shore aging twice as fast as the person onboard a space ship. That's not fair for either party. The Katz solution was to approve any personal relationship that developed on board a starship. If one of the parties in the relationship was up for promotion, then the action had to be approved by two higher ranked supervisors of the parties."

"Admiral Killa indicated that Commodore Bloodworth and Commander Lundberg would be prime examples of this problem. He has supervision of his XO and under current rules they couldn't have a personal relationship. In fact, being the Commodore of a fleet he couldn't have a relationship with anyone crewing the ships."

Admiral Killa said, "These starship cruises are long and stressful and can get quite lonely without a personal relationship. Currently the overall gender makeup on the ships is about 60 percent female, so the males have a greater selection for a mate. However, that is without consideration for those who prefer their own gender as a mate."

Vice Admiral Randall looked at the two officers and smiled, "Commodore Bloodworth, I know without asking that you would never break Navy rules; however, what are your personal thoughts on this proposal?"

Bloodworth's face flushed with embarrassment, but then he looked into his XOs eyes and seeing the hope they both desired, said, "I think it's a good idea. It might need to be tweaked, but considering the alternative, I think we should give it a try."

Randall asked, "Commander Lundberg what do you think?"

Without her saying anything the smile on her face said volumes. "Sir, I vote we give it a try."

Vice Admiral Randall said, "Board Members, what is your vote by a show of hands? Vote for the proposal… good. Let the records show there was a unanimous vote for the proposal. I am going to issue a General Order that the Bloodworth Battle Fleet initiates a two-year test involving two starships of the fleet that would implement this vote. Commodore you will be the controller of this implementation."

Commodore Bloodworth replied, "Yes, sir, thank you for this trust."

Vice Admiral Randall said, "The Governing Board will now

consider releasing all pertinent information regarding the Katz and their help in defending Earth. We should also release news of the great victory we've achieved by defeating the Xones' Fleet."

One of the Board members stood and said, "My name is Geraldine McPeters and I'm part of senior management of the XYZ Corporation that is currently building new starships. Commodore Bloodworth is there any changes you would make in their construction?"

Bloodworth stood and walked down the table and shook the hand of Ms. McPeters. "Madam, I've been carrying this list since I began the return trip home."

He then pulled a flash drive from his pocket and handed it to her. "If you need clarification please contact me through the Vice Admiral."

Vice Admiral Randall smiled as he shook his head. "Now back on subject, I call for a vote on both news matters. A show of hands again, vote Aye? Good, let the records show the Board voted Aye on both matters. Before we get into a discussion about awards for bravery during this battle, let's dismiss the military members who were involved. The Commodore has already submitted his recommendations, so commodore, commander, and Admiral Killa you may now leave."

They stopped outside the conference room and the two Earth officers breathed a sigh of relief. Bloodworth looked at the admiral with arched eyebrows, but then smiled his gratitude. "Admiral you have been a great friend to both of us. How can we repay you?"

Killa smiled and gave a hiss of approval. "I couldn't stand to see so much love for each other go untapped. I don't know how much longer I'll be attached to you, but I would like to attend your mating ceremony if possible."

Commander Lundberg smiled at Bloodworth. "Let's not rush the mating ceremony just yet, he's not even kissed me yet. That's important to me, that first kiss."

He turned to her and raised her chin with a finger while Lundberg looked at his face with wide fascinated eyes, until his lips pressed against hers teasing them open ever so slightly. She completely lost control as she hungrily met his aggression with her own.

When he stepped back slightly while still holding her in an

embrace, he said softly, "Well, Hanna did that kiss meet with your satisfaction?"

"Humm?" She replied while still not completely aware of her surroundings. Then, her eyes refocused on his face while her tongue licked her lips. "Wow! You bet. How about you?"

"Yes, that was even better than I fantasized. We need to introduce ourselves to each other's families before we deploy again."

She smiled at him as she said, "We can shuttle down to an airport near them."

He replied, "Let's wait until tomorrow after the news of our exploits, so they won't think we're crazy people."

"That's a plan, but admiral what about you? Is your fleet leaving soon?"

"I don't think we're ready to leave just yet. We want to gauge the Earth population's response to our involvement and your victory. However, I'll be staying on one of my own ships now. Try not to dally before your mating ceremony."

Both officers gave a short bow of honor to the admiral before they all left for the shuttle port. When the two senior officers arrived on board the UES Thunder, they were both greeted with honor. Unknown to Lundberg she had been promoted to captain of the Thunder, the flagship of Commodore Bloodworth.

Captain Lundberg's face had turned white at this promotion and what she considered enormous responsibilities. But, she took a deep breath and as the pipes stilled she saluted the flag and asked the OD's permission to come aboard, followed by the commodore's salute and request.

They didn't speak a word until they reached the Bridge and the marine guard yelled, "Captain on the deck!" and everyone came to attention. Lundberg approached the Command Chair, which Lt. Commander Conner had just vacated. She looked around the Bridge as if seeing it for the first time, and then said, "As you were!"

Conner had just relaxed, but then quickly stiffened to attention when she saw the steely-eyed look her captain was giving her. "Sir, have I displeased you in any way?"

"Yes, I expect my XO to be in proper uniform at all times, commander!"

Conner replied in a high squeaky voice, "XO...commander, Sir?"

"Yes, commander, it seems we are both without the proper uniform."

Commodore Bloodworth said, "Maybe I can help here. I'll give the new captain my old collar Pips, while the captain gives her new XO her old collar Pips. Captain I'll do the honor for you...and now you do it for your new XO."

Captain Lundberg said, "Comm, inform the ship that Commander Conner is my new XO."

She then said, "Commander Conner the commodore intends to a have a captains' conference here ASAP. Please inform them to bring their XOs. The commodore and I need to make preparations so continue as before, you still have the Bridge."

"Aye sir, I have the Bridge.

The two senior officers left the Bridge and returned to their former shared quarters to find their baggage had been moved to the captain's cabin. Their steward answered the buzzer and showed them inside their now expanded quarters. Yue He congratulated Lundberg on her promotion and pointed to where he was altering her jackets to add another stripe on its sleeves. He held up an altered jacket for her to trade out the old rank designation.

Once she donned the proper jacket she posed for Bloodworth, "How does it look?"

He smiled at her and turned his finger in the air, and she responded by turning around for him. "Now you really look like a captain with that extra stripe. How about you? Do you feel like a captain now?"

"Oh Eric. It feels surreal, almost like a dream."

"Well, it's a better dream. Let's get our story straight on how we're going to sell this to the other captains."

After the other fleet personnel arrived the commodore and Captain Lundberg walked to the podium. He said, "Captains and your XOs, I want to introduce the new captain of the Thunder."

Lundberg stepped forward and nodded her head at the applause from the gathering. She held up her hand to quiet the gathering. "The commodore has an announcement that is going to startle everyone, so pay close attention. Commodore..."

"The captain and I have just returned from a meeting with Vice

Admiral Randall and the Governing Board. Upon the urging of Admiral Gamma Killa, based upon their own experiences with starship travel at warp speed, I have been given the authority to alter the restrictions regarding sexual relations within the chain of command."

The commodore then went through what the new rules would be. When he finished he asked for questions. At first there was total shock, but finally Captain Inez Macchi of the UES Surprise said, "You're saying the change would allow a captain to marry, say her XO?"

"Yes, but if the XO is promoted it would require two higher ranking approvals other than his/her Captain."

"What about Captain Lundberg's promotion?"

Bloodworth's face flushed, but he quickly answered. "Captain Lundberg's promotion was approved by Space Headquarters and was before these changes went into effect. I was given authority to supervise two ships as test cases that will operate under these revised rules for two years and then decide if it will apply to all starships. This ship is one of the two; do any of you want to be the other ship?"

At first they all looked at him in shock, then Captain Macchi held up her hand, saying, "I volunteer."

Then one more hand, two more, and finally they all held up their hands. Bloodworth asked, "Are there any captains who are married to non-starship crew? Remember, the reason for this change is because those left on the ground age twice as fast as those travelling at warp speed. It would soon kill most marriages."

One captain held up his hand, Captain Jason Schmidt of the UES Berlin. "Sir, upon reflection I should request transfer rather than continue in this duty."

Bloodworth thought a moment before saying; "We need a Home Fleet to protect Earth when we're gone. Let's start with the Berlin. You other captains ask your crew if they would want to transfer to Home Fleet, and, Captain Schmidt, ask your crew if they would prefer to stay on a starship. After we get the results of this survey and resulting transfers I'll make a judgment on the other test ship. Check with me or Captain Lundberg before leaving if you have other questions."

CHAPTER 8

A week later the crew of the UES Berlin was complete for the lead ship of the Home Fleet. Commodore Bloodworth's fleet was now nine with the addition of three new starships, the UES Wasp, Enterprise, and Eagle. The Home Fleet had the Berlin and four others, and was currently in maneuvers near the warp gate the enemy would most likely use to enter our solar system.

Vice Admiral Randall was happy he had an experienced ship to train the new Home Fleet ships in the Bloodworth strategies. With everything going as planned he approved a three-day shore leave for the newlywed Bloodworths. Both Vice Admiral Randall and Admiral Killa attended the on-board wedding. Admiral Killa was still in system, but she didn't know for how much longer.

A shuttle from the Thunder had just landed at the Hamburg International Airport, causing some delays until it was no longer disrupting traffic patterns. Hanna put away her cell phone and smiled at her new husband, "Mom is here to pick us up, if we can figure out how to get to the terminal."

"I don't think you need to worry about that, here comes the welcoming committee."

Commodore Bloodworth checked with the pilots who verified they would return in twenty-four hours, so they popped the hatch and each carried a bag down to the tarmac and waited for the arrivals.

After the welcoming committee realized that one of the fleet heroes was a native, they pulled out all stops to welcome them. An hour later they were in the rear seat of an SUV driven by one of Hanna's sisters while her mother questioned her daughter about this new husband she was bringing home.

Hanna acted as his interpreter when Hanna's mother, Alice, asked how they met. He winked at Hanna and said, "Go for it."

She stuck her tongue out at him and then told her mother how things worked aboard ship. As Hanna explained, her mother's eyes got big and shifted toward him in fascination before finally smiling while shaking her head. Hanna said, "I think she understands now because she said, *it's a wonder you got married while in the military.*"

It was almost two hours later before they arrived at Hanna's home on the outskirts of Hamburg. It was a duplex with a single attached garage on each side. The residential construction was new in this area since the end of WW 2 because of the firebombing during the war.

Eric carried both of their bags as they entered the house and he was directed to a spare bedroom that used to be for Hanna's middle sister, Clare, now married. The youngest sister, Lucy, who drove them here was in her final year of college.

Eric dropped the bags on the bed before rejoining them; he suddenly remembered that Hanna's father had died several years before. He walked into the living room, where they still stood. Hanna pointed out a chair where he should sit, then the others followed suit and immediately started talking among themselves.

Eric thought his subterfuge had gone on far too long, so he interrupted in halting German, "Hanna may not know this but my family was originally from Southern Germany and while a child my Grandmother taught me her language. It's mostly come back to me while I've been listening to your conversations. Can you understand what I'm saying?"

Hanna jumped up from her seat and hurried over and sat on the chair's arm giving him an awkward hug. "Honey, you speak German well enough, you just have a southern accent."

He smiled, "I'm told that I also have a slight southern accent when I speak English."

Hanna gave him a quick kiss and then sat with her mother again. Alice gripped her daughter's hand and asked, "Eric, tell us about where you live in America?"

"I'm an only child and grew up in Springfield, Missouri that is located in the South-Central part of the United States. Springfield is the third largest city in Missouri and has been untouched by war since the civil war of the 1860's. We lived in a quiet residential area where my parents still reside."

Lucy quickly jumped up and hurried out of the room and shortly returned with a world atlas in her hands. She quickly turned to the United States where she traced her finger first to Missouri and then slowly to Springfield. "I see where it is – see mother it's right here just like Eric said."

Hanna leaned over where her sister was pointing and smiled. "I guess I never really realized how big the United States was."

Eric said, "Yes, it's about the size of Europe or Russia."

Hanna suddenly said, "Mama, have you started something for dinner?"

"No. But, I was considering having chicken."

"I want to cook something for Eric. Where we were at I can't cook and I want him to see that I can cook a good meal if I had to."

Eric started to say something and then reconsidered, as he realized she had to prove to herself that she could do this. Alice looked his way and he nodded his head, whereupon she said, "Hanna come with me and we'll plan a menu."

When they left, Lucy motioned for him to join her and they started to talk about his life on a starship. He quickly realized that she was star crazy and wanted to join her sister in space.

He asked, "What's your major in college?"

"Pre-med."

"What schooling comes next for a medical degree?"

"I'll have to go four years for that, then another two years internship before I'll get my M.D. What can I do to get onto a ship now?"

"If you want to be an officer, you'll need a profession, a talent, or practical experience that is needed on the ship. Besides medicine what are you interested in?"

Lucy looked at Eric and thought a few minutes before frowning. "Oh my, I'm going to have to take the long route aren't I?"

"Yeah, your sister and I lucked out. We had practical experience and a talent for tactics. You're going to work for a profession. It won't take you as long as us to get on a ship, but you'll find it just as rewarding. When you're ready let either of us know and we'll get you up there."

She quickly kissed him on the cheek before going into the kitchen to help. He used his cell to call his parents and arrange a pickup at the Springfield/Branson Air Terminal tomorrow morning, before checking what was going on in the kitchen.

The next morning they left Hamburg for Springfield on a three-hour sub-orbital shuttle flight. They landed on a large vacant tarmac area near the old terminal building. On the trip Hanna confessed to Eric that she had learned English on the ship's learning machine. They didn't have to wait long on the tarmac before a welcoming committee arrived, including lots of press coverage thanks to his mother's phone call to the mayor.

After the festivities were over they were driven home with a police escort. Hanna jabbed Eric in the ribs with a finger while saying, "Don't ever give me any trouble about how Hamburg treated us, after what happened here."

"What! It was only a little PR for the space program," he said with a wide grin.

His mother turned around and smiled at them. "This is really something, my son and his new bride coming home and they're on the news as the greatest heroes since ever!"

His father shouted back at them, "Eric, you lucky dog. How in the world did you find a woman that beautiful?"

Hanna blushed a little, and then said, "Your son was like catnip to the women, so I had to work fast."

Eric shook his head while saying, "Dad, she's pulling your leg, you know nothing how shipboard life really is."

"Adam, you stop that. She'll get the wrong opinion of us," Sarah said as she gave his shoulder a playful whack with her hand.

It took less than forty minutes to get home with the escort, which brought out all the neighbors as they pulled into the driveway. The space heroes had to give a short speech before they were able to go inside and sit down with a sigh. Sarah took a breath and quickly made her way into the kitchen calling back, "Come on in here I made us some tasty lemonade!"

Hanna and Eric looked at each other, and then with a sigh they both followed his parents into the kitchen. After glasses were filled with ice cubes, then lemonade, they sat at the table and sampled the tart drink. Before Hanna could take her first taste, Eric placed his hand over hers while he took a sip and grimaced, saying, "You better add some sugar or it will gave you lockjaw."

Sarah's eyes got big in surprise as she said, "Oh I'm sorry, I like it tart. Here add some of this sugar."

Before Hanna did anything she took a small taste and shuddered. "Yes, it needs a little more sugar for my taste."

Hanna asked Adam, "What was your profession before you retired?"

"I taught woodworking in high school for thirty years and Sarah taught English."

Sarah said, "That's where we met. Hanna, I'm so glad you two got together. I was afraid that Eric was going to remain alone after his divorce. His military service wasn't conducive to a long-term relationship."

"Yes, previous to my starship service I was with the German Army. I couldn't maintain a relationship for the same reason. However, now we are together all the time."

Sarah looked at her son and his new wife and hesitantly asked, "Have you discussed having children?"

Hanna replied, "Not really, but I'm going to freeze my eggs to keep that option open."

Eric took her hand and smiled. "Honey, I'm glad that you've thought ahead. We need to do that before we leave Earth again."

Sarah smiled at Hanna. "Did you notice that he said 'we.' That's very important in a marriage, that you do things together."

Hanna nodded her head as a tear slid down her cheek. "Yes, I'm finding that out."

Sarah asked, "Son, do you want to eat in or out tonight?"

Hanna interrupted, "I know he wants his mother's home cooking and maybe I can help in the kitchen. I should warn you that I'm out of practice."

"Well, first let's have lunch before we worry about tonight's meal."

The next day they returned to the Space Headquarters' hospital for Hanna's procedure to safeguard her eggs, before returning to the Thunder. Upon their arrival at the Thunder, they were both inundated with messages awaiting their arrival. They both answered those that couldn't wait until tomorrow, and then they retired to their cabin. Eric was waiting when Hanna finally arrived mentally exhausted.

She removed her clothing and surrendered herself to his magic fingers massaging the tension out of her muscles. When he was finished she crawled up beside him and snuggled against him with a smile. "Honey, you don't know how much I needed that."

"I know," he said with a smile. "What time do you need to be up?"

"Six, if I'm going to make time for a run. Please run with me?"

"Okay, I need exercise too. I've left a message for Yue He."

The next morning they were both running with the marines, who kept them honest, before a joint shower and breakfast. After eating and while enjoying the last of his cup of coffee Eric said, "Hanna, after you get things settled this morning, I need to go over consumables you will need for a possible six month cruise. I'll send the same request out to the fleet. Admiral Killa left star charts of their past sightings of the Xones that I'm going to study before we leave."

"Has Vice Admiral Randall given any hint as to when that's going to be?"

He shook his head and considered a moment. "I'm guessing we're going to be leaving within a month, that's why we need to resupply."

"What have you heard about the Home Fleet's readiness?"

"They haven't been at it very long, but according to Captain Schmidt's reports they're coming along. Randall hinted that we should ease back into our system with caution when we return."

She looked at him with surprise. "If we're gone the full six months, a year would have passed here. Surely, the Home Fleet wouldn't be that gun happy!"

Eric shrugged his shoulders. "I wouldn't think so, but it wouldn't hurt to be cautious."

They kissed before leaving their stateroom together, but going in different directions. Eric had taken over the captain's office where he would generally stay unless they were under General Quarters. Today, the new captain was visiting with all her department heads, while her new XO was getting used to command at the Bridge. Later, Commander Betty Conner as the ship's XO would visit the department heads.

Three weeks later Commodore Bloodworth called for a pre-departure meeting on the Thunder for all captains and their XO's. This would be his first face meeting with his three new ship captains.

When the captains and XO's of the eight other starships began to arrive they were greeted at the conference room doors by the commodore, and then the new captain and XO of the Thunder. There were three ships or thirty percent now captained by females in the fleet.

Bloodworth met his first new ship captain, Captain Allison Collins and her XO Commander Derek Bischof of the UES Wasp. She shook his hand and smiled up at him from her petite five foot four inch frame. She made up for her small stature by a strong voice as she introduced herself. Her XO was a little over six feet tall and had the physical appearance of a linebacker.

Following her was another new captain, Captain Drew Melton and his XO Commander Jocelyn Lowry of the UES Enterprise. He shook Eric's hand and said he was looking forward to some action. His XO looked similar in appearance to Eric's wife and seemed alert and anxious to meet the other XOs.

Last to enter was new captain, Captain Christopher Eiberger and his XO Commander Lauren Hinnershitz of the UES Eagle. Eiberger strongly gripped Eric's hand and said he's impressed by the strategy of the fleet's first battle. His XO looked at him with a smile and asked in German, "I hear we have a language in common."

After everyone took a seat, the commodore, and Thunders captain and XO took the stage. Commodore Bloodworth stood before the podium and held up his hand for quiet. "Ship captains and their XOs of the Bloodworth Battle Fleet, welcome to another journey into the fray with our enemy, the Xones. Our initial entry into their territory will be at our last battle site. If no one is there, we will exit that system for another. However, we are going to be cautious. At the last battle site we will send a probe through to test the waters, if safe or not it will send back a message torpedo. If it's an ambush we'll know how many ships and how far from the gate they are positioned. Does anyone have questions?"

The first hand up was from Captain Collins from the Wasp. "Sir, I assume we are going to be doing practice maneuvers before we reach the combat area?"

"Yes, you can count on it. We now have nine instead of seven ships, so I'm going to try a shift from a horizontal firing line of nine to a three stack of threes. We previously had a two – three - two stack. As before we will move our formation after the enemy loses control of their fired missiles."

Captain Eiberger of the Eagle asked, "Sir, what if they wise up and copy our tactics?"

"I think we will have at least one more battle before that happens. We left no enemy survivors at the last battle. If there are no more questions, I'm sure that many of you have questions from the two ships with revised relationship regulations, The Thunder and Surprise. Their captains and XO's will answer your questions."

Bloodworth stepped to the side as most of the officers lined up between the two ship Captains. He started to smile at them when he realized a third line was starting to form for answers from him.

CHAPTER 9

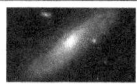

Nearly four months later, they were approaching the warp gate into the system where the last battle occurred. The ships were 80,000 miles from the gate and spread out for maximum coverage against anything coming out of the gate. They waited until a returning message torpedo from their probe showed nothing in the system other than the expanding debris field from the previous battle.

Still at Battle Stations they quickly transited the gate in single file and assumed a firing formation. Ten minutes later Commodore Bloodworth informed his fleet that they were alone and that Battle Stations were cancelled. The fleet was ordered to follow the Thunder to the next gate located four days distant.

After the fleet made an adjustment to their headings, Commodore Bloodworth informed the captain he was standing down until needed. Captain Lundberg said, "Commander Conner, you have the con."

"Yes, sir, I have the Bridge."

Conner smiled as the commodore and her captain left the Bridge holding hands, thinking *I never thought I'd ever see that when I signed up.*

When the couple left the Bridge they decided to have dinner before taking a shared sleep period. Arriving at the Officers Mess they discovered they were not the first with this idea, two other mixed pairs were dining together. They took a table far enough away from the others that they could converse without disturbing anyone.

Hanna smiled at her husband and quietly said, "I never would have paired Lt. Commander Alice Beeker with Lt. Jason Gleason. They appear to be so opposite in personality."

He replied, "Maybe it's not his personality that she's interested in?"

She looked at Eric with surprised wide-open eyes, and then shook her head. "No, I don't believe that."

She continued to think about it for a few moments before dismissing it and looking at the other couple.

"Lt. Commanders Alice Sumter and Robert Bruce. They aren't in the same departments. I wonder how they got acquainted?"

Eric smiled at his wife and shook his head at her. "You could always ask them?"

She looked at him in shock. "I couldn't do that! That's wrong in so many ways."

He laughed and she kicked his leg under the table before turning her attention to her food. After dinner they returned to their stateroom for some quality time for themselves and later some rest.

Four days later, while at Battle Stations they waited at the next warp gate for a message torpedo from their probe. When it arrived they discovered that the enemy was present on the other side. The probe's sensor readings noted that there were two groups of twelve in ball formations about 200,000 miles from the gate and 50,000 miles apart.

Commodore Bloodworth thought through his options before he asked, "Commander Conner, this gate requires a speed of 2.5 gravities speed when transiting. At our null speed and distance from the gate, what speed would a missile have when it entered the gate?"

"Sir, from this distance it would cross through the gate at 2g's. To reach the required speed it would need sixteen additional miles from the gate."

"Comm, connect me with the captains of the Surprise and Wasp."

"Sir, they are both connected."

"Captains Macchi and Collins, I need you to get into firing

position 66 miles from the Warp Gate. When in position I want you each to fire a nuke missile through the gate upon my command. Captain Macchi, I want you to fire first and have your missile programed that after transiting the gate, to veer ten degrees left and to shut down its engines after 60,000 miles. Captain Collins, thirty seconds after the Surprise launches its missile, your programed missile should veer ten degrees right and shut down after 60,000 miles. Both missiles should be programed to restart when they are 30,000 miles from their targets and aim toward each target's center mass. Captains repeat my instructions to me starting with Captain Macchi."

After they both repeated his instructions he said, "Captains, this is a Hail Mary play, so let's hope it works. Now get into position and let me know when you're ready."

Forty minutes later both ships were in position and repeated what they had programed their missiles to perform. Bloodworth then notified all ship captains of his plan.

"Comm, get me Captain Macchi."

"Sir, Captain Macchi reporting."

"Captain Macchi, you may fire your missile."

"Yes, sir, I have authorization to fire my missile. Sir, missile fired!"

After both missiles were fired Bloodworth asked, "Commander Conner how long before the missiles reach their targets?"

"Sir, target one will be in thirty-two minutes, target two will be thirty seconds later."

"Start the clock please."

"Yes, sir, clock started."

"Commander, prep another probe to launch on my command."

"Yes, sir, probe ready at your command."

Thirty-one minutes later all the Bridge personnel watched the clock count down to zero, and then thirty more seconds. Commodore Bloodworth waited another ten minutes before he said, "Launch the probe."

"Sir, probe launched."

Twenty minutes later a message torpedo came back through the gate. The download revealed two huge debris fields with no discernable ship hulls.

"Comm, to all ship captains. It appears that our ploy worked.

The Thunder will transit the gate, first followed by the Surprise and Wasp, and then the remainder of the Fleet will proceed in Ship alpha order. We will regroup on the other side before proceeding."

After all ships cleared the gate and no other ships were noted in the system, they slowly passed the two debris fields taking sensor readings that they would analyze later. The next gate was about two days travel at 2g's, but Commodore Bloodworth elected to use a nearby heavy atmosphere planet to replenish their reaction mass before continuing on to the next gate.

As before they stopped before the gate and arranged themselves in a defensive position before sending a probe through. Twenty minutes later a message torpedo returned with only one contact noted from the probes scan and it appeared to be heading for the next jump gate.

Commodore Bloodworth thought for a few moments before turning to his captain. "Captain Lundberg, we seem to have a fleeing sentry that we have no chance of catching. I propose to enter the gate to give the sentry a sensor reading of our numbers, and after he warps out of this system we return to Earth to increase our strength before we return. What are your thoughts?"

"Obviously, we run the risk of an ambush if we continue to follow him. I agree on the return to Earth to increase our force. However, we may need to stay there longer than last time to achieve a significant increase in our fleet."

"I agree, but I don't want to get too far out here unless our force is bigger. I don't like two to one odds every time we meet the enemy. Comm, notify fleet we will transit the gate at 2g's and reform before following the enemy sentry. When he transit's out of this system we will reverse thrust to return to Earth."

"Captain, you may discontinue Battle Stations."

"Aye sir, Battle Stations discontinued. XO you have the Bridge."

Commander Conner said, "Yes ma'am, I have the Bridge."

The captain stayed and watched her XO command the ship through the warp gate without any problems before she followed her husband off the Bridge.

When she returned to her stateroom she found her husband wearing a robe while propped up on the bed listening to his favorite country/western music. He quirked an eyebrow at her as she entered the room, "Dear, did you have a hard day at work?"

She jumped upon the bed and gave him a hug and kiss before asking, "Did you already shower?"

"Yes dear, did you let her take the ship through the jump point?"

"Yes, Conner did it without a problem. However, our new science officer is good, but she's not up to her standard yet. Let go, I want to get cleaned up." Hanna said as she left the bed and started to strip off her clothing.

The last he saw of her as she entered the head was her delightful rear, which she gave a shake for his delight. He decided to order their dinner while she showered. *Now what would she like after a stressful day at the office?*

* * *

Nearly five months later the fleet approached the warp gate to its home system and stopped. They first sent a message torpedo through informing the Home Fleet that they were returning home. After waiting thirty minutes, a message torpedo came their way out of the gate inviting the Bloodworth Fleet home.

Commodore Bloodworth then commed the Fleet to follow him through the gate in alpha order of Ship's name. They passed ten ships of the Home Fleet after transiting through the gate. Their commander, Captain Schmidt, welcomed them home and wanted to buy the commodore a beer at his convenience.

EARTH ORBIT
JANUARY 2023 (SHIP TIME)
MAY 2024 (EARTH TIME)

CHAPTER 10

Three days later they made Earth orbit. Commodore Bloodworth gave the other ship captains the authority to give a quarter of their crew's shore leave on a rotating basis, before he took a shuttle down to Space Headquarters to report to Vice Admiral Randall.

His shuttle was met by an honor guard and was given an escort to the new Space Headquarters' building. Eric thought it pretty impressive, twenty stories of chrome and glass. Much better than the converted warehouse they originally operated out of.

When Commodore Bloodworth stepped out of the limo a commander met him who introduced himself, "I'm Commander Robert Becker, a special assistant to Vice Admiral Randall. I've been ordered to stick with you and provide whatever assistance you need while you're on the ground."

"Very well, I was ordered to report to Vice Admiral Randall, so lead on."

Commander Becker led the way to a bank of elevators; two tough looking armed marines guarded one elevator door that opened as they approached. Bloodworth was a little surprised that the elevator descended once they entered, but even more when the car stopped twenty floors down.

He followed Commander Becker out of the elevator to a nearby armored door guarded by four armed marines. They each presented their ID's to a seated officer who ran them through a reader before handing them back. He then stood and saluted both Space Navy Officers, before pressing a series of numbers on the door. When the last number was pressed the door emitted a loud klaxon sound for five seconds before ending when the door started opening.

Commander Becker led the way though for a short distance where they encountered another security checkpoint manned by a tough looking marine major. She gave them a steely-eyed look as she asked, "What is your business?"

"Commodore Bloodworth and staff reporting to Admiral Randall as ordered."

She punched in his name on her computer where his picture flashed on her screen. After reading what the screen displayed she stood and saluted them. "Yes, sir, the Admiral is expecting you. Please wait one moment."

She pushed a button that started the klaxon sound again before the door started closing. They didn't move until the door was completely closed, whereupon she said, "Please follow me."

The corridor soon made a left turn where they encountered another checkpoint manned by another marine officer. Our marine guide said, "Commodore Bloodworth and staff reporting as ordered for Vice Admiral Randall."

The two marines saluted each other; the major left and the lt. colonel opened the doors to the vice admiral's office. She announced, "Commodore Bloodworth and staff reporting as ordered to the admiral."

Vice Admiral Randall hurried around his desk saying, "Commodore Bloodworth, it's amazing news you've brought back with you. I've been reading what you encountered out there and how your fleet destroyed a large enemy fleet lying in ambush. That's two battles without suffering a single casualty. Come sit down over here and let's hear what's needed now."

"Sir, I need a larger fleet if I'm going to venture out any further into the Xones' territory. They know we are out there and have already kicked their butts; now we have really given them a black eye with this last battle. I've let them know we've done it with only a small fleet of nine ships and that's got to have given them a scare. I'm guessing that they'll either mass a huge fleet to throw at us, or they'll try to avoid battle with us. I don't want to go out there again unless I have at least fifteen ships. At the last battle they used twenty-four ships, which was apparently two battle groups in their attempt to ambush me. How many new constructs do we have now that I can add to my fleet?"

Vice Admiral Randall looked at the frustrated Commodore Bloodworth for a few moments before replying; "You want at least six more ships before you'll feel safe enough to take the enemy on again. Since you left, all new constructs have added the things you requested, at least those that we could alter the original ship design without creating problems. We gave Home Fleet three new ships, and we have twenty almost ready for you now. They should all be ready within three months to commission."

"Wow! Sir, I'll just take fifteen of those ships. Home Fleet needs the other five to better protect the home system. By the way, how has Captain Schmidt performed as commander of the Home Fleet?"

"I'm very happy with how he has trained his captains. He's using the same tactics that you initiated with such success, but with the addition of these five ships he now rates a commodore rank. Do you think he can handle the job?"

Bloodworth considered the question for a few moments before answering. "Sir, Captain Schmidt was with my fleet on our first voyage and he performed well, but you're considering him for a much tougher command job. From what you've said he's performed the duties of commander of the Home Fleet with distinction. For me to give my approval I'd need to interact with him. If he meets my approval can I give him the word of his promotion?"

Vice Admiral Randall smiled at the greatest hero of modern warfare. "Yes, I think you would be a good judge of his abilities, Rear Admiral Bloodworth."

"What! I wasn't hinting about a promotion."

"I know you weren't, but you deserve the promotion. In addition, you should probably move your flag to one of the new ships to determine if we should tweak the design."

"I'd do it if I can move my captain with me; however, since the Thunder's crew is one of the two ships under the relationship experiment, I'd have to move the whole crew to the new ship."

Vice Admiral Randall's eyes widened in surprise, "Yes, but that's not really a problem. In fact it's a benefit because the crew would be aware of the differences. How is our little experiment doing?"

"For the Thunder we have had no problems yet, but we have a little more than a year to go. The Surprise has reported no problems at all, not even a lovers' spate. We will have to interview all crewmembers of both ships when the two-year experiment ends."

Randall looked at the Home Fleet schedule before saying, "Captain Schmidt's ship is due to return to Earth orbit for supplies and shore leaves next week. I'll have him contact you when he reports in. In the meantime go to the quartermaster and get yourself new uniforms, you look underdressed."

"Aye, sir. Thank you sir."

The new Rear Admiral and his staff retraced their steps and eventually found themselves outside. "Well Commander, are you my permanent staff?"

"Sir, yes, sir, unless you prefer someone else."

"No, I think you'll do fine. Where do I go to get new uniforms?"

After the two had finished at the quartermasters and Rear Admiral Bloodworth was wearing his new uniform and a collar pip of a single star, they took a shuttle to visit one of the new ships. It seemed strange to be on a ship with only a skeleton crew, but he was pleased with the changes made. They now had a dedicated missile storage area with its own shuttle bay access, and an automated mechanism for movement of missiles to their tubes. He checked this ship's number of 1248, so he could inform the admiral of his new ship.

When his shuttle landed on the Thunder, it was to the pipes of an admiral arriving. It was a pleasant surprise as he departed the shuttle and approached the welcoming committee headed by the ship's captain, his wife. He saluted the flag and asked, "Permission to come aboard?"

The captain answered, "Permission granted admiral."

Commander Becker repeated the same entry protocol and followed behind his admiral. "Captain, this my chief of staff, Commander Robert Becker."

She looked at her husband with pride, "My, it was a surprise to get news of your promotion. What other news are you bringing?"

"Well, for starters we are going to move the Thunder's crew to another new ship."

"What! No, don't tell me now. I want to savor the news a bit before the whole crew goes nuts."

Commander Becker was a little surprised at their close relationship, but he remembered this was one of the ships where the old rules didn't apply.

Bloodworth showed Becker the small office originally designed for the captain's use. The new ship also had another larger room earmarked for small conferences near the Bridge. It would be the admiral's office when they moved.

The three officers stood in the small cramped office. Bloodworth said, "Captain, we're moving my flag because Star Headquarters wants my take on the changes I recommended. They're even calling them the Bloodworth Class. We're not moving until there is a crew ready to take over here when we leave. I recommend we move a department at a time, with our assistant DH's staying here until the new crew is settled. What do you think?"

The captain and admiral were sitting on the room's small desk with their shoulders touching. To give them more room she placed her arm around his waist. "Yes, I think that will cut down on most of the confusion when we move. Has the ship been supplied with provisions and missiles?"

"No, but as soon as Food Service moves they will start with provisions."

She frowned in thought. "Well, we better start with that, and then Engineering."

Admiral Bloodworth said, "Commander Becker, you will supervise the move and answer their questions. Defer to the captain if you have serious problems to resolve. Captain, any thoughts?"

"No, now if you two will leave my office I'll make the announcement that will cause the uproar I'm expecting."

After the admiral and his chief of staff left the office, Bloodworth said, "Let's see about getting the replacement crew here."

* * *

Three weeks later the former crew of the UES Thunder were in their new home, the UES Conquest. Captain Lundberg Bloodworth had named the ship the day everyone was moved from the Thunder. So far the move was almost seamless, with very little actual problems. Lt. Commander Alice Beeker was especially happy about her Weapons Section. When she saw her new missile storage area with its automated transfer of missiles to the tube sections, she laughed with glee.

By eliminating one small storage room on one level everyone else received more room. The captain called for a meeting with all her DHs a week after the move.

The ten Department Heads arrived to find their captain standing at the snack table filling her plate with raw vegetables and dips. She motioned for them to join her and added a cup of tea before sitting at the oval table. When everyone was seated, the admiral and his chief of staff arrived, which caused some confusion until he said, "As you were. I'm only here to observe and maybe answer questions at the end of the meeting."

Captain Lundberg asked each DH about the plus and minus features of their new ship, especially regarding their own department. Lt. Commander Beeker was the most vocal about how happy she was with the changes in her Weapons Department, with everyone voicing some minor criticisms of the changes. However, all the departments seemed happy with their new ship.

The captain asked the DHs, to interview their crew and send her a list of the likes and dislikes of their new ship. The purpose of this survey is to make changes in future ships. Who knows, maybe a small change will bring great rewards in the future.

The new captain and XO of the Thunder were Sara Bazyn and Rachel Oglesby. This is the first ship where both the captain and XO were female. Captain Hanna Bloodworth invited them to the Conquest for an informal dinner tomorrow evening.

The Conquest's captain's stateroom was larger than the Thunder and included a dining table. Their shared steward, Yue He, had already readied it and was awaiting the captain's nod before serving dinner.

Eric stood before a mirror adjusting the fit of his jacket when he asked, "Hanna, do you know anything about these two officers?"

"Nothing, other than they scored high on their tests – especially their analytical ability, and neither are from a wet Navy background."

"Hey, that's pretty good. Where did you get your information?"

"I asked Commander Becker."

Eric glanced over at his wife and grinned at her complete innocent behavior as she finished her makeup. She finished and turned to him holding her jacket saying, "Eric, help me with this, I don't want to muss my hair and makeup."

He helped her slide into it and straightened the shoulders. "Turn around and let me see how it looks."

She gave him a raised eyebrow look as he inspected her uniform. He picked off a speck of white lint on her dark blue jacket, before saying, "Perfect, now all we need is our guests."

He no sooner said the words, than the door buzzer sounded. Their steward answered the door and ushered the two officers inside after they announced their names and that they were expected.

Captain Bloodworth stepped forward and introduced themselves to the two female officers. She pointed to the seating area and said, "Let's talk and get to know each other before dinner. Is there anything you want to know about us, although we are perhaps the best known officers in Star Fleet?"

Captain Bazyn smiled at that comment. "I think that's probably true, but I've wondered, did you know each other before arriving on the Thunder?"

Hanna looked at her husband and smiled, "No, we met each other on the Thunder. You are probably wondering how we fell in love so quickly. Remember, we had just fought a battle together and were both under severe emotional stress. However, I suppose the marriage wouldn't have happened if not for the revised relationship regulations that two of our ships are testing. You are aware of the experiment?"

"Yes, how much longer is the test going to run?"

"When we get back from the next voyage, headquarters will make a judgment about making it permanent for all warp ships. The reason for the regulation was because people on warp ships age slower than people on Earth at about a two to one ratio."

Bazyn cleared her throat nervously, "You mean if I have a

boyfriend or husband on the ground and I'm gone a year, it would be two years for him?"

"Yes! No one has told you about this problem?"

"No! Not in those terms. I didn't understand that to be the case at all."

"Commander Oglesby, how about you?"

"Yes, I knew it in those terms, but I had no love interest on the ground so I wasn't concerned."

Bloodworth asked, "Captain Bazyn is this going to be a deal breaker for you being on a warp ship?"

She looked at him with a haunted expression. "I have a close relationship with someone on the ground, but I'm not sure if I want to marry him. Sir, can I take leave for a few days to make up my mind about him?"

"Yes. If you decide he's a keeper, then I can arrange a transfer for you to Home Fleet. The decision is yours to make."

"Sir, thank you. You have really taken a load off my mind. I'll give it a lot of thought because I really want to command a warp ship."

Later, after dinner and their guests gone, the Bloodworth's lay in bed in each other's arms. Hanna gave her husband's ear lobe a playful nip with her teeth, and then said, "You did good giving Bazyn that option."

"Yeah, remember I was married before. Navy life is hard enough without that kind of stress."

CHAPTER 11

Four months later the Bloodworth Fleet, now totaling 24 ships, broke Earth orbit to begin their third voyage. Captain Sara Bazyn of the UES Thunder remained with the Fleet.

Almost three months later they were stopped before the gate into the system where they had fought their first battle, Rear Admiral Bloodworth commed the fleet. "To all Bloodworth Fleet Ships. We are approaching what we consider hostile territory when we transit this gate. We fought our first battle there and had a great success; however, past successes are no guarantee they will continue. We must be cautious, as they have already attempted one ambush. We've already sent a probe into the next system and are awaiting the results. With our present fleet strength I think we can prevail against anything they've previously sent at us. Rear Admiral Bloodworth out."

Ten minutes later a message torpedo came through the gate from their probe that revealed no ships in the system except the debris from their previous battle, which had disbursed over a wide area.

The fleet transited through the gate with the Admiral's Flagship first, followed by the others in SOP alpha order. After all ships had regrouped they preceded to the next gate that was several days distant. The admiral decided that they should replenish their reaction mass before entering the next system, so they diverted to the nearest large gas covered planet.

Four days later they had stopped before the next gate and were awaiting the results from their probe. They were at Battle Stations not knowing what to expect. Ten enemy missiles almost immediately followed the message torpedo. The fleet was widely disbursed for just such a response and quickly disposed of them with laser fire.

After reading the results from their probe, Admiral Bloodworth said, "Comm send this. Probe shows a loose formation of twenty enemy ships grouped from 5,000 to 50,000 miles from the gate. The one ship closest to the gate must have fired their missiles at our fleet. I intend to shake them up by destroying it first. Captain Bazyn take a bearing on that ship and fire a full broadside through the gate on my command. Captain Collins ten seconds after the Thunder fires her broadside, the Wasp will do the same. Let me know when you are in position."

"Sir, the Thunder is ready."

"Sir, the Wasp is ready."

"Very well, Thunder you may fire."

After both ships had fired their broadsides, the admiral ordered another probe sent through the gate. Twenty minutes later the returning message torpedo revealed only debris where the attacking ship had formerly been. The other ships were apparently moving further away from the gate.

Admiral Bloodworth said, "Comm to all ships. Good shooting Thunder and Wasp, your target was destroyed. Fleet, the other nineteen ships are putting space between themselves and the gate. We will wait three hours and send another probe through the gate. I'm concerned about them laying mines in our path, so I may plot a divergent path to their location. If anyone has further concerns I'm open to your thoughts. Rear Admiral Bloodworth out."

He turned to the captain and asked, "What other steps can I take to clear a potential minefield?"

"Let's ask Commander Beeker if she can rig missiles to explode when near mines."

He nodded his head. "Comm connect me with Commander Beeker."

"Sir, Commander Beeker here."

The Admiral asked the captains question and awaited a reply. "Sir, the bulk of the enemy ships were about 50,000 miles from the gate, so its likely that any mines laid would be from there to where they are now. I could tweak the sensitivity of the missiles to explode when they pass close to a mine. If say three or four ships fire a staggered volley of missiles in a direct line from the gate to where they are now, you should be able tell if there is a minefield and maybe even clear it. I'd turn off the engines early, say 30,000 miles, and approach the suspected minefield at a slower speed. Later, if the missiles are still viable, turn the engines back on to attack the enemy ships."

Rear Admiral Bloodworth smiled as he saw the potential of the plan. "Commander, you just earned yourself an extra week of shore leave. Make the adjustments to the missiles and if any remain as they close on the enemy, have them reactivate when they are 50,000 miles from the enemy."

"Aye Sir. Thank you for the extra leave. I will start the adjustments now."

"When you've made your adjustments let me know and I'll have you tell two other ships how you did it if they run into problems."

"Aye sir, Beeker out."

Bloodworth considered which ships he should call next. "Comm, call the captains of the Enterprise and Eagle."

"Sir, Captain Melton of the Enterprise and Captain Eiberger of the Eagle answered."

"Captains, this is Rear Admiral Bloodworth. After we make the transit, our three ships will fire a staggered volley of missiles at the enemy. Our volleys will attempt to destroy any potential mines between the gate and the enemy ships. Program your missiles to turn off at 30,000 miles and coast until they are 50,000 miles from the enemy ships. Adjust the missiles sensitivity so that they will explode if they pass near any potential mines. Check with me if you have any problems with your programing."

Three hours later after sending out another probe, the returning message torpedo showed that the nineteen enemy ships had stopped 400,000 miles from the gate in a loose attack formation. Admiral Bloodworth gave the order, "Comm to all ships. Transit the gate with the first three ships being the Conquest, Enterprise, and Eagle. The remainder will follow in alpha order."

Captain Bloodworth said, "Helm, transit the gate."

After all ships had arrived in the new system they formed a line behind the three lead ships. The Conquests long range scan operator said, "Sir, there has been an explosion about 50,000 miles between the gate and the enemy formation."

Captain Bloodworth said, "Admiral, one of the missiles fired at the destroyed enemy ship must have found a mine."

Admiral Bloodworth grinned as he said, "Comm inform the Enterprise and Eagle to bracket the recent explosion when they fire their volley. Enterprise you fire first at my command, then Eagle, and finally the Conquest. Captain Bloodworth, review the other ships' hits and make any needed adjustments before firing. Enterprise, are you ready?"

"Aye, sir."

"Enterprise you may now fire."

"Enterprise now firing."

"Eagle observe the results of Enterprise's missiles and make any needed adjustments."

"Aye, sir."

Captain Bloodworth asked, "Science Officer how long for missiles to reach the estimated position of mine field?"

"Ma'am, making allowances for the slower speed of the missiles, it will take an estimated 30 minutes."

"Please, start a clock."

"Ma'am, clock started."

Later, as the clock approached the 30-minute mark, everyone on the Bridge tensed up. The scan officer reported, "Ma'am, one explosion noted...now, three more. Two more noted. Sir, that's all from this volley."

Captain Bloodworth said, "Sir, that's seven down. Now its Eagle's turn."

Admiral Bloodworth said, "Comm Eagle."

"Aye, Captain Eiberger of the Eagle."

"Captain Eiberger its now your turn. Make a bigger hole in the minefield. Are you ready?"

"Aye, sir."

"Eagle you may fire."

"Sir, Eagle has fired."

Captain Bloodworth said, "Start a 30-minute clock."

"Aye, ma'am, clock has been started."

Thirty minutes later the scan officer reported, "Ma'am, three explosions noted. One, two, four explosions. Two more…Ma'am, that's all from this volley."

Captain Lundberg said, "Nine mines from that volley, for a total sixteen mines."

Admiral Bloodworth nodded his head. "We've made a big hole. Captain, let's target a larger ring around that hole with this one."

Captain Lundberg said, "Comm connect me with Lt. Commander Beeker."

"Aye, captain."

"Target our volley around the hole the other two ships made. If you think approaching at a slower speed will help, do it."

"Aye, ma'am. Making adjustments…we are now ready."

The captain turned to the admiral and said, "Sir, our missiles are ready."

"You may fire."

"Fire Missiles."

"Aye, ma'am, missiles are fired."

"Start clock at forty minutes."

"Aye, captain, clock started."

The admiral raised his eyebrow. "Forty minutes?"

The captain shrugged her shoulders. "I guessed because of the slower speed."

He grinned at her discomfort. "Want to bet how accurate that guess is?"

"Okay, if I'm within five minutes, you have to give me a back rub. If not, then I'll owe you one."

"That sounds like I can't lose."

Forty-one minutes later the scan officer reported, "Two explosions…another one, two…three more explosions. Sir, that's all for this volley."

Admiral Bloodworth said, "Twenty-three mines destroyed. We probably didn't get them all, but I can't justify using more missiles to clear mines. Comm, notify all ships to follow the Conquest in single file until I give the all clear, and mark this area as the cleared portion of a mine field."

Captain Bloodworth said, "Aye, sir. Science Officer McBride, comply with the admiral's order."

Rear Admiral Bloodworth said, "Captain, you may proceed toward the enemy."

Captain Bloodworth replied, "Helm, proceed through the center of the cleared area at 2g's."

While the Bloodworth Fleet was moving toward the Xones' Fleet, Admiral Bloodworth and Captain Hanna Bloodworth were discussing tactics that they could use against the enemy as they were now deployed. She said, "Admiral, if I was the Xones' commander I'd wait until we were inside the minefield and then hit us with missiles. It would be hard to mount an effective defense if we can't maneuver."

"I've had the same thought. What if we mount our own missile attack before we reach the minefield? If all our ships fire two volleys at only three of their ships, concentrating on the center of their formation where their commander may reside. This huge volley would take out any additional mines we missed before."

Captain Bloodworth smiled in appreciation of his guile. "We better do it within the hour as we are fast approaching the minefield."

He nodded his head, then said, "Comm all fleet ships. At my command we will reconfigure fleet to formation X-Ray 1."

He waited three minutes, then said, "Reconfigure to X-Ray 1."

The fleet changed from a single file to three levels of eight ships, all ready to fire missiles. Admiral Bloodworth said, "Each level will target one of the three center ships of the enemy formation. Level one will take the left, level two will take the center, and level three will take the right. Configure your missiles to shut down engines after 50,000 miles and restart again when 30,000 miles from target. On the count of three each ship will fire two volley's, one…two…three FIRE."

The fleet sent 240 missiles in two waves, or 480 missiles at the three targeted enemy ships. That meant each of the targeted ships would have 160 missiles heading their way.

Captain Bloodworth asked, "Science Officer McBride how long before missiles are in range?"

"Sir, estimated time is 1.3 hours."

"Start clock for 1.3 hours."

"Aye ma'am, clock started."

"Contact, missiles launched from enemy."

Captain Bloodworth said, "Start clock two for when enemy missiles become ballistic."

"Aye ma'am, clock two started."

Admiral Bloodworth asked, "Did any of our launch strike mines on the way out?"

The Sensor Officer replied, "No, sir, they all made it through the minefield."

"Contact. There have been two explosions from the enemy's location."

Captain Bloodworth quickly looked at the admiral. "Sir, the time is about right for our missiles aimed at the minefield to reach the enemy fleet."

The admiral mused, "I wonder which ship's missiles should get credit for those hits? Sensor, can you determine if the explosions were from any of the three ships now targeted?"

"Sir, the explosions were from one enemy ship on the extreme left side of their formation."

Captain Bloodworth asked the admiral, "Sir, would you like to take a coffee break?"

He looked at clock two and saw it had another twenty minutes to run. "Yes, I think I do. I'll be right back."

"Admiral off the Bridge," was sounded as he made his way to the captains' office. Ten minutes later he was back with a cup of tea for the captain.

The two senior officers watched clock two count down to zero. Captain Bloodworth asked the admiral, "X-Ray 2?"

"Yes, it's time. Comm, contact all ships. At my command, formation X-Ray 2 will be made."

Admiral Bloodworth waited fifteen seconds, and then said, "Execute Formation X-Ray 2."

The Bloodworth fleet moved 10,000 miles to the right of their former position. Once in position, they had a different angle from the enemy position and hopefully were out of range of the minefield.

Admiral Bloodworth said, "Comm to all ships. Target the two enemy ships on either side of those just fired upon. Use the same missile adjustments and be ready to fire two salvoes; all ships target the two ships of the left with the first salvo, and the two ships of the right with the second salvo. Fire on my command."

The admiral waited a minute before speaking again. "All ships fire."

After both salvoes were fired, Captain Bloodworth ordered, "Start clock for time to second missile attack."

"Aye, ma'am, clock started for second missile attack."

* * *

Both the admiral and his captain looked at the first clock for the time remaining until their first attack missiles reached the three-targeted ships. Captain Bloodworth thought to herself, *Forty-eight more minutes. It seems like hours since we've begun our attack.*

When the captain turned to look at the admiral, he smiled and winked at her, which caused a warm comforting feeling to flow over her. She returned his smile and then concentrated on how the Bridge crew reacted to the stress.

Commander Becker, the admiral's chief of staff, was pushing a cart with refreshments among the Bridge crewmembers. Since he had no duties during the attack phase, he was doing this to keep himself busy. He could replace someone injured on the Bridge, but he wasn't thinking of that at this moment.

* * *

As the clock counted down its last minutes until their first attack missiles reached their targets, the tension racked up for everyone on the Bridge until suddenly the scanning officer said, "Explosions! Our missiles are being intercepted…one of ours got through, now two more; all three ships have now been hit. One has exploded, now another, and there goes the last. Sir, all three have been destroyed."

Rear Admiral Bloodworth said, "Now we will see how they react."

Five minutes later, scan said, "Contact! Fifteen enemy ships have launched missiles at our current location."

Captain Bloodworth said, "Start clock on when these missiles become ballistic."

"Aye, ma'am, clock started on this launch."

Ten minutes later scan said, "Contact! Fifteen ships have left their former position and are moving toward the next gate."

Admiral Bloodworth considered several possibilities before

making his decision. "Comm, to all ships, aim two salvoes to intercept the enemy ships when they are reversing thrust to slow before entering the next gate. Configure your missiles to shut down after 50,000 miles and to restart when they are 30,000 miles from target. I will send you the aiming point after its calculated. Stand by."

"Science Officer McBride I want to intercept them when they have been in reverse thrust for forty to sixty minutes. Calculate when we need to fire our missiles and the intercept point. Another factor is we may have to move our ships to avoid incoming missiles, which is now in sixty-eight minutes."

"Aye, sir, I will begin my calculations."

"Sir, we will have to delay fire until much later than the time we need to move to avoid missiles. I will calculate from a position 50,000 miles to our right if that meets your requirements?"

"Very well, I will notify fleet of our plans."

"Comm, to all ships. When we move to avoid incoming missiles we will use X-Ray2. We need a greater angle for our next salvoes."

Captain Bloodworth took a comfort break, along with all other critical Bridge stations, leaving it to their assistants to cover their absences. Ten minutes after the approaching missiles went ballistic, Admiral Bloodworth ordered all fleet ships to move to X-Ray2.

Science Officer June McBride verified the fleet's current location and that it fit her calculations before saying, "Admiral Bloodworth, the fleet needs to fire its missiles in thirty-six hours toward this intercept point."

Admiral Bloodworth said, "Start a new clock for thirty-six hours. Comm, to all ships. We will launch two salvoes in thirty-six hours aimed at the following coordinates. We will remain at our current location until we see the enemy leave this system."

The Bloodworth Fleet launched their salvoes at the scheduled time and then downgraded their Battle Stations condition to only a Battle Ready status. It would be about thirty-four hours before their salvoes reached the enemy, so until just before zero hour, conditions aboard the ships were near normal.

The Bloodworth family enjoyed their first normal sleep period in days. Hanna laid her head in her husband's arms. "Eric, your idea to hit them while they were decelerating was brilliant. They would have to break away in order to maneuver and that would preclude them from entering the gate, at least to the location they wanted."

He squeezed her firmly against his body. "Yeah, I don't think their normal commander made the decision to leave in this manner. Whoever made this decision didn't think it through."

"So, you think we made the right choice on which ships to target initially for the commander's ship?"

"I figured it was one of the centrally located ships and we lucked out."

"Honey, enough of this. Show me how much you love me and I'll try to beat you."

The next day the couple enjoyed a leisurely morning meal in their stateroom and was finishing their coffee before dressing, when the Battle Stations klaxon sounded. They quickly dressed and hurried to the Bridge.

XO Commander Conner said, "Ten enemy ships just transited into this system."

Admiral Bloodworth said, "Crap! How far apart are the two enemy fleets?"

Conner said, "The original fifteen have just started to decelerate and the new ten ships had 2.5 gravities speed as they travelled through the gate. They may join forces before heading our way."

Science Officer McBride just entered the Bridge when she heard Conner's statement. "Sir, it's possible that they may join together at our original target point, at least close enough that our missiles targeting program will be able to engage all of them."

Admiral Bloodworth said, "Check it out and give me your best estimate."

Ten minutes later McBride said, "Sir, the missiles will automatically restart in fifteen minutes and they will be close enough to acquire both groups of ships; however, the kill rate on the new group will not be as good as the ships decelerating."

Admiral Bloodworth said, "Its just luck we had those missiles there when we needed them. Let's hope for the best and see what happens when they deal with our surprise."

When the missiles restarted, there was an almost immediate reaction from the new group as they tried to form a defensive posture. The decelerating ships showed no change; it was as if they didn't see the approaching missiles. Ten minutes later it was much too late for the decelerating ships as the missiles swept through them like a sickle cutting wheat, before continuing on to attack the others.

When it was all over only three ships remained, and they were powerless. When their sensors detected the Bloodworth Fleet, they all self-destructed. The captain turned to the admiral and said, "We did it! We actually pulled it off."

Rear Admiral Bloodworth said, "Lt. Commander McBride please step over here."

McBride hurried over to stand before the admiral. "Yes, sir. Do you have a question?"

"No. However, you have earned a promotion. You now have the rank of commander and I'll want you on my staff as soon as I have a ship big enough to warrant it. It was your work as much as mine to get the results we just achieved and I'm going to put that in my report to Vice Admiral Randall."

"Sir, thank you sir."

CHAPTER 12

The Bloodworth Fleet returned to Earth about four months later. Rear Admiral Bloodworth, Captain Lundberg Bloodworth, and Commanders Becker and McBride were all summoned to report to Vice Admiral Randall.

When their shuttle left the UES Conquest, Admiral Bloodworth asked the pilot to make a pass near the shipyards where the new constructions were parked. Admiral Randall had hinted before they departed on their last cruise that he might have a surprise for him when he returned.

As the shuttle approached the parked ships, one stood out from the others because it was half again as large as all the other cruisers. Hanna gasped at its size. "Admiral, what is that ship? A Battleship?"

"No, I don't think so, but it's bigger than our cruisers. It's got to be a ship of our own design. When we see Admiral Randall I'm sure we'll get all our answers."

After they landed, the four were quickly transported to Space Headquarters. Instead of the Headquarters Building they stopped before a large outdoor amphitheater full of military and civilians, where they were told to exit their vehicle. Vice Admiral Randall met them and motioned Commander Becker to stay behind with him, as the others were escorted to the podium where they stood uncertainly until the Vice Admiral stepped before the podium.

"We are here to honor again a great hero of Earth in its battle against our enemy, the Xones. Details of the Bloodworth Fleet's latest battle with them will be posted so that everyone can wonder at their skill and bravery. Rear Admiral Eric Bloodworth is the first to be awarded the Star Medal for actions against the Xones. Captain Hanna Lundberg Bloodworth and Commander June McBride are each awarded the Silver Star for their actions during this same action. The UES Conquest as the lead ship in this action will receive a Unit Citation. All other ships and their crews of the Bloodworth Fleet will receive Citations."

Vice Admiral Randall turned to Rear Admiral Bloodworth and placed the Star Medal around his head, and then shook Bloodworth's hand. They then saluted each other before the vice admiral moved on to the next honorees. He then pinned the Silver Star on the tunic of each of the two officers, shook their hands after each presentation, and afterwards they saluted each other.

Vice Admiral Randall then returned to the podium. "Now I'm going to put the first recipient of the Star Medal on the spot by asking him to say a few words. Rear Admiral, please step up here." Bloodworth stepped up to the podium and looked out over the amphitheater filled with well-wishers. "Ladies and Gentlemen and fellow members of the Star Fleet. I did what every member of Star Fleet does when he meets the enemy. I tried to do him the greatest harm without undue risk to my own people. So far, I have achieved this goal and I will continue in this effort when I return to space. Thank you, and God Bless us all."

Vice Admiral Randall escorted everyone back to their transportation and they returned to the Space Port, where they followed Randall onto another shuttle. The shuttle took them back to the large new starship in parking orbit where they entered its docking bay. A marine guard met the shuttle and presented arms when the vice admiral stood in the doorway. Randall turned to Bloodworth and said, "Admiral Bloodworth, come see your new flagship. It's the first in its class, a Heavy Battle Cruiser, so its captain will have to find its plus and minus points. Come along Captain Bloodworth and greet your new ship."

* * *

For Hanna it was love at first sight. She'd never been enamored by an inanimate object before, but she was hooked by this ship. *What was she going to name this beast of a ship? She smiled to herself as she realized she had just named her personal Beast.*

She hurried to catch up with the group and asked Vice Admiral Randall, "Sir, has the ship been named yet?"

He smiled at her. "No, that will be your privilege."

She smiled as she proudly proclaimed, "Everyone, this ship is my Beast, the UES Beast."

Rear Admiral Bloodworth smiled. "Aptly named. She certainly looks like a Beast. Vice Admiral may the crew of the Conquest transfer to the Beast?"

"Yes, it only has a skeleton crew aboard now and I think you will find that you may not need any additional crew other than that found on the Conquest. You will find your armaments have been improved as well; also you have additional space for storage and crew quarters. Captain, I'm anxious to hear your comments after you've tested her in battle."

Later, after they toured the Beast, the shuttle returned Randall to Earth's Space Port. After saying their goodbyes to Vice Admiral Randall, the shuttle then returned to the Conquest where they received a huge welcome because of the honors bestowed upon their senior officers and ship.

When the officers made their way to the Bridge, Admiral Bloodworth said, "Comm to all crewmembers. Attention to the crew of the UES Conquest. I'm moving my Flag to a new bigger ship designated as a Heavy Battle Cruiser named the UES Beast. I've been given permission to transfer any or all crewmembers from this ship to the Beast. I anticipate that most of the crew will want to follow their captain to our new ship. Any that have reasons to stay on the Conquest please notify your Department Head. Rear Admiral Bloodworth out."

XO Betty Conner immediately came to Captain Bloodworth to ask her about the new ship. "Sir, just how much bigger is the Beast?"

"I don't know the exact dimensions, but its at least half again the size of this ship. A real beast of a ship, she added with a smile."

"Noo!" The XO said with a grin. "You didn't name it that because of her size?"

"Wait until you see it. Everything about it is bigger including its missile salvo of twenty tubes on each side."

* * *

A month later the UES Beast was fully manned and the crew was accustomed to their new surroundings. Their former ship needed a crew of 2,850. The Beast while considerably larger only needed 150 more crew due to more automation.

Weapons DH Commander Alice Beeker was in heaven with all the improvements in her department. A double throw weight in missile salvoes was just the beginning. She also had missile storage capacity for fifteen salvoes for both defense and offense missiles. Everything was automated from storage to the tubes, and if battle damage knocked out the automation, then they could be loaded manually as well. Half of the extra ship crew was for her department to handle possible battle damage.

The wattage of their defensive laser weapons had been doubled so that they were now effective out to 10,000 miles instead of their former 5,000 miles. This meant the lasers would be a formable offensive weapon if an enemy ship became close enough.

Rear Admiral Bloodworth now had a dedicated Fleet Commanders Bridge separate from the ships main Bridge. It could also be used to control the ship if the main Bridge was incapacitated. Captain Bloodworth would follow all orders addressed to the fleet or to her ship individually. Admiral Bloodworth would have the assistance of Commanders Robert Becker and June McBride. Both Bridges were buried deep within the center of the ship and were separated some distance from each other.

The experiment of relaxing the Space Fleet's fraternizing regulations was deemed a success and was now in full effect for all warp ships.

Now that the move to the Beast had been accomplished and the ship provisioned, Captain Bloodworth thought it time for her and her husband to visit their families. This last trip had been over a year and half for their families, while only about eight months for those aboard the star ships. They made arrangements with their families for times convenient for the visits and would leave the

Beast to arrive in Hamburg, Germany tomorrow morning.

This time Hanna had made arrangements with both cities for the arrival of a space shuttle. They both watched a monitor as they departed their ship and marveled at its magnificence as it quickly shrunk in size as the shuttle headed toward Europe. Forty minutes later they grounded at a small aircraft airport near Hamburg. They had made arrangements for police protection of the shuttle while the crew and passengers left the craft. Hanna's sister Lucy was waiting to drive them home, while the crew found their own transportation.

Lucy hugged her sister and Eric before they started driving. "Hanna, Clare made arrangements to visit while you're home. She said she's got to see this guy from America you've married."

Hanna shook her head at Lucy while grinning. "Not the guy who's one of the most famous men on the planet."

"No silly. Heck, you're almost as famous as Eric. She wants to see if he's really such a hunk in person."

"Lucy! He's right here."

"Oh, right. I keep forgetting he can understand what I'm saying."

Eric smiled at Lucy, who didn't appear sorry at all. "Hanna says that Clare has a child."

"Yeah, he's a three-year old – a real terror. Mom is about at her wits end. It would have been better if Jasper had come with Claire, but he couldn't get off work. Hey, I heard that you both got some medals, Cool!"

Eric asked, "Lucy, how's school?"

"I start medical school next month. Is there such a thing as Space Medicine?"

Hanna said, "By the time you graduate there will be. We have a small hospital aboard our new ship, the Beast."

"What! That's its real name? You named it, didn't you?"

"Well, I am its captain, so I got to name it."

Eric laughed. "Lucy, don't be too hard on her. It really looks like a Beast."

Lucy giggled some more as she shook her head. "Eric, I'd really love to see what its like aboard a starship."

He looked at Hanna and smiled. "Well, maybe something can be arranged on our next trip home. Wait a moment. How much time before school do you have?"

"Three weeks."

He asked Hanna, "What do you think? She comes with us to Missouri, then back to the Beast for ten-twelve days, and then we take her back to Hamburg."

Hanna thought about it for a moment, then said, "How about it Lucy, you'll get a taste of space and living aboard a star ship?"

Lucy pulled off the road and turned to look at them both. "You're not pulling my leg are you?"

Hanna smiled at her sister's excitement. "No, but for now we better keep this between us. Later, you may be able to show this as some Space Medicine training."

Lucy looked at them with such excitement she could hardly concentrate. Hanna said, "You want me to drive while you talk to Eric about the trip?"

"Yes, I can hardly see straight I'm so thrilled."

Hanna continued the drive home while Lucy sat in the backseat and talked with Eric. When the SUV stopped before her home, Lucy ran inside telling everyone she was going into space with Hanna.

Clare led her mother out of the house to welcome them. Hanna was ecstatic in her greeting with Clare. It had been years since they had last seen each other. Looking over Hanna's shoulder while hugging her, Clare whispered, "Is that hunk of a man a good lover?"

Hanna winked at her while saying, "You better believe it."

After all the greetings the Lundeberg's gathered the visitors luggage and went inside where they continued catching up on each other's news. Ian, Clare's young three-year old, made his presence known by running through the living room with a space ship in his hand. Upon seeing the visitors from space he had heard the grown ups talking about, he stopped before them with his mouth open in fascination.

He shouted, "Mama, they spacemen?"

Clare came over and sat on the floor with him in her lap. "Ian, they just now came down to Earth to visit us. They are your aunt and uncle. Just think, you have relatives who live in space."

"She ant and he unkle to me?"

"Yes, now go in the other room and play while the grownups

talk."

"Kay, bye ant and unkle," he said before leaving buzzing the space ship into the next room.

Hanna raised her eyebrow at her sister. "That seemed too easy."

"Yeah, let's cross our fingers," Clare said.

Lucy came down the stairs and sat down next to Clare. "Hanna, how much should I pack?"

Before Hanna could respond, her mother said, "You really are going back with them into space?"

Hanna replied, "Just for about ten to twelve days. She has to get back home to prepare for medical school."

Alice looked between her two daughters before saying, "Well, I guess she'll be in good hands and she's not going out there to fight someone."

Clare said, "Whoa, Lucy you're really going back with them into space?"

At her nod, Clare said, "I'm jealous. I get to stay here and raise kids while they have all the fun."

Hanna replied, "You wouldn't want to leave Ian and your husband. You have responsibilities here on Earth."

"Yeah I guess. Lucy, you better tell me all about your adventures when you come back."

"Oh, I will. Now Hanna, what should I pack?"

Hanna smiled at her eagerness. "Three changes of clothing and something fancy in case of a dinner party. You'll wear a standard ship suit while in the hospital."

Alice blurted, "So Lucy is going to learn medical stuff while she's on the ship?"

Hanna said, "Yes Mother. Learning space medicine may help her later in medical school."

Lucy left them and returned to her room to pack. The family continued their conversations and Eric and Hanna answered their questions regarding the medals they were recently awarded.

Clare said, "So those medals were for heroism in your latest battle with the Xones?"

Hanna said, "At the time we were more interested in killing them before they killed us. It worked out that we did an excellent job of destroying them."

Clare persisted, "So you weren't scared when they shot at you?"

"No, I didn't even consider them hurting me until after the battle was won."

"Hanna, you are a brave woman," Clare said and then sat next to her giving her a tight hug while struggling to hide her tears.

Eric said with a smile, "What about me? Don't I get a hug too?"

Clare said, "Is he like that all the time, looking for sympathy?"

"No, Eric is the bravest man I've ever known."

Clare responded, "Says the woman who loves him beyond all reason."

* * *

Two days later they were at the shuttle preparing to leave for Springfield, Missouri, Eric's hometown. Lucy was looking at the open shuttle door with stars in her eyes as they approached, then jumped back as a crewman appeared.

She was as surprised as Lucy, but recovered quickly and asked, "An additional passenger, Sir?"

Captain Bloodworth responded, "Yes, a VIP, my sister Lucy. She's going back to the ship with us for a short visit."

"Very good Ma'am, may I give you a hand with your bags Lucy?"

She handed over her bag and stood aside as the other two did the same. Once the doorway was cleared Lucy easily climbed aboard, followed by her sister and brother-in-law. Hanna pointed at a row of seats. "Take one of those and watch that monitor when we take off."

Lucy followed their lead as Hanna and Eric buckled up. The crewman shut the doors and notified the pilots that they were ready for takeoff. There was a muffled roar and suddenly they were pushed back into their seats by their extreme acceleration, as the shuttle seemed to leap into the air. Lucy watched the monitor in fascination as the ground shrunk beneath them until they passed through a cloud layer blanking out the ground entirely. Then even that sight shrunk until she was looking at the curvature of the Earth.

Hanna interrupted Lucy's thoughts. "It's fascinating isn't it?"

Lucy looked at her sister with wide eyes. "How can you get used to something like this?"

Eric smiled as he shrugged his shoulders. "You do though. It took me five trips to make it commonplace. Wait until we approach our ship later, that still gives me a thrill."

Lucy looked at the monitor again and noticed that they seemed to be getting lower. She turned to Hanna and asked, "How long does this trip take?"

"Not long, about forty minutes. It will take longer to get to Eric's home after we land."

Eric said, "My mother may be rusty with her German since she hasn't had anyone to talk to since her mother died. Start off slowly until she's comfortable with it. My father doesn't speak German."

They soon landed at the Springfield/Branson Airport near its old terminal where its tarmac wasn't used. Eric noted that they were being met with a reception committee as they approached touchdown.

Lucy asked, "Who are all those people?"

Hanna smiled at her husband. "They are here for Eric. They make it a big deal every time he comes home. You better stay aboard until they finish their reception festivities. You won't be able to understand what they say anyway, they only speak English."

"You understand English?"

"Yes, I used the learning machine on-board the ship. You'll have to use the machine to learn Universal, which is the language used aboard all ships."

The shuttle landed with barely a bump. The crewman quickly opened the door and stepped back, allowing Rear Admiral Bloodworth and Captain Hanna Bloodworth to step down to the tarmac. Immediately, band music started playing until the two reached a hastily provided podium. The Springfield Mayor stepped up to the elevated podium motioning for them to follow. The mayor gave a short welcoming speech, and then turned over the microphone to the admiral.

Bloodworth smiled at the gathered crowd. "Ladies and Gentlemen, my wife and I appreciate this welcome back to my home town. I don't get this opportunity as often as I would like. My fleet of ships has been fortunate to destroy the enemy when we find them. I now have an even more powerful weapon at my disposal, the UES Beast. Believe me that the name fits this ship and I expect good results. I am now anxious to visit my family, so if you will excuse me I must go."

The two left the podium and Hanna motioned for her sister to join them as they walked to Eric's family car that was sandwiched between two police cars. The crew and Lucy arrived with their baggage and once loaded they left in a convoy toward the Bloodworth home. The shuttle crew took a cab to wherever they wanted while the local police guarded the shuttle.

Once on the move Lucy looked around at her surroundings and said, "Wow, Eric you really get the royal treatment."

"I know. It's all my mothers fault. She has an in with the mayor who is only happy to cause this dog and pony show every time I come home."

Hanna giggled into her hand. "It embarrasses Eric, but he continues doing it for the PR it affords Star Fleet."

Adam, Eric's father, was driving and he chuckled, as he understood part of what was being said. "I've tried to tell Sarah, but she keeps saying that you deserve the recognition this gives you."

"I know Dad. That's one of the reasons I still do it. By the way, this girl I've brought with me is Lucy Lundberg, Hanna's sister. She can't speak English yet, so you'll have to talk to her through us."

"Tell her I'm glad that she is visiting. Maybe Sarah can talk to her."

When the convoy pulled into their neighborhood the police pulled off to the side so that Adam could drive into his driveway. They had just gotten out of their vehicle when their neighbors came over to wish the space heroes well. Sarah came outside to greet her son and his wife, when she stopped and asked, "Eric, who is this young woman?"

He put his arm around Lucy's shoulders. "This is Hanna's younger sister, Lucy. She's going with us when we go back to the ship. She's to start medical school soon and wanted to observe Space Medicine in action. She only speaks German, do you remember how?"

Sarah smiled at the young woman who was looking at her uncertainly. "Lucy, my German may be a little rusty, but hopefully you will understand that you are welcome in my home as part of

Hanna's family. Come inside so I can welcome you properly without the whole world watching us."

Lucy quickly moved to Sarah and they hugged before everyone moved inside. After everyone had been properly greeted, Sarah had everyone take a seat and tell her what adventures they've had since they were last here. Lucy quickly asked to use their toilet, which caused a run on the two available in the house.

While their quests were busy, Sarah prepared lemonade being mindful not to make it as tart as she preferred. Later, when they all had a glass of the tart drink, Sarah proposed a toast to future successful voyages. Lucy sipped her drink cautiously being warned by her sister. Liking the flavor, she drank down almost half before stopping and licked her lips in appreciation.

Sarah laughed, and then spoke in German, "That's someone who appreciates the way I make it. So there!"

Later, after they had a good talk, Lucy was helping Sarah in the kitchen while Eric and Hanna were upstairs in his old bedroom storing their bags and changing out of their uniforms. Sarah was quizzing Lucy about Hanna's favorite foods and her family. Soon they were fast friends and exchanging stories about each other's backgrounds. That evening Sarah and Lucy prepared a typical German dinner, much to everyone's surprise.

CHAPTER 13

They were back into the shuttle and were returning to the UES Beast. Lucy was looking at the monitor as the Earth's surface shrunk before her eyes, but then she was told to look at another monitor that showed several starships growing from a single white light to huge ships, with the largest one apparently their destination.

Lucy now appreciated why her sister named her ship the Beast. It was huge, and they were headed toward its side where a door opened before them letting the shuttle enter and softly settle. She looked at her sister who suddenly appeared very serious as she told her to stay inside the shuttle until after she and Eric got through the entrance routines.

She heard the ship playing its welcoming pipes and watched as Rear Admiral Bloodworth and Captain Hanna Bloodworth were welcomed aboard their ship. They both saluted the Flag and asked permission to board which was granted by a female officer. The female crewman tapped her on the shoulder motioning for her to leave the shuttle.

She jumped down and retrieved her bag before joining her family waiting on her. She followed behind as they led the way to an elevator where they dropped two levels. It was another twenty minutes before they arrived at their destination where Eric touched a buzzer and an Asian man answered the door.

When he saw who they were, he opened the door wide and gave

then a short bow. Eric said, "Yue He, this young woman is the captain's sister, Lucy. Can you fix a bed for her in our quarters for a few days while she visits?"

"Yes, sir, it will be done. May I take charge of your luggage?"

"It will be delivered here shortly. You may store Lucy's bag after she gives it to you. Please acquire several ship suits in Lucy's size. She will be working in the ship's hospital while staying here."

"Yes, sir. Lucy please stand over here while I get your measurements. You will require ship shoes as well, what is your size?"

After Yue He had gotten all her measurements he left the room. Lucy asked, "Who was that?"

Hanna smiled at her sister. "Yue He is our personal steward."

"Wow! Do all officers get one of those?"

"No, only the captain and if we have an admiral on board. Yue He was Eric's steward when he was captain. He's doing double duty with us."

"Wow, you guys have got it made. I don't need to take up your personal space, although this is really nice. You didn't mention this about your other ship."

"Our stateroom here is twice the size we had on our other ships. I've got to admit I really like the extra room. I need to talk to the doctor about having you watch or help in her department. She has control of everything in the hospital, so keep a low profile and don't piss her off. Before you do anything, you need to use the learning machine to be taught the Universal language. That's the only language spoken onboard ship. Do you want to learn English as well?"

"Yes please. I want to be able to speak to Eric's father. Maybe I can get some medical knowledge as well?"

"Very well, I'll get you on the schedule for the learning machine, and then I'll talk to Doctor Joyce Yutesler."

"Come with me, I might be able to get you started on the machine right away."

Lucy asked, "What about my clothing? Is this alright?"

Hanna went to her closet and pulled a one-piece white coverall out. "Try this on; it should work until Yue He gets you your own clothing."

When Lucy came out of the head, Hanna had her turn around

slowly, and then stand still. "The legs are too long; don't move while I mark them."

Using some quick stick tape she soon had the problem fixed. "Okay, now let's see about the learning machine."

As they were ready to leave, Eric said, "Honey, I'm going to the Admiral's Bridge Station, so I'll see you later."

When they arrived at the learning machine, Lucy got right in. Captain Bloodworth asked, "How long is her session going to be?"

"Ma'am, eight hours."

"Please escort Lucy to my stateroom when she is finished."

"Aye, ma'am."

* * *

Captain Bloodworth pulled her handheld out to check how to get to the hospital. She then reversed her course to the nearest elevator where she went up one level. Five minutes later she walked into the ship's hospital reception area.

The corpsman looked up from his game machine to find his captain looking daggers at him. His face turned white as he came to attention as he said, "Yes ma'am, how can I help you?"

"I need to see Dr. Joyce Yutesler."

"Yes ma'am, her office is right over there. She has no scheduled patents, but she may be on her rounds."

"Do you have anyone to guide me to where she might be?"

"Ma'am, I'm not busy. I'll place a notice on the counter that I'll be right back."

As they were walking down the hallway, she asked, "What's you rank and name corpsman?"

"Ma'am, Petty Officer Third Class Derek Geeslin."

"Is this as busy as you normally are?"

"Ma'am, yes ma'am."

"Petty Officer, I'm curious what illness your patients are generally checked in for."

"Ma'am, it's usually broken bones."

"Accidents or fights?"

"Ma'am, so far its just accidents."

They approached double doors that he opened by pushing a knob on the wall. There was one patient in a room with ten beds. A woman wearing a white lab coat was playing chess with the patient. She looked up when Geeslin said, "Captain on Deck!"

She quickly stood at attention as the Captain approached them. Bloodworth said, "At ease doctor."

Captain Bloodworth looked at the female patient and smiled. Hanna picked up the patient's chart and said, "It appears you are ahead in your game Lance Corporal Haden. Marine, how did you break your foot?"

"Sir, it's my own fault. We were doing a practice rappelling of enemy boarders when it happened. I just stepped wrong."

"Doctor, is she going to be alright."

"Ma'am, the new bone healing machine is doing great on her ankle; she'll be on crutches tomorrow and back to duty in a week."

"Wow, that is fast. Doctor, I have a problem that you may be able to help me with. Can we go back to your office to discuss it?"

Doctor Yutesler looked at her in surprise, but nodded her head. "Yes ma'am, please come this way."

When they got back to her office, she closed the door and motioned to a chair by her desk. After they both sat, the doctor asked, "What can I do for you?"

Captain Bloodworth then explained about her younger sister wanting to be a doctor aboard a starship. "She's starting medical school next month and wanted some basic understanding of Space Medicine. Right now she's in the learning machine being taught Universal language, English, and the medical devices on this ship."

Dr. Yutesler said, "Her native language is German?"

At Captain Bloodworth's nod, the doctor continued, "I foresee no problem in taking her under my wing, especially if we remain in dock. She'll be here, what ten, twelve days?"

Suddenly, the Battle Stations klaxon started sounding. They looked at each other in alarm, and then the captain began to run toward the Bridge.

When Captain Bloodworth entered the Bridge her arrival was noted when the marine guard yelled, "Captain on Deck!"

She responded with, "At ease, continue as before."

Her XO, Commander Betty Conner, looked relieved that she was back when Hanna announced, "I have command, what is happening?"

"Sir, Admiral Bloodworth stated that the Home Fleet has

detected an incursion from another warp gate and that they were investigating. We and the rest of our fleet have been ordered to prepare to break orbit to support the Home Fleet."

"How many of our crew is on shore leave?"

"Sir, about a quarter of our crew – 500 crew members, including twenty-eight officers."

"Any DHs?"

"Sir, only one Department Head - Food Service, is missing."

"Very well, I'm going to assume every fleet ship is in the same condition as we are. The Beast is shorthanded, but able to fight. Comm, get me Admiral Bloodworth."

"Admiral Bloodworth here. What is your status?"

"Sir, this is Captain Hanna Bloodworth. The Beast is short 500 crew, but able to answer to the helm."

"Very well Captain. Please question each DH for any critical short comings including provisions and report back to me."

"Aye sir. Captain Hanna Bloodworth out."

"Comm to all Department Heads. Report all critical short comings including provisions to the captain ASAP."

Fifteen minutes later the captain had received answers from all the DHs. She made a note of who were the last responders. She turned to her XO. "Betty we seem to be ready to sail, how about backups to the Bridge crew?"

"We are missing three, but because of cross training we can function at 100 percent."

"Comm to Admiral Bloodworth."

"Admiral Bloodworth here."

"Sir, the Beast is ready to sail."

"Very good! Currently, we have twenty of our twenty-four ships ready to sail. The Beast will break orbit in fifteen minutes and join the Home Fleet at the following coordinates."

"Aye sir. Good luck to us all."

Fifteen minutes later the UES Beast broke orbit leading nineteen ships away from Earth to meet whoever had entered our system. Thirty minutes later scans reported the ten ships were of Katz origin. The Home Fleet passed on a message from the Katz ships that they needed to speak to Admiral Bloodworth ASAP.

Three hours later the Beast was close enough to receive communications directly with the Katz ships. Admiral Bloodworth looked at a monitor showing the surprised face of Admiral Killa, who started the conversation. "Admiral Bloodworth how fortunate we are to find your fleet here. We need your ships to help defend a new race of people we found in the direct path of the Xones. They are about the same evolutionary level as you were when we gave you the ability to defend yourself. I would like to transfer to your flag ship to consult on how best to achieve our goals."

"Admiral Killa, at our present location and speed we will be at nil speed with you in twenty-eight hours assuming we both reverse course in fourteen hours. I anxiously await your arrival. Admiral Bloodworth out."

"Comm to Home Fleet."

"Sir, Commodore Schmidt of Home Fleet here."

"This is Admiral Bloodworth. All our ships are short crew. We left five ships on Earth when we sortied, but expect them to eventually join us here. Would you ask for volunteers from your ships to join our fleet for this emergency? They would rejoin Home Fleet upon our return to Earth. You could replenish your people who volunteered from the crew we left behind."

"Admiral, I would be happy to help in this emergency. When I have numbers for you I will get back to you. In the meantime my fleet will join you at your rally point. Commodore Schmidt out."

Captain Hanna Bloodworth eventually checked her time and realized that Lucy would soon be finished with her time in the learning machine. She thought for a moment before saying, "Comm connect me with Marine Major Blevins."

"Ma'am, Major Blevins here."

"Major, my sister, Lucy Lundberg, is aboard using the learning machine. She is currently a civilian. Please send a female marine to her location and escort her to my stateroom when she is finished with the machine."

"Aye, ma'am, do you want her to be informed of the ship's current situation?"

"Yes, please. I don't know how long it's going to be before I'm available to talk to her. Please have the marine escort take her to the chow hall. She's been in that machine eight hours."

"Aye, ma'am, I'll take care of it. Major Blevins out."

* * *

Lucy was a little unsettled when they opened the hatch of the learning machine. She didn't have a sense of the time she spent in the machine, but when helped out of the machine she did feel hungry. A very tough looking female marine stepped up to her and asked, "Is your name Lucy Lundberg?"

"Yes, did my sister send you to escort me?"

"Captain Hanna Bloodworth asked that I fulfill that task. She said that you were in the tank for eight hours and you'd need food."

The marine held out her hand to Lucy, who took it and shook a hand she'd never felt so callused in a woman. "My name is Gunnery Sergeant Victoria Hull and I'm also tasked with bringing you up to date on the condition of the ship. We have just been downgraded from Battle Stations caused by a fleet of starships entering our solar system. They turned out to be friendly, the Katz. Apparently, we are going to help another alien race endangered by the Xones."

"I'm not sure I understand. Are you saying that this ship is going to leave this system to go help other aliens?"

"Yes, but before we leave we're trying to get volunteers from the Home Fleet to help run our ships. We left almost a quarter of our crews on shore who were taking leave."

Lucy rubbed her stomach. "You said something about getting me something to eat. I think I can eat a horse the way I feel."

"Okay, follow me. I think I could eat something too."

Lucy closely followed the Gunnery Sergeant whose pace almost made Lucy run to keep up. They stopped before a large room with a small line of people waiting to fill their trays with food.

Hull said, "Pick out what I do. I've eaten here before and know all the good food."

Lucy picked the same items as the Gunnery Sergeant, but not every item, nor the size of the portions. After they were seated, she asked, "How can you eat so much. If I did I'd be a real porker."

Hull laughed. "Honey, the way I exercise I'll burn this off in no time flat."

"Oh. I'm sorry. Maybe I should exercise too."

"Honey, if you are part of the crew you'll be required to exercise every day. The captain runs with us grunts every morning and she keeps up. Of course the admiral is running with her and she has to keep up with him."

Lucy grinned as she pictured in her mind her sister running with her husband. To get that image out of her mind she said, "I originally was going to work with Doctor Yutesler while here to gain some insight into Space Medicine before I returned home to start medical school. That plan is dead now. Maybe I can work for her and get some practical experience while I'm here."

"You want to be a doc? That's cool. Doctor Yutesler is good people."

After eating, the marine escorted Lucy back to the captain's stateroom. Yue He let Lucy inside and showed her the clothing and shoes he had acquired for her. She decided to take a nap while waiting for her sister to return.

CHAPTER 14

Captain Hanna Bloodworth felt she had the time to check on how Lucy was doing, so she had her XO take over the Bridge. As she approached her stateroom she looked at the time and realized it had been almost five hours since her sister had been released from the machine.

Yue He answered the buzzer and held his finger to his lips as he ushered her inside. She found Lucy asleep on the couch, but when she started to move past her to the head, Lucy raised her head and muttered, "Hi sis, you taking a break?"

Hanna sat down next to Lucy and asked, "Are you feeling alright, no adverse reaction from the machine?"

She gave Hanna a wan smile before responding. "You mean the tank, that's what Gunnery Sergeant Hull called it. No, I'm okay. What am I going to do while I'm on-board?"

"The real problem is the uncertainty of how long this trip is going to take. It can be a few months or maybe a year or more. That means when we get back to Earth it will be twice the time we were in Space."

"That means I won't be starting medical school for awhile."

Captain Hanna Bloodworth thought through a possible solution before saying, "Lucy, you can't function properly aboard this ship as a civilian. I propose that I give you the rank of Ensign while aboard ship. You would be Doctor Yutesler's assistant and have quarters with the other young officers. To fit in you need to take classes in military etiquette and learn how to live the life of an officer in the Space Navy. When we get back to Earth you will have the option of staying with the Navy on detached duty while attending medical school or being released as a civilian."

Lucy looked at her sister in gleeful wonder. "Wow! You can arrange that? That's the best deal I can imagine happening. I accept, o'boy do I accept!"

Hanna looked at her sister's glee and smiled. "Okay, in a few hours I'll take you to Personnel and get you started. I hope you don't live to regret your decision to join the Navy."

Hanna took a shower and changed into a fresh uniform before she took her sister to breakfast in the Officers Mess. Lucy was not very hungry, but had coffee and a pastry while watching Hanna eat a large meal. "Gunnery Sergeant Hull eats large meals too. She said she burns it off with daily exercise."

Hanna smiled. "Regulations require that all crew exercise daily, and that includes officers. So you better get into the habit. I usually run with the marine women at six a.m. every morning in storage bay 3B. Those women are tough so don't give them any sass."

She then took Lucy to Personnel, explained what she wanted done and if there were any problems to contact her. Hanna hugged her sister and said, "I probably won't see you for a few days because you're going to be very busy, but I'll check up on you to see if you're surviving. So good luck!"

Captain Bloodworth quickly made her way back to the Bridge. She took command from her XO, who then took some personal time off.

The Beast was now doing reverse thrust slowing their speed to null for their meeting with the Katz. The clock showed another ten plus hours before the meeting. Captain Bloodworth was happy with the way the ship was performing, and so far nothing major had broken.

She checked with her DHs on how they were performing with their short crews. So far, they haven't had any major problems. Admiral Bloodworth hasn't yet received any word from the Home Fleet on volunteers for replacements; however the five fleet ships left in dock were now thirty hours from our meeting place. Reportedly, they were carrying some of the Battle Fleets' missing crew.

Suddenly, there was an announcement, "Admiral on Deck."

Bloodworth said, "As you were."

He walked up to her Command Chair and asked, "How's she performing?"

She smiled at her husband. "Like a kitten. No major problems. However, I hope we get more crew replacements from volunteers and late comers."

Admiral Bloodworth said, "I wonder what these new aliens are like. This may turn out to be a big can of worms."

She told him about her solution with Lucy and he responded, "Hey, that seems like the best solution to a problem I caused by suggesting she visit us aboard ship."

"Hey, I thought it was a good idea at the time."

"Yeah, maybe her being here will have other positive effects. I guess I had better get back to the Admiral's Bridge, the clock is down to thirty minutes."

The shuttle carrying Admiral Killa arrived forty minutes later. Both Admiral Bloodworth and Captain Hanna Bloodworth were present at the shuttle bay to welcome her. She and three of her officers greeted the Earth's senior officers and then moved to a conference room to discuss matters.

Admiral Killa had one of her officers display a star chart to show where Earth's system was located, and then where the new aliens' system was located; and finally where the approaching Xones were last encountered.

Bloodworth asked, "How many warp gates is our system from the new aliens?"

Admiral Killa said, "Four gates that will take you over three months to reach."

Admiral Bloodworth shook his head in disappointment. "Admiral that would put a strain on our food provisions. We only carry enough for a year and that doesn't leave us much margin. How far away are the Xones from the new aliens?"

"About the same distance as you are, but they don't know their location yet."

"You indicated earlier that the new aliens are not yet space capable. Do you have one of those space yard ships you gave us?"

"No, it will take at least six months for one to reach them. We need you to delay the Xones until it gets there."

Admiral Bloodworth shook his head in frustration. "If we can't resupply from the new aliens we will be limited to three months on station. That's not going to be enough time for us to do any good. Even if your ships brought us additional food from Earth, your ten ships will not carry enough to last us more than three months. Can you think of a solution?"

Admiral Killa asked, "How many ships are in your Home Fleet?"

Bloodworth looked questioning at Captain Hanna Bloodworth. She replied, "I believe they now have twenty ships."

Bloodworth said, "I think I understand what you are suggesting. Your ten plus ten of the Home Fleet ferrying food supplies to the new aliens. That should give us the margin we need until the ship builder arrives. Any Earth new builds will be taken by the Home Fleet until we return."

Admiral Killa smiled at Admiral Bloodworth. "Can you get this plan approved by your Star Headquarters?"

"I'll send the request by a message torpedo. We should get a response in twelve hours."

"Very good admiral. While you are doing that I would very much like Captain Hanna Bloodworth give me a tour of this wonderful ship. What have you named it?"

While the captain was providing the tour, Admiral Bloodworth was composing their plan to help the new aliens. When the message was sent he went looking for his wife and Admiral Killa. While walking down a hallway, he encountered a familiar looking young female Ensign who gave him a smart salute. He stopped and smiled at Lucy. "Ensign Lundberg you look smart in your uniform. Have you been assigned quarters yet?"

"Sir, yes, sir. I share a room with another officer who I haven't met yet, but I've been issued all my clothing and kit that I've stored and I was on my way to my duty station to meet Dr. Joyce Yutesler."

"Ensign, walk with me. I want you to meet someone interesting who your sister is hosting a tour of the ship."

"Sir, I would be happy to accompany you." She turned around and followed a half step behind the admiral as he continued his quest.

Bloodworth consulted his handheld before they took an elevator up two levels. Ten minutes later they found the captain and her charge, Admiral Killa. When they approached them, Ensign Lundberg gave both officers a smart salute. Admiral Killa realized that the young officer looked a lot like the captain, when she asked, "Admiral, who is this young officer?"

"Until your fleet showed up she was a civilian. Captain Bloodworth's youngest sister was visiting the Beast hoping to gain some knowledge of Space Medicine before starting medical school. May I introduce Ensign Lucy Lundberg, a new crewman assigned to the ship's hospital?"

"So, you have no interest in driving a war ship, but instead want to heal any injuries its crew suffers. That is a noble task you have set for yourself."

"Madam, thank you madam. All Earth is a little space happy, but I'm even more so because of Hanna's position as captain of the largest ship in the fleet and the battles she's participated in."

"Yes, they both have gained a following even among our own Navy, and they don't even know about their most recent victory and this magnificent ship. The name of the ship brings to mind something that waits to spring out at the enemy. It makes me shiver with anticipation until we have some like it too."

Bloodworth smiled. "I'm sure that Vice Admiral Randall will provide you with one if you let him know how much you desire one of the Beast's twins."

Captain Bloodworth asked, "Admiral Killa, would you like to adjourn to my stateroom for tea and refreshments?"

"Ah, I very much would like to see what you have done for your personal space, and tea would be perfect. Ensign, can you join us?"

Admiral Bloodworth said, "Yes, she would be happy to join us."

Twenty minutes later, Steward Yue He answered the door and bowed for them to enter. Admiral Killa took two steps inside and stopped while looking around the room that was easily twice that of the other Cruisers. It also had a large seating area and a dining space. "Yes, I would very much enjoy a ship like this as my Flag Ship."

Captain Bloodworth led the way to a large couch and three

matching chairs, where she offered the Katz Admiral her choice of seating. While Admiral Killa was settling back onto a soft chair, the captain ordered the steward to provide tea for everyone and make some sweet snacks available.

Later, after everyone had been served tea, Admiral Bloodworth asked Killa how their battles with the Xones were progressing?"

"Better, much better, but not as well as you have brought the war to them. We are using your tactics which has confounded them, but they are now changing their tactics as well."

"Yes, at our last battle they were lying in ambush at a gate. When we sent a probe through to see who might be there, they fired a salvo of missiles through the gate following a message torpedo sent back to us. The missiles were easily destroyed without any damage to us and we killed the ship that fired at us, but this was definitively a change in their tactics. If your ships are not sending probes through the gates before entering them you are likely going to be ambushed."

"I heard that your fleet destroyed thirty ships in that battle. You have done very well for such a young fleet against an enemy who has been operating hundreds of years without much opposition."

"Yes, but I have a feeling that we are forcing them to change their tactics. Future battles may be harder to win."

Admiral Killa turned to Ensign Lundberg. "Ensign, tell me about your family. Are there other military members in your past?"

Lucy nodded her head. "Neither of my parents were, but now two of us are. There have been two world wars in the last 100 years, so it's likely that others in our past were in the military."

Killa asked Bloodworth, "How about your family admiral?"

"I'm from America and we went to war about 300 years ago to gain our independence.

We have been fighting ever since to retain that independence and helping others in our world to gain their own freedom."

"So, your cultures have been developed by conflict. Your world populations have seen conflict for many years and learned how to survive despite it."

Admiral Bloodworth asked, "Does this new world you've found have a similar background?"

The admiral appeared uncomfortable, but answered. "Their appearance is more similar to you than us. They didn't appear to trust us as their savior, but more like an overlord. They have war weapons, but apparently have been at peace with each other for over 400 years. They have a space station, but no space ships capable of leaving their system. We were the first aliens to approach them and they seemed not to understand the threat the Xones represent to them. This is the reason we came for your help."

Bloodworth asked, "What name do they call themselves?"

"They use several, but the most common name is Peacekeepers. Yes, I can see that you agree that we have a problem with these people."

The Home Fleet arrived and Commodore Schmidt reported that they had 500 volunteers ready to transfer to their fleet. Admiral Bloodworth thanked him and his crews and asked which of his ships he should send shuttles. After getting this information shuttles began distributing the crew to where it was needed.

Ten hours later, the Bloodworth Fleet's remaining ships arrived with additional crew that was ferried to where they belonged. Admiral Killa remained aboard the Beast to guide the Bloodworth's Fleet of twenty-four ships to the system containing the Peacekeepers.

Eventually, Vice Admiral Randall gave his permission for Bloodworth's plan and Earth's Battle Fleet began its journey toward the warp gate, while the Home and Katz Fleets started their return to Earth to fulfill their portion of the plan.

Later, after transiting their first gate they headed toward the nearest Gas Giant Planet to replenish their reaction mass fuel before traveling toward the next gate. During this down time, Captain Bloodworth escorted Admiral Killa toward the ship's visiting VIP stateroom, which was almost as spacious as the Captain's. The Katz Admiral's Steward had already arrived and met them at the door.

Admiral Killa was happy with her stateroom as she exclaimed, "This ship just gets better the more I see of it."

Captain Bloodworth smiled at the Admiral. "If you need anything or wish to join me on the Bridge just ask the marine stationed outside your stateroom."

CHAPTER 15

Ensign Lundberg was working under the supervision of Doctor Yutesler. They only had two corpsmen, so the hospital crew was the smallest on the ship. The only patient today had been a Petty Officer Second Class from the Engineering Section who came in with a second-degree burn on his left arm.

The doctor stood back and watched Lucy handle the injury. The male Petty Officer was trying to flirt with Lucy while she applied a soothing lotion to the affected area. She smiled at him before saying, "Petty Officer, this pip on my collar indicates that I'm an Ensign, so unless you want to be reported you better treat me with the respect due my rank."

"Sorry Sir, I thought you were a corpsman. I meant no disrespect."

"Very well, I thought that might be the case. Now apply this lotion daily and try to keep it dry. Come back if you develop a rash from the lotion."

After the Petty Officer left, Lucy looked at her Mentor for any suggestions regarding her performance. Yutesler smiled and then used her hand to smother a laugh. "I thought he was going to wet himself when you told him you were an officer. But, what was that business about a rash?"

"Well, he was pretty good looking. I was just wondering what hoops he would jump over to see me again."

She shook her head. "Don't do that. There are plenty of officers if you want a date. Messing with an enlisted man will bring both of you nothing but trouble. Besides that, remember whom you are related to. Don't cause her any embarrassment."

"Yes, ma'am. Thanks for the advice," she said with a red face.

That evening she arrived in her berth just as her roommate started to leave. Lieutenant (jg) Amy Fursa, who worked in engineering, stopped and asked, "Do you want to join me at the Officers Club?"

She said, "Sure, just let me freshen up and we'll be on our way."

They were soon sitting together with a beer in front of them, but were disappointed that there were no young officers in the room. Lucy asked Amy where she was from.

"Oh, don't let the last name fool you. I was born in Kansas City. My family originally came from Turkey. Are you any relation to the captain?"

"Don't freak out, I'm her younger sister."

"So you're from Germany?"

"Yeah, I was going to get some exposure to Space Medicine and was in the learning machine when the Katz Fleet showed up. By the time I got out of the tank the ship had already left Earth, so I'm stuck until we return to Earth. Since I'm going to be a doctor after I graduate from medical school, Hanna suggested I serve here and get a detachment from the Navy to attend school when I return to Earth."

"Talk about being in the right place and time. You really lucked out. You start your Navy career early, get some training, and then attend medical school on the Navy's dime."

"I didn't think about the Navy paying my way. Hey, that's really great!"

After they finished their beer they decided to go to the Officers Mess for Dinner. Amy saw two other officers she knew and they were invited to join them. They were both officers of Amy's rank in the same Engineering Section.

Chuck Williams and Bradley Hackler introduced themselves and where they worked. Lucy said, "My name is Lucy Lundberg and I work in the hospital as a doctors assistant."

Bradley asked, "Why are you only an Ensign?"

Amy Fursa said, "Lucy is the sister of our captain and she was aboard as a civilian inside the learning machine when we left

Earth. She wants to be a doctor, so our captain gave her the opportunity to join the Navy, gain some experience, and later when we return to Earth she can get a detachment to attend medical school."

Chuck said, "You're the captain's sister?"

"Yeah, but if you think I can put in a good word for you, forget it. Hanna believes everyone should forge their own future. The only reason I'm an Ensign is because as a civilian I can't function on a military vessel. However, my plan was to join the Navy after medical school. I wanted duty aboard a starship."

Chuck smiled as he said, "Wow! Talk about falling into it and coming up smelling like a rose. Can I touch you so maybe some of your luck rubs off on me?"

* * *

Three months later they transited through the warp gate into the Peacekeepers' system. Their home planet was the second planet from their sun and had two small moons orbiting it. They called their planet Aqua because it had even less land mass than Earth, making it another water world.

The fleet approached Aqua and made orbit, while communicating with its world government. Admiral Bloodworth asked to speak with someone who would have the power to make a treaty with them. After a day, they agreed to make available a person who would speak with them and the coordinates where they may be picked up.

Commander Robert Becker, the Admiral's Chief of Staff, would be on the shuttle that picked up the delegation from Aqua. Twelve hours later the shuttle left the Beast for the trip down the gravity well to the coordinates on Aqua. When their craft settled on a hard surface that appeared to be an airfield, several land vehicles met them.

Commander Becker stepped down from the shuttle and waited empty handed. He noted that the gravity on this world was similar to Earth's. One person soon exited the lead vehicle and walked toward him. They each gave the other a short bow. Becker said, "I'm Commander Becker and will accompany your delegation to our Flagship, the UES Beast."

The individual who appeared to be a female, answered, "I'm the delegation's interpreter. You are not the same race as we had contact with earlier. Are you a male of your species?"

"Yes. We've had contact with the Katz for several years now and are their allies against a common enemy. That is why we are here now. I intend no disrespect, but you appear female, am I correct?"

"Yes, what is your rank in these treaty negotiations?"

"I am Rear Admiral Bloodworth's Chief of Staff, and yourself?"

"Just an interpreter. I will gather the delegation of six. Can your craft handle this many?"

"Yes. We are ready to leave if you are."

As the interpreter left he tried to gather his impressions of her appearance. She was his height, slim of build and the body structure of a female human. She wore loose clothing that concealed her form, a face and coloring that resembled an Italian heritage. In short she looked like a human, a beautiful human female.

The interpreter returned to the lead vehicle and talked for about ten minutes with its occupants, when suddenly the occupants of two vehicles exited and followed the interpreter back to the shuttle. Commander Becker helped the people into the craft and once everyone was seated, with the help of the interpreter, demonstrated the use of the seat belts. When everyone was buckled up, he pointed at the monitors, saying, "You should watch their journey through the planet's atmosphere and to the ship where the discussions will take place."

He asked the interpreter to determine if everyone was ready, who nodded her head and said, "We may proceed."

Becker told the crewman to shut the door and then told the pilots to takeoff, whereupon the shuttle lifted off the ground in a smooth steady acceleration, while Becker watched their faces as they were pushed back into their seats. When they were above the atmosphere the monitors showed the twenty-four ships of the fleet with the huge Flagship at the center of the formation.

The interpreter asked in awe, "That big ship is our destination?"

"Yes, that is our largest ship in our fleet, the UES Beast."

"Beast, does that have the same meaning in our language?"

"Probably, it means a large dangerous animal, a Beast."

"Yes, it looks like you describe. What does UES mean?"

"That is our planet's designation for starships. United Earth Ship Beast."

"So, your ships from Earth, your home planet, represent all your peoples?"

"Yes, until the Katz arrived, it was not so. Now we are combined in our efforts to defeat the Xones, who are destroyers of everyone not themselves."

"You have personally fought the Xones?"

"Yes, our commander, Rear Admiral Eric Bloodworth is a great tactician. Even though the Xones' ships have similar weapons, he has managed to defeat them in every battle where they have met, without any losses to ourselves despite being outnumbered."

When the shuttle approached the side of the ship, the visitors watching the monitor gripped their arm rests in panic until the shuttle bay door opened for them. When the shuttle settled onto its pad and its engine stopped, they seemed to relax. The shuttle door opened to pipes playing and the announcement, "Delegation from Aqua arriving."

Becker quickly stepped down to the deck to help the others leave the craft. When everyone was grouped together they followed Commander Becker toward Rear Admiral Bloodworth and Captain Hanna Bloodworth who were waiting near the entrance to the ship. Becker saluted the Flag and asked permission to Board. Captain Bloodworth smiled as she granted permission and then turned to the delegation and asked, "Who is your leader?"

The Interpreter stepped forward and said, "Our leader is Sire Grantsman, who does not speak your language. I am the only person in the delegation who has this ability."

Captain Bloodworth said, "We have a machine that can teach him our Universal language in four hours, if this would speed up our discussions."

The Interpreter consulted with their leader for a few moments, before turning back to the captain. "Our leader would like to learn the Universal language and have the others in the Delegation follow along by the use of our Interpreter."

Captain Bloodworth responded, "Commander Becker can escort Sire Grantsman to the machine while the others will be shown the room where the discussions will be held."

* * *

The parties entered the ship before separating into two groups. Commander Becker consulted his handheld to find the quickest path to the machine, and then motioned for the other two to follow him. Fifteen minutes later they were at the room containing the learning machine. After the technician programed the machine, Sire Grantsman was helped into the machine and connected before the lid was closed.

Commander Becker turned to the Interpreter and asked, "What is your name. I can't call you the Interpreter all the time."

She looked at him in surprise a few moments before nodding her head. "Very well, my name is Mae Fieldspire. Do you have a first name?"

He looked at her in surprise, and then said with an embarrassed smile, "My first name is Robert, Robert Becker. Are you married or mated with anyone?"

"No, no attachments. How about you? Any attachments?"

"No, not anymore. I was seeing someone before this assignment, but being on a starship is not conducive to maintaining a relationship."

"How long are your trips outside your system?"

"Anywhere from six to fourteen months, but for those waiting on Earth it would be doubled."

"I don't understand. What do you mean by double the time away from Earth?"

"Time is slower while in warp space, so it generally equates to about double the time in space to time on Earth. Six months in warp space equals twelve months on Earth."

"Oh, that would be terrible for the people left behind on Aqua. How do you manage?"

"Not well. Generally, people find relationships onboard the ship they serve. Time is constant for them."

* * *

After Sire Grantsman left the tank, Commander Becker led the pair to the conference room where the rest of the Delegation was waiting. Admiral Bloodworth addressed the head of the delegation when he entered the room. "Sire Grantsman welcome to the meeting. Are you feeling well and do you understand my words?"

"Yes admiral, I understand you and I feel well with no ill effects from the machine. Now, what do you propose?"

"The benevolent Katz when they first made us aware of the danger the Xones represented to all other peoples, offered to arm us with the same weapons they themselves used against the Xones. They informed us that this race would not abide the existence of any other race and destroyed all they encountered, whether a threat to them or not. They told us that they had encountered us previously, but at the time thought we were too aggressive, but now considered us a good ally against the Xones. Their own efforts were ineffective against the Xones. We accepted the challenge and have defeated the Xones handily in four battles without any damage to our ships. They prefer to attack immediately if they encounter an opponent of lessor numbers, and withdraw when their opponent has a stronger force. The Katz stated that the Xones are of reptile origin, which we have verified."

"I should add that in no instance have the Xones attempted to parlay before attacking. We believe our best defense is a strong offense, and we offer you the same deal the Katz gave us. Ships to defend your system and the capability to build more as needed."

Sire Grantsman said, "We are a peaceful world and have no desire to harm our neighbors, even if they are disrespectful. I can't believe anyone would attack us without provocation on our part."

Admiral Bloodworth nodded his head. "I thought you might have this idea. We have people like you on our world too. Others of us who do not wish them harmed protect them. Your beliefs work for you until someone else comes along and attacks you because you are an easy target. If you won't help yourself when warned of the consequences, then why waste our resources defending you."

Grantsman's eyes widened in surprise, "You would leave us defenseless against this horde?"

"No, we offered you the ability to defend yourselves. If you don't have the will to defend yourselves, then you're not worth saving."

"Our people are not aggressive, how can we find people to man your ships if they don't have the will to kill our enemies."

"I can record a meeting with the Xones fleet and show how they react to what they assume is a weaker opponent. Do you think that will bring you volunteers to man your ships?"

"That would depend on how the Xones react. I would like to witness this meeting as well."

"What size of ship do you use in system? Could it fit into a Shuttle Bay?"

The delegation quickly consulted one another and Grantsman answered, "Yes, they are all about the same size and we believe one would fit inside."

"Very well, does the entire delegation wish to observe or only you?"

Grantsman looked at the others and started to speak, when Mae Fieldspire raised her hand, saying, "I wish to observe."

"Very well, it will just be the two of us."

Admiral Bloodworth smiled. "Please compose a message so that we have the use of one of your space ships for this demonstration."

"Will sending the message with the delegation returning to Aqua be acceptable?"

"Yes, but haste is recommended."

Soon a shuttle was returning the remainder of the delegation back to Aqua. Two hours later the Beast received a message that a ship would be ferried to them. Four hours later the ship was helped into the Shuttle Bay and locked down. Its crew was available for technical support when they converted it to remote control from the Beast.

The Bloodworth Fleet soon broke orbit and headed toward the gate closest to the Xones territory. Admiral Bloodworth elected to replenish the fleet's reaction mass at the nearest large gas planet before heading toward the gate. It was going to be a three-day journey, so their guests were shown guest quarters. Mae Fieldspire asked if she could share quarters with one of the officers, rather than be alone in a quest room.

Captain Bloodworth smiled as she thought of someone who might enjoy sharing her quarters with an alien. She asked comm to contact Ensign Lundberg.

"Ma'am, Ensign Lundberg."

"Ensign, please report to the Bridge ASAP."

"Ma'am, yes ma'am."

Fifteen minutes later an out of breath Ensign reported to the Bridge. The captain stepped down from her Command Chair and looked at her sister. "Lucy, would you do me a favor? I have a female alien who would prefer staying with someone rather than in a quest room by herself."

"Let me guess, I'm elected as her roommate. What do I do with my other roommate?"

"She'll have to stay elsewhere for the duration, and she's already been moved."

"Do you want me to fetch her from someplace and show her around?"

"Yes, that would be wonderful. Her name is Mae Fieldspire and she already knows Universal. She's now taking a nap in my stateroom, so gather her up and have fun."

"Ma'am, yes ma'am, thank you ma'am. I'll be on my way now."

* * *

Lucy took her time walking to the captain's stateroom to catch her breath after her run to the Bridge. When she pushed the buzzer, Yue He answered the door and let her inside. She asked, "Where's the girl?"

"In the head. Maybe you should check on her, it's been over thirty minutes?"

Lucy knocked on the door and asked, "Mae! Are you alright?"

"Yes. I'm sorry, but could you help me in here?"

Not knowing what to expect, Lucy entered the head and found her sitting on the toilet. "What's wrong?"

"I did my thing but couldn't find any tissue. Where is it located?"

Lucy briefly considered playing a joke, but instead told her how to access what she needed. After Mae stood and rearranged her clothing, Lucy introduced herself, "I'm Ensign Lucy Lundberg and you're going to share a room with me."

"Oh, am I putting you out by my request?"

"No, but you did cause my roommate to be moved, and I couldn't hardly turn down my sister, who's the captain."

"Lundberg, your last name is Lundberg, which is a family name you share. Oh, this is even better than I hoped."

"You're not going to kidnap me, are you?"

"Mae blushed, "No, nothing like that. I'm hungry, is it alright if we go someplace to eat?"

"Sure, but are you certain what we eat might not agree with you?"

"Oh, I didn't think about that. What do you suggest?"

"Leave it to me. I'll help you order."

When they got to the Officers Mess they found a table away from the other officers eating. "Mae, what kind of meat do you eat?"

"Meat…do you mean like animal flesh?"

"Yes, we eat beef, pork, poultry, and fish. You live on a water world, so you must eat fish?"

"Yes, I like fish from the ocean and fresh water."

"Okay, we'll try fresh water fish. I'll order a variety of things and you can try small portions and see if you like it or in case it doesn't agree with you."

After ordering, Mae took a small sample of fish and tasted it by holding a small portion inside her mouth for a few moments before swallowing. Lucy asked, "How was that?"

"It tasted like fish."

"How do you feel?"

"Hungry. I'm going to try something else. These mashed potatoes look good, what's the yellow stuff on top?"

"Probably butter, that's made from milk of cows. Do you have cows?"

"Yes, but if it's the same type of animal, we call them noms. I'll try a little. Hey this is good, what is it?"

"It's a root vegetable. Any adverse reaction?"

"No, I think I'll order fish and mashed potatoes and fill up on that."

Soon they were both eating and enjoying their meals. Mae asked, "Do you know a Commander Robert Becker?"

"Sure, he's the admiral's chief of staff. What about him?"

"He met the delegation when he came to take us to the Beast.

He said he was unattached. Does that mean he currently does not have a girl friend?"

Lucy paused with a fork of food at her mouth. She placed it back onto her plate and gave Mae her full attention. "You find the commander attractive?"

Mae's face colored as she flushed in embarrassment. "Am I that obvious?"

"Well, you are a woman and you asked if he's available. To me that means you have a sexual attraction toward him. Are you sure you're physically compatible? After all you each were born on different worlds. You might not be able to make babies."

"I know! Sometimes I think I'm crazy. I've only met him once, yet I continue to think about him with this awful yearning. You people don't have powers over others, do you?"

Lucy frowned at her new friend. "No, not that I'm aware of anyway. Have you felt this way with your own people?"

"No. Not even a twinge. Do you think something's wrong with me?"

"Yes, it sounds like you're in love."

"How about you? Have you loved anyone?"

Lucy shook her head. "No, not even puppy love. But I have hopes of finding someone that I'm compatible with."

"What's compatible mean?"

"You know, have the same interests and can't live without them being close to you. Like that."

"Oh. Robert Becker told me that people aboard starships don't age as fast as others who stay behind. If we were lovers I'd have to travel with him or die a slow death while waiting for his return."

"Did you know that my sister and the admiral are married?"

"Is that like being mated?"

"Yes, they are both the most famous people on our planet."

"Oh my, so they found a way to stay together. That's something to consider. Lucy, what do you do on this ship?"

"I'm a doctor's assistant. I plan on attending medical school when we return to Earth."

"You want to be a doctor. What about later?"

"After finishing school I want to come back here to this ship, if possible."

"You like ship life?"

"I love it, even if there are more women than men aboard. I'm going husband hunting when I come back after school."

"You want to find a mate eventually?"

"Yeah, there are a lot of dreamy looking men aboard. Surely I will eventually find myself a mate."

CHAPTER 16

The Beast approached the third gate from Aqua where they stopped and sent a probe through to see if the enemy was in the next system. While waiting the ship went to Battle Stations. The message torpedo returned and reported a small fleet of ten ships that were about 600,000 miles away and were heading toward this gate at a speed of 2g's. The Admiral ordered the Beast to immediately transit the gate at 2g's where it remotely launched the small Aqua ship toward the approaching fleet.

The Beast then reversed thrust to stop their advance. The small unmanned Aqua ship was broadcasting messages toward the approaching fleet in an attempt to get some kind of response.

Suddenly, one of the advancing ships launched a salvo of ten missiles at the Aqua ship. Sire Grantsman asked, "Why did they fire at our ship? It's small and unarmed, no possible threat to them."

Captain Bloodworth ordered, "Helm move the Beast 50,000 miles to the right of the missile track and rotate ship to attack position."

Admiral Bloodworth said, "The missiles aimed at your ship will become ballistic after 100,000 miles. The clock for that is down to eighteen minutes, after which I will remotely move the Aqua ship out of the missiles' track. I'm curious at what they will do then."

After the Aqua ship moved from the enemy missile track the

admiral watched for their response. When ten minutes expired without a response, he said, "Maybe the Commander of that fleet is concerned what our ship is doing down here by the gate. If I was him I'd shoot a spread my way to try to illicit a response."

Five minutes later the ten ships each launched a salvo of ten missiles at the Beast. The admiral said, "Captain launch five salvoes with the standard early cut-off and restart when 10,000 miles from enemy. Allocate the missiles equally among the fleet."

"Aye sir. Comm connect me with Weapons."

"Weapons, Lt. Commander Beeker reporting."

"This is the captain, at my command launch five salvoes of missiles at enemy evenly disbursed, standard cutoff at 80,000 miles and restart when 10,000 miles from enemy. Reply, when ready."

"Sir, Beeker reporting. Launch is ready."

"Very well, you may launch missiles, I repeat launch missiles."

The ship quivered slightly as it fired twenty missiles, then the ship spun placing its starboard side missiles' ports facing the enemy where another quiver was felt. This was repeated until the ship had completed five salvoes, a total of 100 missiles, a number equal to those fired at the Beast.

Captain Bloodworth said, "clock on incoming becoming ballistic is twenty minutes, clock on our missiles impacting enemy is fifty-eight minutes."

Sire Grantsman said, "That's amazing! This one ship fired the same number of missiles as their ten ships. Admiral, you have an amazing ship here."

Mae said, "Sire, remember those ten ships have the ability to maneuver that one ship cannot match."

Commander Becker smiled at her. "Very good. If you were their Commander, what would you do next?"

"I'd move my ships out of the line of fire that is coming at me, but apparently he doesn't know about your missiles ability to maneuver. If he doesn't move far enough out of the missiles' track he's still going to get hit."

Becker replied, "From our experience, they don't move away from the missiles' track. After several battles they start to copy our tactics, but not the missiles turning off and then back on. I hope we can continue with this tactic. You have a talent for tactics, if your world decides to put together a fleet of your own you should apply for a captain's position "

Captain Bloodworth said, "The incoming missiles are now ballistic, so its time to move position. HELM, maneuver ship upward 50,000 miles."

"Aye sir, maneuver ship upward 50,000 miles."

"Sir, maneuver was successful and ship is now 50,000 miles from its previous position."

Admiral Bloodworth looked at the clock timing the missiles arriving on target. "Less than thirty minutes and they haven't taken any evasion movements. Each of their ships has a total of ten missiles in five waves targeting them. If we have any early kills, then extra missiles will attack the remaining ships."

Commander Becker went over to the admiral and softly said, "Watch Mae Fieldspire's face."

Mae was watching the clock count down and her face was changing into a feral expression of a huntress waiting to ponce upon her enemy. Becker said, "She's a killer. We want her in the fleet regardless of any bias against women in command."

"I agree. I wonder if women are their more aggressive sex?"

The attacking missiles arrived with flashes of explosions against both defensive missiles and ships, then a much brighter flash that could only be a ship, followed in quick succession by three more, then a short break before the second wave hit them which immediately killed two more ships. The third wave arrived with only half of the enemy left and the remainder of the enemy disappeared with a flash.

They watched as the fourth and fifth wave passed through them with only an occasional flash noted as a missile hit debris. Admiral Bloodworth said, "Captain, send a message torpedo back though the gate to have the fleet join us here. Also have the Trojan Horse reverse course so that we can return it to Aqua."

Becker edged close to Mae and asked, "Was this exciting for you?"

Her face was still red with excitement. "Oh yes. I can see why you do this. I love the excitement of the chase and using tactics to defeat your enemy. From what you and the Katz say, this enemy is numerous and has expanded over a vast area. This presents us with endless hunting potential as long as we can stay ahead of them in tech and tactics. However, I would want our ships to be like this one, is that possible?"

"This one is the first of its kind. Our people modified the original Katz designs, so why not. I'm sure we can give you the plans for it and afterwards maybe you can figure out improvements."

Mae gave him a puzzled look. "You called our ship a Trojan Horse, what did you mean?"

"Back in our world's early history, two countries were fighting each other and the Trojans built a hollow wooden horse. They filled the horse with soldiers and rolled it before the city gate, hoping they would bring it inside as a tribute. They did and after everyone slept, the soldiers left the horse and burned the city. It was a tactic to win a battle."

"I like that story," she said. "Did it really happen?"

"I'm not sure, it was recorded. But, did it happen, who really knows? However, it is a good example of tactics in action."

"We don't have examples like that. I'm sure we must have had such examples, they just weren't written down."

Admiral Bloodworth asked Sire Grantsman, "Sir, do you think your people will support a fight against the Xones after watching a recording of this battle?"

Grantsman looked at Mae Fieldspire in fascination and a little awe. "If there are more people like her we couldn't build enough ships to meet the demand. All we can do is try and see what develops. Fieldspire! You are going to help me sell this proposal. I think we need to sell it to save our world from these evil jackals."

After the Bloodworth fleet gathered, they advanced to the debris field to take recordings of the carnage, including recovering bodies of the Xones to show the people of Aqua what their enemy looked like.

Before returning to Aqua the Beast recovered the Trojan Horse to return it home. Mae Fieldspire was thinking of a story to tell her people that would use the Trojan story to her own benefit.

When their fleet arrived back in Aqua orbit they found both Katz and their own home fleet ships already in orbit with additional food supplies for an extended stay. The two peacekeeper people aboard the Beast had already proven that they could eat the food from Earth, at least in the short term. Tests would have to be conducted to determine if the exchange of food met all the requirements needed by both the peacekeepers and humans.

* * *

Two months later, after a blitz campaign by the leaders of Aqua they achieved victory in convincing their people they needed to mobilize to fight against the Xones. Before the Katz shipbuilding yard arrived, they were training crews for ships not yet constructed. When the first crew was trained, Admiral Bloodworth gave them one of the Home Fleet ships to train in. They left the Department Heads behind to make sure no accidents happened, but the rest of the human crew was transferred to other ships.

The ship was renamed the UAS Trojan Horse by its Captain, Mae Fieldspire. Commander Robert Becker was her advisor as they left orbit for maneuvers. After a month they returned to Aqua orbit and its Captain and XO were asked to attend a meeting aboard the UES Beast.

* * *

When her shuttle touched down in the Beast's Shuttle Bay, she could hear pipes playing welcoming her aboard. Captain Fieldspire, her XO, Commander Jorge Platerman, and Commander Becker stepped forward and saluted the Flag, before asking for permission to Board.

After being granted permission, Commander Becker led the way to the ship's conference room where all the Bloodworth Fleet Captains were gathered. When Captain Fieldspire entered the room, everyone stood and clapped their welcome. Admiral Bloodworth motioned for her and her XO to join him at the podium.

She was dressed as they were, having adopted the military trappings of the Earth Star Fleet with minor differences. The main difference was that their uniform was black instead of blue, and they wore a beret instead of a hat. In addition, the ship's captain wore a white beret, while the other officers wore black. In their Navy, everyone knew who the ship's captain was by the white beret. Admiral Bloodworth called everyone to attention.

"Captains, I wanted you to recognize someone who is the first ship's captain of her planet. She is someone who is going to lead her planet's Navy in the fight to defeat the Xones in her sector of space. She is innovative as well. She wears a white beret so that everyone knows she's a starship captain, one to envy in her Navy. I believe our own Navy should adopt this distinction and will recommend the change when we return to Earth. I give you Captain Mae Fieldspire of the Aqua Space Navy."

Captain Fieldspire smiled as she took the podium. "Fellow captains, I thank you. I have the distinction of being a captain in a one ship Navy. However, that will change as our Planet builds its own Star Fleets; a Home Fleet and a Battle Fleet like your own. Admiral Bloodworth has been persuasive in making us aware of the danger from the Xones. I do appreciate that your fleet has our backs until we get up to speed. Our one ship fleet will eventually become one to reckon with and the Xones will feel our wrath if they approach too closely. I thank you for your help."

As she stepped away from the podium she received enthusiastic applause from her audience. Admiral Bloodworth asked, "Captain, is there anything we can provide you before I reduce my force here and return to Earth for shore leave and resupply?"

"Sir, I'm not privy to your ultimate plans, but when is the construction ship due to arrive?"

"At any time now according to Admiral Killa. We won't pull any ships out until the Katz arrive."

"Sir, I've really appreciated having Commander Becker as a source of information and advice while I'm learning my job. Is it possible for him to remain longer with me?"

"I would have to ask him if he's willing to stay detached for a longer period. How long do you need him?"

"Six months to a year, if possible."

Admiral Bloodworth looked over to where Becker was talking with others and said, "Commander Becker can you step over here?"

Commander Becker approached them and smiled at the captain. "Yes, sir, what can I do for you?"

Bloodworth started to ask his question when he suddenly realized the almost longing gaze the captain was giving Becker. He took Becker by the shoulder and walked him out of her earshot.

"Commander, Captain Fieldspire is asking me for an extension of your time with her. How do you feel about that?"

Becker looked quickly at her and as their eyes met it was almost like an electric spark between them as he quickly inhaled air into his lungs. Becker turned and looked into his admiral's eyes. "Sir, I don't know what's come over me with her. I'm like a bug to a bright light with her and I think she feels the same about me. Is this love?"

"Son, I felt the same about Hanna. Stay with her as long as you like. If you decide to be their commodore I'll put you on extended duty. I hope you find as much happiness with her as I have with my wife. Go on over and tell her you love her and you'll stay as long as she wants."

"Sir, thank you very much."

Bloodworth watched as Becker walked up to Fieldspire and took her hand as he spoke. Suddenly, she put her arms around his neck and they kissed before everyone. There was some clapping and applause before they broke apart, but maintaining their cool they held hands and bowed to them before moving to a corner and talked with their heads close together.

The first graduating class of Aqua Space Marines was last week and the Trojan Horse would receive its allotment of 900 Marines in two weeks. Aqua had no standing army; so fifteen human Gunnery Sergeants started a Marine Boot Camp. Surprisingly, they had more volunteers than openings and there was now a waiting list.

The Katz construction ship arrived with an escort of fifteen ships, ten of which would be used by the Aquas as crews were trained. Captain Fieldspire was pleasantly surprised to find that all new constructs would be of the Beast's class. It would take at least six months to get construction going and the first ship completed.

Admiral Bloodworth decided that the time was right for half his fleet to return to Earth for resupply and shore leave. They would return in six months to relieve the remaining half. Commander Becker also remained behind as Aqua's Star Fleet advisor. Captain Fieldspire was lobbying for him to join her Navy as an on-loan commodore.

Admiral Killa joined Admiral Bloodworth and Captain Hanna Bloodworth on the Bridge as the Beast and twelve Cruisers left Aqua orbit. The Katz Admiral said, "You have done well to bring these people into our cause against the Xones. I stayed out of their view because we looked too strange for them to trust our motives. However, they were so similar to you that their first captain mated with your Commander Becker. I am curious how this relationship will fare."

CHAPTER 17

Slightly more than three months later they were back in Earth orbit. Admiral Killa transferred to one of her ships, but before leaving she patted the ship's hull and said, "Admiral Bloodworth I'm going to be traveling in a ship like this when I see you next."

He saluted her and said, "Good fortune to you and your new ship."

Rear Admiral Bloodworth shuttled down to Star Fleet Headquarters to report to Vice Admiral Randall. After reporting to the admiral he noticed that he was sporting another ring on his jacket.

"Admiral Randall, congratulations on your promotion. When did this happen?"

"Almost nine months now. It's been my career goal, now what have I to seek?"

"Well, for one, the defeat of the Xones."

"Spoken just like a fleet admiral."

Admiral Bloodworth smiled uncertainly at him. "Yeah, when pigs fly. Do you think we can get approval to lend Commander Becker to the Aqua Navy?"

Admiral Randall smiled and shook his head. "It's not up to me anymore. The new fleet admiral has that authority."

Bloodworth's face paled as Randall's words registered. "They jumped me from a low Rear Admiral to a Fleet Admiral? How is that possible?"

"Well, for one, you've been doing the job ever since you were a Commodore. We only have one Battle Fleet, yet you indirectly supervise the Home Fleet, and now have your fingers into another world's fleet. You deserve it and we need your authority to match your responsibility. We haven't had a fleet admiral since WW 2, so here are the cuffs and stars. Wear them proudly as you deserve them."

Fleet Admiral Bloodworth stared blankly at him for a few moments, and then shuddered as a heavy weight settled upon his shoulders. "Yes, sir. Please let the board know that I appreciate the confidence they have shown me. Now, I really need a chief of staff to help me."

Admiral Randall gave him a list of names. "Any of these five commanders will make an excellent chief of staff."

"Which of them is immediately available and close by?"

Randall took the list back and then consulted his computer. Commander Chandler Hall is located in this building, second choice is Commander Diana Williams, also nearby."

"Can you arrange an office where I can interview them this afternoon? I would like to be in proper uniform before the interview."

Admiral Randall smiled and commed his yeoman, who made the arrangements for an office and appointments with the two candidates. He again thanked Admiral Randall before he left for the quartermaster's office.

After being properly dressed he went to the Communication Building and commed his wife. "Captain Bloodworth speaking."

"Honey, they promoted me to Fleet Admiral!"

There was dead silence for a long count of three, but before he spoke again, she said, "What! Did you say Fleet Admiral?"

"Yes Dear, I was as floored as you are."

"Okay, okay, what changes is this going to require. Five Stars...I'll have to look up what we need to do. Oh honey, you got promoted five grades to fleet admiral. This is hard for me to adjust my thinking. Is there anything you need me to do?"

"Well, I'm going to interview for a new chief of staff. Tell Lt. Commander June McBride to arrange a bigger room for my staff.

I'm going to need maybe three more people for a five person staff."

"Honey, don't worry about that. Your chief of staff will do that for you. If you pick a woman, she better not be pretty."

"Yes dear. There's no one as beautiful as you."

"That's the response I was looking for. See you later."

Bloodworth decided to go to the Officers Club to have lunch and kill some time. When he arrived, he caused such a stir he regretted his decision. Biting the bullet, he asked the OIC for a private room, who quickly obliged. While waiting for his lunch order to arrive he looked around the room and found today's newspaper. He'd been out of touch for so long that he wanted to see what was happening. His lunch arrived with as much fanfare as you would have expected for a person of his high rank. He looked at his chef salad with expectation. On-board ship anything fresh and green hadn't been seen in months unless it was ship grown. Since he had another hour before his first appointment, he savored his alone time with his salad.

Finishing his meal, he scanned the newspaper looking for any mention of starships
and found that his fleet was expected to arrive in orbit today. There was nothing about his promotion, but he didn't really expect it. He signed his chit and decided to walk slowly toward his first appointment. Outside the building where he was heading sat a female Commander on a park bench. She sat with her eyes closed seemingly enjoying the sun.

He sat at the other end of the bench and watched to see a reaction, if any. Three minutes passed before she said, "If you sat there to try to pick me up, you're out of luck. I'm just divorced after a messy marriage and I'm not interested."

Bloodworth replied, "How about a job as my chief of staff?"

Her eyes opened wide in panic as she stared at Bloodworth. "Crap, I'm sorry admiral. I must be out of my mind to say what I did without even looking at you."

"You are Commander Dana Williams aren't you?"

"Yes, sir. Can we please start over? I would be ecstatic to be considered for the position as your chief of staff. My God, you're a fleet admiral! I didn't know we had a fleet admiral."

"We didn't until a few hours ago. This position requires that you serve aboard a starship that may be away from Earth for many months. Apparently you are recently divorced. Do you have children or any attachments that would make such absences problematic?"

"No sir. You must be Rear Admiral Eric Bloodworth – they just now bumped you up five grades to fleet admiral – that's unheard of in this modern Navy. Only in wartime have we had that rank."

"You got it in a nutshell. How about it, do you want the job?"

"Sir, what happened to your previous chief of staff?"

"He stayed back in another star system to help them develop their own fleet to fight the Xones."

She looked at the man who in a very short time had grabbed all the headlines with his spectacular battle victories against the Xones. "Did your wife warn you about picking a pretty woman?"

"Yes, but I told her she was beautiful and had nothing to worry about."

She looked at this hunk of man flesh and shook her head in frustration. *Why couldn't her husband been more like him?* "Sir, I would be happy to be your chief of staff."

"Very good. Your first assignment is to cancel my next interview with Commander Chandler Hall. Report to the UES Beast shuttle tomorrow at 10:00 hours with all your gear and be prepared to hit the ground running. Any questions?"

"Sir, no sir."

"Very well. As a point to consider, you have only one other person on your staff. Think about what you need to fulfill your job position."

"Yes, sir. Thank you sir."

CHAPTER 18

Fleet Admiral Bloodworth's shuttle arrived with great fanfare. When the shuttle door opened the sound of the welcoming pipes somehow seemed sweeter. He stood in the door looking at a double line of marines standing at attention, with his captain standing at its end.

Eric sucked it up, standing tall before taking a step down and walking toward the love of his life. He could see tears in her eyes as he stood before her and saluted the Flag, and then asked for permission to board. She granted permission and they walked the short distance into the ship where a marine guard turned his back to them and blocked the view of others as the admiral and captain embraced and passionately kissed.

After they broke apart, he took his finger and gently wiped a tear off her cheek and softly said, "How was it kissing a fleet admiral?"

"About the same as kissing a rear admiral. Did this promotion come completely out of the blue?"

"Yeah. I almost passed out when Randall dropped that surprise on me. I've got another surprise for you. I picked out a pretty woman for my chief of staff who's recently divorced. Is that good or something else?"

"I'll tell you after I talk to her. Honey I trust you, but if I consider her a threat I'll kick her butt off this ship."

"Babe, let's go to our stateroom where we can converse privately."

The following day was eventful with the expected arrival of the admiral's new chief of staff. Lt. Commander June McBride had appropriated a nearby storeroom to the Admirals Bridge for the chief of staff operations room. Office furniture and equipment was still being added when Admiral Bloodworth entered. McBride caught sight of him and yelled, "Attention on Deck!"

"Belay that." He responded.

"Lt. Commander I see that you've gotten this room almost ready for action. Good work; my chief of staff left the ground at 10:00 hours and should be here shortly. Go down to shuttle deck H3 and help her aboard."

"Sir, yes, sir. I'll leave now," McBride said as she hurried out of the room.

He noted that the far end of the room was enclosed with a clear material and contained a large desk and chair. Behind the desk were two flags, the Earth Flag and the Star Fleet Flag with Five Stars.

Bloodworth smiled as he wondered who had put that Star Fleet Flag together so
quickly. The work party had just brought in the last of five desks that were arranged in two rows of two facing each other. One desk was facing the others and the Admiral's office. Behind this desk was a counter that blocked access to the room. Outside the room were two armed marines. He considered that McBride had done a good job, but he'd see what Commander Williams thought when she arrived. Bloodworth went down the hall to the Admirals Bridge where he found an officer he didn't recognize.

The officer came to attention when the Admiral walked through the door. "Who might you be, Lt. Commander?"

"Sir, my name is Arthur Nguyen. I'm your comm officer when at Battle Stations."

He smiled at him and said, "How long have you been aboard the Beast?"

"Not long, I'm a transfer from the UES Skipper. Captain Bloodworth said I'd be a better fit here than on her Bridge."

"You've had a chance to review the comm station?"

"Yes, sir. It seems like standard equipment and is in working order."

"Very well. My Chief of Staff Dana Williams is reporting for duty soon. Why not come down to her duty office and wait for her arrival? Follow me."

They had just walked into the office when Williams and McBride arrived together. Bloodworth made introductions and then Dana Williams looked at the incomplete office. She pointed at her two officers and said, "Why don't you two take a seat while I consider what we have here."

Admiral Bloodworth said, "Commander Williams I'm heading to the Bridge to talk to the captain, comm me if you need anything."

When Bloodworth arrived at the Bridge, the marine sentry called out, "Admiral on Deck!"

He replied, "As you were."

Bloodworth moved to were Hanna was sitting in the Command Chair talking to her XO, Commander Betty Conner. After the XO left Bloodworth said, "Commander Dana Williams arrived and is assessing what needs to be done. What's the story on Lt. Commander Nguyen?"

"Oh, you've met him. He transferred here from the Skipper because of some disagreement between himself and a female Commander. Apparently, he's good at his job but I didn't have a vacancy in his specialty, while you did."

"Do you think I should stick my nose into the beef between him and the Commander?"

"Not unless he complains to me or you. Eventually, I want to have a woman-to woman talk with your chief of staff, but not until she settles into her job."

"It's going to take us two months to rotate our ship crews shore leaves before we can return to Aqua. Have you taken care of Lucy?"

Hanna turned to him and frowned with sadness. "Yes, I promoted her to Lieutenant (jg) and placed her on detached duty to her medical school in Berlin, whose next term starts in a week. She wears her uniform, gets paid, and Star Fleet pays costs of the school. All she has to do is make good grades, graduate, and spend another four years aboard a ship with Star Fleet doing her internship and duties as a Navy officer."

"Was she happy to leave the ship?"

"Not really. I think she was really enjoying herself here."

"Maybe we can get her back here when she graduates."

"God, I hope so. I miss her already."

"I checked with Fleet Construction, and they are currently constructing thirty percent of their production in the Beast Class. The Home Fleet picked up ten smaller ships to replace the ones we borrowed as well as one Beast Class for its Commodore. We keep the ten borrowed from Home Fleet, plus four new Beast Class ships. We still need to exchange crews from the borrowed ships for those who want to travel in starships."

The admiral thought a moment. "That gives the Battle Fleet five Beast Class and thirty-five standard size ships. I have to figure out who gets what portion of the remaining ten standard sized ships. It's only fair that Home Fleet gets half of the ten. That gives the Home Fleet one Beast and twenty-five standard ships. The Battle Fleet will have five Beasts and forty standard ships."

Hanna replied after a moment of thought, "Home Fleet will need another Beast when they split their ships between the two gates."

"Yes, and they need at least another twenty ships to properly defend Earth. I think I'll give them another Beast now and I'll let them know that they will get the majority of the new constructs until they get their twenty ships. So, Battle Fleet is down to four Beasts. I can split Battle Fleet in half, giving them each two Beast Class Heavy Battle Cruises and twenty Cruisers. Each of these Battle Fleets would be a formable foe when they encounter a Xones Fleet, even if slightly outnumbered."

She shook her head in frustration. "Do you have someone in mind for the commodore position of the other Fleet?"

"Not a clue. I'm going to put my new chief of staff on that problem. Before I split the fleet, I'll have her recommend the top three candidate's from among the forty ship captains."

"Don't include me in that selection. I want to stay with you."

Fleet Admiral Bloodworth grimaced. "I'm sorry dear, that was a good catch. But you would be excellent in that position except for that one reason. I better go see how Commander Williams is doing putting her section together."

As Bloodworth approached the Admirals Bridge area he immediately noted additional security. There was now marine security at the Bridge door as well as the office. When he entered the office, the marine said loudly, "Fleet Admiral on Deck!"

Everyone immediately rose to attention until he said, "As you were."

He stood still and looked for any changes in the room since he left. Instead of two rows of two desks, there was now a loose circle of desks around a central desk. The counter desk at the room's entrance remained. He walked toward his office at the back of the room and said as he passed the others, "Commander Williams, please follow me."

He entered his office and sat behind his desk while Williams entered and shut the door, then advanced and stood at attention before his desk. "Sir, how may I help you?"

"Commander, I have your first task. I plan on dividing the Battle Fleet into two entities. We currently have four Heavy Battle Cruisers, three not yet crewed, and forty Cruisers. I want your section to cull performance reports and other data to arrive at what you consider the best three candidates of Battle Fleet's captains for the position of commodore of the Second Battle Fleet. You should start with the forty Cruiser captains, then add the three Heavy Battle Cruiser captains as they are named. Do not include this ship's captain as she has already declined. Any questions?"

"Sir, what is my time limit?"

"ASAP! But no later than a month. If all captains of the Heavy Battle Cruisers haven't been named within that time frame, submit your conclusions regardless of that fact."

"Sir, yes, sir. Is that all?"

"No. I have another minor job that you may be able to work on while doing the other. While at Aqua, their Space Navy's first selected captain came up with uniforms similar to our own except their uniforms were black instead of dark blue, and instead of a cap they wore a beret. What I thought was significant was that the captain's beret was white instead of black like the others. I would like all Space Fleet personnel begin to wear a dark blue beret except for the ship's captain, who would wear a white beret."

"Yes, sir. Sir, I noticed we have two extra desks in the office. Does this mean we have a manning staff of five?"

"Yes. Talk to me first if you think you need more than five."

"Yes, sir, thank you sir. I'll get right on these tasks."

Williams quickly left the office with tasks to perform. She sat at her desk thinking, *important tasks that I'll need additional help on. Now whom can I get to help me?*

She turned to her staff and told them what they were going to do and then asked, "Whom do we know in Personnel that can help us?"

Fleet Admiral Bloodworth knew several of his ship captains personally, so he commed Captains' Inez Macchi, Vlad Pavlova, Allison Collins, Marcus Frank, Christopher Eiberger, and Drew Melton to meet with him tomorrow at 07:00 hours for a breakfast meeting on the Beast.

He took the list he had compiled and handed it to Commander Williams, saying, "These six captains are meeting with me tomorrow for a breakfast meeting to fill the three slots for captains of the Heavy Battle Cruisers. I want you there as well to observe and give me helpful hints to ask them questions as needed. My picks may be good candidates for commodore as well."

Commander Williams smiled at her Admiral. "Yes, sir, I'll be there. What dining room is it going to be?"

"You arrange it and the menu for 07:00 hours."

"Yes, sir, I'll get right on it."

After he returned to his office, Williams turned to McBride and said, "You arrange it. I don't even know where the Officers Dining Room is."

McBride replied, "It's almost time for lunch so let's all go together and I'll show you around. Commander, have you been assigned a room yet?"

"Yes, it's probably in this packet they gave me when I arrived. Let's see, here it is – room 3176 and a code."

McBride said, "You're on deck three, room 176. The code is to gain access to your room. That little device there, you can use it to find things like your room or a person. Just push that button and talk at it with your question. Everyone ready, let's go eat, I'm hungry."

The next morning, Fleet Admiral Bloodworth dressed carefully and then asked Hanna if he looked presentable for his captains?"

She looked up from her makeup mirror and said, "Turn around slowly, wait, stop right there."

She got up and approached him saying, "Now turn a little more,

Stop!"

When he stopped his motion she came up to him and put her arms around his neck, giving him a passionate kiss. She wiped her lipstick off his lips, saying, "You're perfect, go get them."

He arrived at the Officers Dining Room at 06:30 hours to find Commander Williams already present speaking to three ship captains. Captain Inez Macchi spoke as he walked up, "Admiral Bloodworth, you have a very impressive chief of staff here. She appears to know my complete history."

He replied, "Yes, you should have seen her when we first met. She impressed me so much I hired her on the spot."

"Well, I'm not surprised. What are we here for? Something big I bet."

"I'll wait until everyone is here; oh, here comes the last of them. Captain's let's take our seats and while we wait for our food to be served I'll tell you why I called you together."

"Captains, our Battle Fleet is getting three more Heavy Battle Cruisers. You six are going to try to convince me that you are my best pick for one of them. Of course, if you'd rather stay on your current Cruiser, I'll understand. Now compose yourselves and after we eat I'll ask you some questions."

The six individuals looked at each other in confusion, then understanding. Steak and eggs was the main dish and they attacked it with gusto. Later, while they were drinking coffee and considering each other, Admiral Bloodworth said, "captains, who wants to go first?"

Captain Inez Macchi held up her hand, "Ladies first?"

"That's fine with me, so Captain Collins you come after her. Captain Macchi, tell me why you deserve one of my Heavy Battle Cruisers?"

"I was one of the first captains when our fleet was formed and have been at every battle we've fought. I've followed your orders and my ship has performed well without any injuries or loss of life. Morale is high mainly because of the relaxation of the fraternization rules for starships, and no requests for transfer have been made to shore or the Home Fleet."

"Captain Allison Collins you're next. What makes you better than Captain Macchi?"

"Actually, I can make the same claims as Captain Macchi,

except I'm a newer captain and haven't been present at as many battles as she. I run a taut ship and morale is high, mainly because we have had no battle damage from the enemy. Our success is because of your excellent tactics."

The other captains' justifications appeared to duplicate the first two testimonies. Admiral Bloodworth turned to Commander Williams. "Do you have any questions?"

"If you were the admiral, is there anything you would have done differently at any of the battles?"

Captain Vlad Pavlova held his hand up. Admiral Bloodworth said, "Yes, Captain Pavlova, do you have a comment?"

"Yes, sir, no one has mentioned it, but the admiral and myself have both come from a wet Navy where the tactics are completely different from space warfare, but he adapted quickly and won his battles. I might have adjusted as well, but maybe not as fast. Our admiral is a genus at what he does and I've kept a log of every battle that I study for their logic."

Commander Williams said, "Captain, our War College teaches his tactics as well. The key factor is the ability to adapt to changing conditions. From what has been said here, you all have been students of the admiral."

Fleet Admiral Bloodworth said, "captains thank you for coming and I'll let you know of my decisions. Something else you can think about. I plan on splitting the Fleet into two Battle Groups. Initially, one fleet will be from Earth and the other from Aqua. Both fleets will be increased by constructions from Earth and later from Aqua."

CHAPTER 19

Commander Dana Williams held a meeting with her staff when she left the captain's breakfast conference. She began, "I heard something this morning I wasn't aware of. What is meant by the relaxation of the fraternization rules for starships?"

The two looked at one another for a moment, before Nguyen answered. "Starships no longer have to abide by the rules that forbid dating within the chain of command. The reason is that your time in space is about half the same time on Earth. This would kill relationships where only one of the two is in space. However, under the new rules any promotions or demotions where one has supervisory powers over the other has to be approved by two of a higher rank."

"You're saying if I had a personal relationship with either of you I wouldn't be breaking any rules?"

McBride replied, "Not unless you used your position to harass or promote me that was subsequently found to be unsupportable by two higher ranking officers."

Nguyen said, "I was in such a relationship until she cheated on me numerous times. I elected to remove myself by transferring to this ship."

Williams looked at him with sympathy. "I recently divorced my cheating husband, so I know how you feel. I wasn't aware that warp time was having such a profound effect on personal relationships. Now, back to business. The admiral's meeting was informative, but I don't think he is ready to make any decisions regarding the captain positions for the three Heavy Battle Cruisers, at least not right away."

McBride pointed at a desk covered in personnel files. "We got these files from Personnel while you were gone. Where do we start?"

"Well, each of you take thirteen files and compile a list of positive and negative things about our candidates. Once we finish with the first one, let's compare what we consider a positive and negative feature. Okay, let's go to work."

* * *

Admiral Bloodworth saw the captains off after the meeting ended, and was thinking of the specific talents on his Bridge he needed to function properly in case of an emergency. Command, need two – check, Comm – check, Science – check, I think that's it for me. Now, my chief of staff will have to fill her needs. What she doesn't have is someone who knows the ship and all the DH's, and someone who knows how to scrounge for equipment or information. He pulled out his hand held and asked for the location of Master Chief Petty Officer Patrick O'Malley.

Bloodworth found O'Malley in the Weapons Section dressing down a rating that seemed to shrink with every word hurled at him. The rating saw the Admiral first and yelled, "Admiral on Deck."

"At ease Master Chief. What's his problem?"

"Lazy. But he's one of the good ones. Wait a moment and I'll get him back to duty."

Bloodworth stepped back and watched a master at work. When he finished and sent the rating off, he motioned for the admiral to follow him to his office. Once inside, O'Malley offered him his chair, while he stood at attention, saying, "Aye sir, what can I do for you?"

"Master Chief I need a really smart scrounger on my staff, rank or gender is not important."

The Master Chief slowly smiled. "Admiral, I forgot you were formerly wet Navy. So you know the value of a good scrounger, but you want a smart one as well. There's only one aboard the Beast. Let me call him down here and let's see if you can use him."

"Comm call for Gunnery Sergeant Jason Mao to report to

Master Chief Patrick O'Malley ASAP."

Bloodworth was expecting a small oriental man, but what walked into the room was a giant. At least seven feet tall and built like a weight lifter. Mao immediately came to attention when he saw the admiral. Master Chief O'Malley said, "Gunny Mao, Admiral Bloodworth wanted to meet the smartest scrounger the ship had, and I told him there was only one smart one."

Mao still stood at attention, but he must have a guilty conscience because sweat was starting to form on his forehead before he responded. "Aye sir, what can I do for the admiral?"

"Gunny Jason Mao, you must be very good because I haven't heard of you before now. How would you like to work for me on my staff?"

"Sir, what would be my duties on your staff?"

"You would work for my Chief of Staff, Commander Dana Williams. Do you have a problem working for a woman?"

"Sir, not if she has a strong stomach and can abide me breaking a few regulations."

"Well, I don't know her that well to make that judgment. Let's go ask her and see if you and her are the right fit."

"Aye sir."

The two, an admiral and a huge Marine Gunnery Sergeant soon entered the office of the Chief of Staff, where the three Navy Officers stood at attention. Gunny Jason Mao seemed to enjoy the Navy officers coming to attention at his arrival. Bloodworth said, "At Ease. Staff, this is Gunnery Sergeant Jason Mao. He is the smartest scrounger on the ship. You want something you can't find whether equipment, people, or information, he will find it. His concern is are you going to quibble about whether it's according to regulations? Commander Williams, what is your response?"

Commander Williams walked up to him, where the top of her head barely reached his chest, and looked up at his face. "Gunny, don't kill anyone unless you clear it with me first, otherwise you do your job as you would normally. Who do I call to get you detached to me?"

"Sir, Major Roger Blevins is my commanding officer."

"Very well, when I need your services I'll comm you. Right now we are working profiles on all our fleet ship captains."

"Sir, I can get you the unofficial skinny on your captains. How soon do you need it?"

Williams looked at him with renewed interest. "Very good Gunny. Get it ASAP. We'll add it to our official recap. Do you need a list of the captains?"

"No Ma'am, that won't be necessary. Do you also want it for the Beast's captain?"

She looked at him with a knowing smile. "Why not? She's not the focus of this profile, but I'm curious anyway."

"Aye Ma'am, will that be all?"

"Yes, thank you Gunny."

Commander Williams turned to her admiral and asked, "Sir, where did you find him? He's going to be very helpful."

"I know a certain master chief."

After the admiral went to his office and shut the door, McBride said in awe, "That guy was huge."

Three weeks later found several changes. The captains for the three new Heavy Battle Cruisers were named and were now ready for their shake down cruisers. Captain Inez Macchi commands the UES Miracle, Captain Vlad Pavlova commands the UES Growler, and Captain Christopher Eiberger commands the UES Raptor. The Space Navy changed its uniform head covering to a dark blue beret for everyone except the ship captain, who would wear a white beret. The berets would also carry a badge from their ship predominantly displayed.

The chief of staff also submitted to her admiral a list of the top three candidates for Commodore of the Second Fleet. They were Captains Vlad Pavlova (28), Drew Melton (22), and Sara Bazyn (18). She also gave each a point value according to how the captains were rated.

When Commander Williams gave Admiral Bloodworth the staffs' commodore recommendations, he asked for how the point system was derived. After a thorough review he decided to go with their recommendation. However, he decided to wait until the ship trials were over before making his decision public.

Three weeks later the three new Heavy Battle Cruisers were back in Earth orbit after making successful shakedown cruises. None needed additional shipyard time, but the UES Miracle needed some minor electrical repairs. Fleet Admiral Bloodworth commed all the fleet ships in orbit to send their captains and XOs to the Beast for a conference at 10:00 hours tomorrow.

At the appointed time everyone was seated and a little uneasy on what was to be announced. Fleet Admiral Bloodworth took the podium and looked out at his captains.

"Ladies and gentlemen we have come a long way since we first left Earth on our own. However, things change and we now have the strength to field two Star Battle Fleets under my overall command. Commodore Vlad Pavlova will command the Second Fleet and will be in charge of two Heavy Battle Cruisers and twenty Cruisers. Commodore Pavlova you will have to wait until I relieve the ships at Aqua before you will have your full allotment of cruisers. Both of us are going to be short-handed for a period of time, you when I leave and me when I send the ships at Aqua home for leaves and resupply. Your second Beast Class Cruiser will be the UES Miracle, captained by Inez Macchi. Second Fleet will initially operate out of Earth and First Fleet out of Aqua. After eighteen months we will trade places. Each of you captains will receive notice of which fleet you will be assigned. Those assigned to First Fleet should schedule all leaves to be ready for departure in forty-five days. In addition, on a lighter note I have approved a change in Star Fleet Uniforms. All crews will wear a dark blue beret with the unique badge of their ship, except for ship captains who will wear a white beret. I will try to answer your questions before you leave. Commodore Pavlova please stay until after everyone else leaves."

Later, after the other captains left, Pavlova sat with Fleet Admiral Bloodworth discussing their plans for the future. Pavlova said with a rueful smile, "I really didn't expect to get one of the Heavies, let alone be named Commodore of the Second Fleet. Why me and not one of the others?"

"Because you are a thinker. I didn't want someone who would do something rash, like getting his fleet wiped out by doing something stupid. Be cautious in your actions. Just because something worked once doesn't mean it always will. My fear is that when I send a probe through the gate I'd immediately get a salvo in return. I'm going to put my heavies within their 10,000-mile laser range of the gate and have the other Cruisers hang further back. I can't see anything getting past our new lasers."

Pavlova nodded his head in agreement. "Sir, I agree that we

should use our strength of the heavies and not try to protect them. On a personal note, I transferred my XO from the Striker to the Growler in the same position. We plan to marry, much like you and your XO did. Is this going to be a problem for you?"

"No. I hope the arrangement works for you as well as it does for Hanna and myself. We would like to attend your wedding if we are still in the system."

"Thank you sir. We plan the wedding for next week and I'll have Annalisa send you and Hanna the information. Do you have any idea what cruisers you're leaving here?"

"Yes, you're going to get the nine cruisers we borrowed from Home Fleet. Their crews are still in a state of flux because of the transfers of crews back to Home Fleet. That should be resolved before First Fleet leaves. I'll let you know of any other ships, but don't count on them. You'll get more when I relieve the ships at Aqua."

CHAPTER 20

Fleet Admiral Bloodworth and his wife, Captain Hanna Bloodworth were watching the monitors as the UES Beast left Earth orbit, wondering what was going to happen before they were scheduled to return in eighteen months. He hoped that Commodore Pavlova and his wife would have as much happiness in their marriage as he and Hanna.

The Beast was leading nineteen Cruisers and one Heavy Battle Cruiser. Captain Christopher Eiberger was in command of the Raptor, the new Heavy. During the trip to Aqua the First Fleet conducted maneuvers trying to determine how two Heavy Cruisers changed their mix using standard tactics. Eventually, they came up with several plans to handle expected Xones' strategies.

A little more than three months later they entered the Aqua System and were immediately challenged by its Home Fleet. It was well the First Fleet was friendly because the defenders were only three Aqua Cruisers. Fleet Admiral Bloodworth was informed that the Battle Fleet was on patrol, but was expected back at any time. The First Fleet made orbit around Aqua and were pleasantly surprised to find three new Aqua Heavies and four Cruisers in parking orbit.

After sending a request to Aqua Space Control for a resupply of consumables they waited for Aqua's Battle Fleet to return.

Bloodworth sent a message to all First Fleet ships to begin delayed repairs to their vessels, and to send any parts lists to him for relay to the Aqua Construction Yard.

Upon First Fleet's arrival, the remaining Katz Cruisers soon left the Aqua System. They wished us continuing good luck in our battle with the Xones. Ten days later the Aqua Fleet returned to their system. According to Aqua Space Control they had been gone almost six calendar months. This seemed about right for a three-month cruise for their Battle Fleet.

Later, after the Aqua Fleet made orbit near Earth's First Fleet. Bloodworth invited its commander to the Beast for a conference at their convenience. Commodore Becker replied, "Captain Fieldspire and I would be happy to attend at 19:00 hours today. Please make it a Dinner Conference as I have a great desire for a beef steak."

Fleet Admiral Bloodworth showed his wife the reply he just received, who smiled her appreciation of his request. "Honey, how much beef did we bring with us?"

"Only another three months' supply. I guess we're going to have to find something here that is similar to beef. I don't want to resort to Spam."

That evening they welcomed back Commander Becker, now acting as Commodore for the Aqua Battle Fleet, and his wife Captain Fieldspire. When the admiral and Captain Hanna Bloodworth met them at the shuttle bay, Hanna immediately noticed a change in Mae and Becker's attention to her welfare, as he helped her down from the shuttle. When the welcoming pipes began playing he held her hand until it was finished, and then they began the walk toward the Flag. Becker saluted the Flag and asked permission to board from Captain Hanna Bloodworth, who granted them permission to Board.

Hanna immediately approached Mae and hugged her, asking, "How far along are you?"

Mae looked at her wanly, "About three months. I have morning sickness, but it is starting to get better. My doctor is concerned because we aren't of the same race, but I'm determined that I'm going to have this child."

Hanna put her arm around Mae's shoulder and as they walked into the ship she asked, "Our ship has a doctor and several medical machines that might give you a better idea of your health. Why not stay here after our meeting and have him examine you?"

Mae looked over at her husband and asked, "Robert, do you think I should have the doctor here examine me?"

Becker, who exhibited all the symptoms of concern for a wife carrying his child, nodded his head. "Yes, maybe the doctor has some insight in helping you."

Admiral Bloodworth commed the doctor and put her on notice that they would visit her at the hospital in about an hour. They went to their stateroom where Yue He immediately helped the expectant mother to a chair at the table, while the others took their own seats.

The others had steaks, while Mae received clear broth and crackers. Mae studiously avoided looking at what they ate, and sighed in relief when the dishes were removed from the table. Commodore Becker's face colored in embarrassment as he suddenly realized that Admiral Bloodworth had been promoted to the rank of Fleet Admiral. "Admiral, forgive me for not recognizing your promotion. Mae, that rank hasn't been used since our last World War, almost a hundred years ago."

Bloodworth replied, "Yes, I was taken aback too when they gave me the rank. We now have two Earth Battle Fleets, Commodore Vlad Pavlova commands Second Fleet out of Earth. I command First Fleet out of Aqua. How many Earth and Aqua ships do you command here?"

"To answer your unasked question, we've had one battle since you left with no damage to our ships. We destroyed twelve of their ships, while two escaped. So, they now know what we look like and how dangerous we are to them. We still have fourteen Earth Cruisers, and the Aqua Fleet now total four Heavy Battle Cruisers and six Cruisers, not including the three in Home Fleet."

"Does that include the ones in orbit here when we arrived?"

"Yes, we are crewing the Heavy Battle Cruisers first. That should speed up once the news gets out of our recent victory."

Bloodworth said, "Great. I'm going to send the fourteen Earth Cruisers back to Earth for resupply and leave. Ten will become part of Second Fleet. First and Second Fleet will change positions every eighteen months. Before the Aqua Battle Fleet expands any further, they should consider beefing up their Home Fleet. Three Cruisers is not enough if there's no one else here. They need a

Heavy and three more Cruisers to have a chance at defending this system."

Captain Fieldspire nodded her head in agreement. "I know! I just wanted a chance to see if I could command a Battle Fleet and succeed. Now, we'll add the Heavy and other Cruisers to the Home Fleet as you recommended; with our combined ships we could do the Xones a lot of damage. If that's all, I think I want to see your doctor now."

Captain Hanna Bloodworth said, "I'll take her and let you know if she needs to stay overnight."

After the women left, Admiral Bloodworth asked, "Robert, how did she do out there?"

"Even handicapped by her nauseous condition she was able to function, perhaps not 100 percent, but she got the job done."

"I hope her condition now is temporary, but eventually she'll have to relinquish her command to have the baby. It would be better if she's not in a battle zone when that happens."

Becker replied, "Let's see what the doctor says before we make any further plans."

* * *

Doctor Joyce Yutesler was surprised to see who her patient was and her condition, but immediately started her examination by first taking a blood sample. Two hours later, she said, "Captain Fieldspire you are still in your first trimester and everything appears normal if you were a human. Your blood work does not show any significant abnormalities from that of a human female. Is the Aqua population all like you, no other beings that differ from you in any way?"

"No, we are all the same race of people. It is strange that you humans and our people so closely resemble each other."

"Yes, I'm beginning to believe that we may have a common beginning. But, that is for others to determine. In your case, I'm going to make an assumption that you're close enough to being human that our medications will work for you. I'm giving you a shot for your nausea that should give you relief. In addition, I'll give you a list of foods to avoid and supplements you need to take with you. When you need a refill or have any difficulty please let me know."

"What about when it comes time to deliver, would you do me the honor of helping me?"

"Certainly, I'd be happy to. You shouldn't be in a stressful situation in your last thirty days before your delivery date. Do you know when the baby was conceived?"

"I think it was shortly after we were married…about 36 days ago."

"Alright, is nine months the same gestation period for Aqua women?"

"Yes. So nine months would make my delivery time to be about February 8th. So, I shouldn't be in a Battle Zone beginning in January. Crap, I'm going to be stuck here until after I've had my baby."

"Maybe longer if you intend to breast feed the baby."

"We have artificial baby milk, but do I want to risk the baby by taking him or her with me?"

"Do you want to know the sex of the child?"

"Maybe I should ask Robert that before you tell us. Hanna can you get them to come here for that question?"

When the admiral and the commodore arrived and were brought up to date on Mae's condition, she asked Robert, "The doctor asked if we wanted to know the gender of our baby, I do if you agree."

Becker nodded his head eagerly and Mae asked, "Doctor is the baby a girl or boy?"

Doctor Yutesler answered, "You're going to have girl."

* * *

Six days later, the fourteen Earth Cruisers previously left in the Aqua System broke Aqua obit for their return to Earth for resupply and shore leave. Ten ships would be reassigned to the Second Fleet and the other four ships would return to First Fleet at Aqua and would be carrying extra provisions with them.

The combined Battle Fleets at Aqua were three Heavy Battle Cruisers and twenty-two Cruisers, plus three heavies and three Cruisers currently un—crewed. Current plans were to crew one of the three heavies and add it to the Home Fleet of three Cruisers.

The combined fleet made plans to leave in forty days to scout inward on their arm of the Galaxy. Captain Fieldspire would remain behind and supervise construction and allocation of crews until their return in about six or seven months Aqua time.

The day for their departure arrived. The three heavies led the way followed by the twenty-two Cruisers. All ships refueled their reaction mass at a Giant Gas Planet before entering the first warp gate out of the Aqua system.

CHAPTER 21

Starting with their second warp gate they tested each system before entering. Their probe at the third gate responded with two separate fleets of ten ships, each positioned about 800,000 miles from each of the system's two-warp gates.

Admiral Bloodworth thought, *the further Xones Fleet was about 80 million miles from this gate and effectively out of position to help their people outside our gate. When we destroy the closer Fleet the others could leave through their nearby gate. Well, we take what we are given. Let's see if I can sucker these guys into attacking us by appearing weaker than we are.*

The Fleet Admiral said, "Comm to all ships from the admiral. Only the two Heavy Battle Cruisers, Beast and Trojan Horse will transit the gate. All others will remain on this side until you receive further instructions from me. My intent is to tempt the ten enemies outside this gate to attack rather than run. The other group may attempt to help, but eventually they will leave through their nearby gate. Wish us luck."

The two heavies slid through the gate and immediately spread apart about 1,000 miles before using their powerful lasers to probe for any minefields left in their path. It was well that they used this precaution as at least 100 mines were exploded. The two ships maintained their 2g speed toward their enemy who were using a horizontal two level spread for their ten ships, five ships on each level about 1,000 miles apart.

Bloodworth said, "Comm to Trojan Horse. If they fail to fire before we reach 500,000 miles from them, we will each fire two salvoes at them evenly disbursed and standard early cut-off and turn-on when 10,000 miles from target, otherwise we fire after they do."

The Xones fired one salvo at them when they were 600,000 miles apart. The two heavies replied with their two salvoes and the clocks were started. When the enemy missiles went ballistic the two heavies moved 50,000 miles to their right and waited for a response from either enemy fleet.

The further Xones' Fleet started to move in their direction at 3g's. The closer enemy fleet made no attempt to avoid the incoming missiles so far. The clock on the heavies missiles reaching their targets was now twenty minutes.

When the clock reached zero, the 80 missiles fired in two waves started exploding from defensive hits or against the sides of the enemy. When the first wave of 40 missiles finished, there were only four ships left. Then, the second wave hit and ten missiles were allocated to each surviving ship. After the second wave passed there was only debris left where ten ships once stood.

Admiral Bloodworth's ship sensors showed that the second enemy fleet was slowing with the apparent purpose of leaving the system. He commed the Trojan Horse to reverse course and approach the nearby gate so they could message the remainder of the fleet to join them.

Later, when their fleet was intact they set a course toward the far gate where the enemy fleet was now approaching. The other ships in their fleet were informed of how the battle was fought including the mines placed in front of their gate and the defensive action taken. Admiral Bloodworth anticipated more mines at both ends of the next gate.

When the Fleet reached a point 200,000 miles from the gate where Bloodworth felt the enemy would position mines, he ordered all three Heavies to spread out and use their lasers to destroy any mines they might encounter. To his surprise they found no minefield. The three heavies spread out to defend against a possible missile attack after they sent a probe through the gate.

No attack was made and their probe reported that the ten ships were still fleeing at 3g's toward the next warp gate. Fleet Admiral Bloodworth commed the fleet, "Captains, I feel that there is no longer any profit in continuing the chase. Follow the heavies back to Aqua."

A little more than three months later they arrived back in the Aqua System. The Home Fleet welcomed them home with a new Heavy Battle Cruiser leading three Cruisers. Later, Captain Fieldspire commed the Flagship UES Beast that there had been no incursions into their system during the fleet's absence.

ONBOARD UES BEAST
OCTOBER 2027 (SHIP TIME)
JULY 2032 (EARTH TIME)

CHAPTER 22

Eighteen months later the First Fleet was heading back to Earth, trading places with the Second Fleet. They left Aqua's Home Fleet in much better shape to defend their system with two heavies and six Cruisers. Captain Fieldspire and Commodore Becker were the proud parents of Karrie, who after a year was accompanying her parents into space.

The combined fleet had three more successful battles with the Xones, with each one further away from the Aqua system. The result was more positive interest from Aqua's populace, and enlistments were up to fill positions on its completed ships.

First Fleet arrived in Earth orbit 98 days after leaving Aqua. As soon as possible the fleet began issuing shore leave passes to its crew and officers, one quarter of each ship's total for up to 30 days.

Fleet Admiral Bloodworth met with Admiral Randall where he turned over his written report for the past eighteen months in the Aqua Zone. Randall looked at Bloodworth with a small smile. "Eric, you look well and I see you've returned home without any losses. Generally, how is the conflict going out there?"

"Better Jim. After our successes against the Xones, Aqua recruitment numbers have increased to a point where the Aqua Battle Fleet now total Four Heavy Battle Cruisers and Three Cruisers. They only build Heavies; it takes longer to construct, but the manpower requirements are about the same as a Cruiser. I anticipate that as soon as two more BC's are added to their Battle Fleet, the remaining three Cruisers will be transferred to Home Fleet. That would give Home Fleet Two BC's and Nine Cruisers. All future additions to the Battle and Home Fleets will be BC's."

"Eric, when Second Fleet left here, Commodore Pavlova commanded Four BC's and Twenty Cruisers. His fleet plus Aqua's Four BC's and Three Cruisers makes a formidable foe for any Xones they meet."

"Yes, sir, how many new constructs are available to add to First Fleet?"

"Like Aqua, we are now only building BC's. There are Two BC's almost ready, and Two Cruisers crewed and ready except for their shakedown cruise."

"All right! That's certainly good news. Hanna and I are going to take some leave soon to visit our families. Anything in the works that I should be aware of before we leave?"

"No, not really. However, that change you made for Star Fleet's uniform headgear has caused a brew-ha with the wet Navy. They now want berets for their people too."

"Crap. I just wanted the Star Fleet uniform to be different from the wet Navy's. I could change the color of the uniform from blue water to black space. Do you think they'd object to that?"

Admiral Randall suddenly looked thoughtful. "Now, that sounds like a really good idea. I'll get the Quartermaster right on it. Give me a call when you get back from leave."

The next morning Eric and Hanna's shuttle landed, as before, at the same small aircraft airport near Hamburg, Germany. Since they were planning on being here a week, the shuttle returned to the Beast. Clare, Hanna's sister, picked them up in her SUV and slowly drove through the heavy incoming traffic that apparently was coming to see a space shuttle that they heard had landed.

Hanna asked Clare, "Have you heard how Lucy is faring at her medical school?"

"Apparently, quite well. She told me she got to skip a quarter of her schooling dealing with space medicine because of her stint aboard the Beast. There was even an article in the local newspaper about her celebrity status being the sister of the captain commanding the Flagship of the First Fleet, and her attending school on detached duty from Star Fleet. Lucy told me that she gets a lot of attention wearing the Star Fleet uniform to class from the male students. Apparently, she's the only person on detached duty from the military at her school."

Hanna smiled at Clare's boastful telling of her younger sister's accomplishments, showing how proud she was of her. Hanna asked, "Is Ian with you?"

"Yes, I swear he can get into things you would think he couldn't reach. His father is back at the house watching him."

After their arrival at Hanna's childhood home, Eric was unloading the car when her family came bursting out of the front door greeting the new arrivals. Eric finally met Clare's husband, Jasper, who was a tall blond haired man in good physical shape despite being a computer IT man. Ian, now an active five-year old, came running up to Eric and hugged his leg.

He reached down and picked the boy up and speaking German said, "Ian, have you signed up for the Star Fleet yet?"

Ian grinned at him. "No, I tried but they said I was too young. Ah, you were funning me."

Eric roughed his hair and put him down. "Ian, you want to help me bring this stuff into the house?"

Jasper came over and picked a small bag for him to carry and they lugged it all inside in one trip.

Clare and Hanna watched this interaction play out. "Hanna, that husband of yours would make a great father for your kids."

"I was thinking the same thing. Now if only the right time and conditions arrive for us."

Clare put her arm around her older sister and gave her a hug before they went inside.

That evening there was a surprise visitor. Hanna was closest to the front door when there was a knock. When she answered the door a young Lieutenant (jg) in Star Fleet uniform was staring at her with a big smile on her face.

"Lucy!" She exclaimed in glee before grabbing her youngest sister in a fierce hug. Both sisters had tears running down their cheeks as they came into the house.

It seemed that it was only an hour's high-speed train ride from Berlin, where she was attending school. It took them another hour to exchange news when their Mother called them to Dinner. Later, while drinking coffee, Lucy congratulated Eric on his promotion to Fleet Admiral. "It's still news even after almost four years. I'll graduate early in less than two months and I hope to spend my internship aboard the Beast."

Eric looked at his wife and smiled. "Lucy, I'll let your sister give you the good news."

Hanna looked at her sister with a twinkle in her eyes. "After your graduation, you will receive orders to report to the UES Beast to begin your internship under Doctor Joyce Yutesler. When you report aboard you will be promoted to the rank of Lieutenant."

Lucy sat for a moment savoring the news, then giving everyone a big smile, said, "Let's celebrate! Mom do you have any wine?"

Clare said, "Mom I'll get it, you stay there and visit. Ian come and help me."

In a few minutes they returned, Ian carefully carrying the wine bottle, while Clare was carrying a tray of wine glasses. Clare held up the corkscrew asking, "Who wants to do the honors?"

Hanna said, "Eric you need to do it for this occasion."

He stood and took the corkscrew and bottle and carefully opened it with a soft pop. After everyone but Ian had a glass of wine, Eric held his glass up, saying, "A toast to my Sister-in-Law for a job well done and for her future in Star Fleet."

After everyone toasted Lucy, Ian asked his mother, "Can I toast her too with a sip?"

At her nod, Ian took a sip of the wine and grimaced before saying, "To Aunt Lucy."

Everyone laughed and his mother said, "Well done Ian."

Lucy soon left to take the late train back to Berlin. Before Ian went to bed, Eric gave him a ship badge from the Beast as a keepsake. He turned the small piece of metal over and felt the raised relief of the depicted creature and the words, UES Beast, under it. "Wow! I'm going to keep this forever. My friends didn't believe me when I told them you're my Uncle – this will show them. Thanks Uncle Eric."

Eric and Hanna spent most of the week visiting and shopping for presents. Eventually, it was time they left for their next family visit.

When they were arriving at the small aircraft airport, they saw the shuttle land with a loud roar. Hanna said, "No wonder people came to see what was going on."

They said their goodbyes to Clare and soon were in the air again headed toward Springfield, Missouri.

CHAPTER 23

Again, the mayor and a crowd of people met the shuttle when it landed next to the old terminal building. This time the local TV stations had set up cameras. After the mayor's welcome speech and Fleet Admiral Bloodworth's obligatory speech they were able to leave. Eric's father met them and the local police escorted them to their home in a normally quiet cul-de-sac neighborhood. Eric and his father, Adam, were unloading their luggage from the car when the neighbors came outside to welcome Eric home. Apparently, the TV coverage and the police cars alerted them.

When a crowd started to gather, Eric took Hanna's hand as they walked to meet the neighbors and shake hands. There was one boy and girl, apparently twins and about fourteen years old, who were staring at them with almost crazed adoration. Suddenly, the boy took the girl's hand and approached them.

Eric and Hanna faced them with a smile and waited for them to speak. The boy said, "My name is Robert Boyd and this is my sister Jessica. What can we do to prepare ourselves to be eligible to get on a starship?"

Hanna looked at the girl as she replied, "Jessica, there are many career paths that can lead to getting on a starship. What are your interests?"

She blushed, but quickly shook that off as she thought on Hanna's question. "I'm very good with numbers and sometimes can get an answer faster than my hand calculator. Robert is mechanically inclined and can fix about anything."

Eric looked at the two eager youngsters for a moment before answering. "You both need to attend schools that will enhance both of your interests and abilities. Jessica would fit very well as a Science Officer with additional schooling, and Robert sounds like he would be perfect in Engineering, also with additional schooling. I can see both of you in ships within eight to ten years. Get a poster of Star Fleet and anytime things get tough, look at the poster – that will be your goal."

The twins looked at each other and smiled. They now had an outline to reach their goal. They both thanked the two most famous people in the world to them.

* * *

After shaking a few more hands the crowd broke up and they returned to unloading the car. Hanna helped the two men bring the luggage inside to Eric's old bedroom. She smiled to herself as she perused his wall posters. There were a few depicting popular music artists of the time, but it was the model of the USS Missouri that showed his interest in the wet Navy.

Eric helped Hanna unload the luggage, and then he went downstairs to visit with his parents. Hanna picked up their dirty clothes and took them to the laundry room where Sarah, Eric's mother, found her and immediately took over the task of washing them. Hanna stayed with her and they talked about Eric's early life in Springfield. How he was active in sports at Kickapoo HS, and his first girl friend that lasted until he entered the Naval Academy at Annapolis.

Hanna asked, "Did he see any action while in the wet Navy?"

"Oh, he was part of several skirmishes, but I don't think his ship was fired upon. You know, he was a captain of a ship before he was transferred to Star Fleet. Now I worry because every time he leaves our system he's been shot at."

"Yeah, I know because I'm with him. Did you know that his tactics are so good that none of our ships have had battle damage?"

Sarah hugged her daughter-in-law tightly before releasing her. "You being with him is a God's send. His first marriage ended because of his long absences and I now feel it was better that they had no children. How about you two? Hanna, you are getting close to the end of your childbearing years. Are you going to remain childless?"

Hanna shook her head. "No, I'm going to talk to Eric about my plan to add a nursery and child care to every Heavy Battle Cruiser. Maybe even the Cruisers, but they are probably too small. The point is that women can remain aboard ship while pregnant and later raise their children aboard. Some problems may occur, but I think it's a doable plan."

Sarah looked at Hanna with surprise for a moment, and then she slowly smiled. "Eric is one lucky man to have married you. Bring my grandkids home when you can, and I want pictures as they grow up. I've got to be able to brag about them to my friends."

Eric stuck his head into the laundry room. "Whose grandkids are you talking about?"

Sarah grinned at him and playfully slapped his arm. "Why yours of course. Your wife isn't getting any younger, so talk to her about it."

After his mother left the room, he entered and shut the door. "I've detected you and the other female members of our family talking quietly about apparently serious matters, but not where I can hear."

"Well honey, I've got a plan that started when Mae Fieldspire took her child along with the Battle Fleet."

Eric started to speak, but stopped when she held up a finger. "I'm not finished. The ships are well shielded against radiation, so that's not a risk. Battle damage has been nil, although that may change. We can place a nursery at or close to the hospital and a 24-hour childcare facility deep within the ship. With this available, women can stay aboard during their pregnancy and later raise their children aboard the ship. Now, tell me why it can't be done."

"You want kids. You want them now!" He said with a slow grin lighting up his face.

Hanna hugged him tightly. "Do you think we can do it?"

"Yes, but only with the heavies. The Cruisers are too small and don't have a hospital. We could do crew transfers to the heavies for women who get pregnant and want to keep her kids with her. We also need to recruit nannies for the childcare facility, either that or have volunteers until there's a need for them. Well-done Hanna. You may have solved a problem for Star Fleet."

"Well, let's not drag our feet on this matter, I want to start our own family."

"Yes Dear. I'll have my staff get on it as soon as we get back to the Beast."

Hannah gave Eric a kiss that would have curled the toes of a lessor man before letting him escape after the washing machine buzzed that it was done. Later, Hannah joined Sarah in the kitchen where they each enjoyed a cup of tea.

Sarah raised an eyebrow at Hanna as she asked, "How did your plan go over with Eric?"

"I think very well. He said he would have his staff start work on it when we get back to the ship. In fact he seemed eager at the prospect of becoming a father."

"Aah. Finally, I have a chance of becoming a grandmother. I can hardly wait until I have a chance to spoil them."

Hanna smiled at Sarah. "You sound just like my mother and she already has a five-year old grandson from my middle sister."

"Do you think she would lend me him until yours arrive?"

"Ian is a future starship man because of two Aunts already in Star Fleet. Eric gave him a beret ship medal representing the UES Beast. You would have thought it was made of gold the way he prized it."

CHAPTER 24

A week later they were back aboard the Beast and attending to business. Commander Dana Williams and her staff took leave at the same time as the Admiral so that when he returned, his staff would be ready to carry out his wishes.

When his chief of staff heard his wishes regarding pregnancies and running a childcare facility in each of heavies, she was at first dumbfounded because it was so in conflict with the wet Navy traditions. But, after some thought and the example of Captain Fieldspire, she threw herself into the project with gusto.

There were presently eight heavies in First and Second Fleet, but she only had to transform the four ships in First Fleet. The doctors assigned to the heavies had to be fully up to date on pregnancies and childhood diseases. In addition, childcare personnel would be a new rating and recruitment effort. Contract workers would be too expensive because of the battle risk and time away from Earth.

Three months later, Star Fleet Command received the first recruits to fill childcare crew vacancies. Initially they recruited the supervisors from similar positions held in the civilian sector. They needed one senior supervisor, an assistant, and six workers for each ship. In other words the Navy ranks would be - one Lt. Commander, one Lieutenant, and six enlisted crew, all with previous experience.

The four Lt. Commanders met with Commander Williams. She initially told them what Star Fleet was starting and why, and then said, "I have a list of storage rooms that I think could be used for a childcare facility. All four ships are similar, so check them out and give me a report later today as to their feasibility."

Three hours later they were back. Lt. Commander Shanell Rullman spoke for the others. "Any of these rooms will do. I assume you picked them because they are all deep within the ship for better protection against battle damage. I would suggest that some sort of air supply be added in case it's shut off because of battle damage, and one marine stationed nearby to assist us if needed."

"I think that can be arranged. Anything else?"

"Yes, what about all the children of the crew that has been left on shore until now?"

Commander Williams' face almost turned white at the thought that she had missed something so obvious. "Crap. I wonder how many that's going to be? Never mind, it doesn't matter. We can always cut a connecting door to combine two rooms. This means we need to bring the other caregivers on sooner than I expected. Okay let's look at that list again for two adjacent rooms."

After a survey of First Fleet for the number of children left on shore and the number of children a parent would desire be kept onboard with them, resulted in thirty-five children less than four years of age. All but three wanted their children aboard ship with them. That would be about eight children per ship, and several transfers to and from other ships to get the parents aboard a heavy. The caregivers had to be aboard and acclimated before the children arrived. However, the transfers of parents could be made immediately.

When new crew arrived, adjustments were quickly made as personnel adjusted to their new quarters. Two weeks later the first caregivers started to arrive and their working quarters began to take shape.

After the caregivers were adjusted to ship life and trained in their new jobs, children were brought aboard each Heavy. They were met at the shuttle by their parent(s) and escorted to the caregiver room where they watched their children become indoctrinated into ship life. They would pick up their children each day/night after their duty shift and return to their family quarters, usually upgraded in size from what they had before.

A month after the last of the children arrived, Admiral Bloodworth and Captain Hanna Bloodworth walked to the Caregiver Unit that is comprised of two rooms. They noted a marine guard outside the unit who immediately came to attention as they approached. Admiral Bloodworth had her stand down and asked, "Lance Corporal, anything unusual happen during your watch?"

She replied with a smile, "Not if you don't count a three-year old girl chase after a ball that escaped the play room."

The couple smiled at the response before entering the room. It was like entering another world seeing all the young children performing various things. School was one item they initially overlooked, but plans were being made to eventually start a one-classroom school.

Hanna asked Lt. Commander Rullman, "How are your charges doing in this environment?"

"We've found that using a normal nap time doesn't work here because of the different times the children are picked up by their parents. I think instead of a three-shift pickup, we try two shifts – pickups at six A.M. and six P.M. Naps midway through their stay with us might work then with less disruption from children who are awake."

"You're saying that ideally the children should be picked up at the same time. This might work now, but as we gain more children, scheduling the crew would be too difficult."

"That's why I suggested shifts. We close off one room for nap time; even better use the planned school room as the nap room when it's not used."

Hanna said, "So, I need to arrange a work schedule change for any parent currently working the 3-12 shift. How many kids are picked up at Midnight?"

"Two. Jefferson and Marlow are the parents."

"Okay, consider it in process, but don't do anything until I tell you its been fixed."

Later, as Eric and Hanna were returning to their stateroom she said, "I think we have a handle on this except for the care of infants. I don't think we can place someone that young in with those kids. When Lucy comes aboard, we need to talk to her about this. Maybe segregate a small portion of the hospital for infants and add personnel to care for them."

"I suppose we can ask for volunteers from the corpsman to act as baby nurses?"

Two weeks later Lieutenant (jg) Lucy Lundberg reported for duty aboard the UES Beast. Captain Hanna Bloodworth met her when she got off the shuttle. Lucy had stopped at the Quartermasters before boarding her Shuttle and was wearing the new black uniform and beret as she saluted the Flag and asked permission to board. She and her sister traded salutes and was welcomed aboard before they embraced.

The sisters were both the same six-foot height as they bumped their foreheads together and held each other tightly for a few moments. Then wiping away a few errant tears they went to the captain's stateroom to catch up on personal matters.

Inside her quarters, Captain Bloodworth handed her sister new sleeve markings and had her stand while she replaced her gold bar with new Lieutenant rank pips. Then she was given the Medical Corps' symbol that was to be added to her sleeve rank.

Lucy looked at her new sleeve markings with surprise, and then looked up at her sister with tears in her eyes. "I was beginning to think I would never reach this point in my life."

Hanna replied, "I never doubted you for a moment. Besides I have plans for you. Eric and I are going to have a baby and I've made arrangements to stay onboard as the captain."

Lucy looked at her aghast. "What! Surely you're not serious?"

Hanna then told her about the changes she and Eric had made. "I hope you've been trained in delivering a baby because in about nine months you are going be delivering mine."

* * *

Later, after Yue He stitched on her new sleeve rank, Lucy reported to personnel to get checked into the computer system and receive her cabin assignment. When she eventually got to her cabin, she found that her roommate was someone she knew. "Lieutenant Amy Fursa! What a surprise. Look at who your new roommate is."

"Crap, it's that kid sister of the captain. Wow, look at you, a lieutenant and you're all grown up. So you finished medical school and you're now a doctor?"

"Almost, I'm an Intern for two more years before that happens. So, what gives with you since I left?"

"Well, for starters I've had this cabin all to myself. But, I was getting lonely so I guess having you here with me is an improvement."

"Have you met anyone who gets your pulse going like a race car?"

"Not yet, but I'm still looking. I want to meet a guy where we both immediately know we were made for each other."

"Yeah, I'd like that. My sister did, so I know its possible."

Fursa suddenly turned serious and asked, "Have you heard that we're now bringing our kids aboard?"

"Yes, the captain told me what she's doing. She's determined to have a child and keep both of them aboard. She's using Captain Fieldspire of the Aqua Navy as her justification that it can be done."

"Wow! That's really going to change things in the Battle Fleet."

"For me too. I'm going to take care of babies and children as well as crew illness and injuries. Have they delivered my luggage yet? I want to get that stowed away before I report to Doctor Yutesler for the morning shift."

"Not yet. Help me move some of my stuff so you'll have your own space."

They had just completed moving Amy's possessions back into her closet when there was a buzz from the door. Lucy said, "I bet that's my stuff now."

Twenty minutes later she was unpacked and her luggage stowed under her bed. Lucy looked at Amy and said, "Let's get something to eat, I'm famished."

"You're not going to wear that dress uniform are you?"

"Oh, sorry. Wait a few minutes while I get my undress uniform sorted out. Show me yours."

"It's the tan ones, like I'm wearing."

After Lucy changed clothing, she posed for Amy's inspection. "How do I look?"

"Better than me. You have bigger boobs. Okay, let's go trolling for men while we get something to eat."

When they entered the officers' mess they didn't see any likely men sitting alone, so Amy steered them toward a table where a single woman sat. Amy smiled as she said, "Betty, may we sit with you?"

Betty looked up at Amy and slowly smiled. "Surely, take a seat Amy. Who is this fresh face?"

After they sat, introductions were made. "Betty Imhof this lovely new face is Lucy Lundberg, sister of our captain. She is our new Intern Doctor. Lucy, this fascinating woman is my DH in Engineering."

Betty looked at Lucy with appraising eyes. "Just now arrived you say. But somehow I seem to remember you being here before?"

"Oh, I was on the first cruise to Aqua. Shanghaied you might say."

Betty laughed. "Oh, I remember now. You left the ship when we returned to start medical school, and now you're back. Well, well. You look all grown up. An Ensign when you left and now a Lieutenant."

Amy said. "I don't see any prospects here tonight Betty."

"No. Lucy, have you reported to your supervisor yet?"

"Not yet. I'll do that at the beginning of the second shift tomorrow. Don't cause any accidents because I want an easy first day."

"Well, well, you do have your sister's bite. But she has much longer teeth. The captain has started something now that's going to cause many changes in fleet policy. What's your thoughts on the matter?"

"Remember, I'm new to the Navy. Besides, I just repair broken bodies, not make policy."

They ordered their meal and talked about everything except the children onboard. After the roommates returned to their cabin, Lucy asked, "What's Betty's problem?"

"I'm not sure, but did you notice that she didn't place any blame on the admiral who actually makes policy."

Lucy looked at her roommate with wide-eyes of disbelief. "She has the hot's for Eric? No, I can't see him coming onto her at all!"

"Maybe so, but that doesn't stop a jealous woman from blaming her rival."

"Well, knowing my sister she'd better cool her jets or she's going find out just how sharp her teeth are. Enough of this crap, it's been a long day and I need my sleep to cope with tomorrow's hassle."

Lucy reported to Doctor Yutesler at 08:00 hours. She was wearing her undress uniform while standing at attention before Commander Yutesler's desk. The doctor stood and walked around her desk and the Lieutenant before stopping beside her. "Lieutenant you look like a Navy Officer, but you're missing your medical tags. I can provide those. Now, stand down from attention and tell me about where you attended medical school."

When Lucy relaxed from attention her supervisor held out her hand for Lucy to shake.

An hour later Dr. Yutesler was showing her what changes the hospital had made preparing for infant and children care. They even had an incubator machine ready for use if needed.

A corpsman interrupted them. "Sir, Lt. Commander Rullman has brought in a male child with an injury."

The Doctor raised an eyebrow at her Intern. "Dr. Lundberg let's see what fate has brought to our door."

CHAPTER 25

Ninety-six days from their arrival, First Fleet broke orbit with four Heavy Battle Cruisers and thirty-one Cruisers. The fleet refueled reaction mass from Jupiter before continuing through the warp gate into the next system.

Before entering the third gate, the four heavies took up dispersed positions 10,000 miles from the gate awaiting a response from their probe. Their own sensors didn't find any mines this side of the gate.

It wasn't long before their message torpedo returned with sensor data from the next system. There was a sparse minefield laid about 5,000 miles from the gate, but no active ships noted within the system.

Fleet Admiral Bloodworth ordered the two newest heavies through the gate to clear the minefield before the others followed. Two hours later another message torpedo arrived giving an all clear signal, whereupon the remainder of First Fleet followed led by the remaining heavies.

They were halfway through the system toward the next gate when two groups of enemy ships lit their engines. Both groups were facing them about 800,000 miles this side of the next gate and the same distance from First Fleet. Each group totaled thirty ships in a loose ball formation and was putting on an acceleration of 2g's toward them.

Fleet Admiral Bloodworth brought all ships to Battle Stations before ordering each of the two new Heavies, the Missouri and the California, to launch one nuclear missile at each group of ships.

When the two missiles were fired, Bloodworth ordered, "Start the clock."

The time to targets was four hours and 28 seconds and counting down.

Science Officer Namio reported, "Sir, missile launch from both groups. One salvo, two salvoes. That's all so far.

Captain Hanna Bloodworth ordered, "Start clock for missiles going ballistic."

"Clock two started for salvoes going ballistic."

Admiral Bloodworth asked, "How long for clock two?"

"Sir, twenty-eight minutes."

"Sensor, monitor their engines and if they cut off early let me know."

"Aye, sir."

At twenty minutes the Science Officer reported, "Sir, the enemy cut its missile engines early."

Bloodworth commed his captain. "Captain, the enemy has cut his missile engines short. We need to move the fleet further than planned, say 50,000 miles in three point five hours."

"Sir, we better make that 100,000 miles."

"Very well, I'll comm that to the fleet."

"Comm to fleet. We will move according to XRAY One, 100,000 miles in three point five hours on my command."

Admiral Bloodworth turned to his science officer. "Has there been any change in enemy movements?"

"None yet Sir. They are still approaching at 2g's."

For the next three plus hours there was no change in either combatants other than they were still approaching each other. At three point five hours Admiral Bloodworth gave the order to move the fleet. When the fleet reached their new position the enemy fired another two salvoes at their new location.

Admiral Bloodworth asked his science officer, "How long before our missiles are on target?"

"Sir, in about ten minutes."

About eight minutes later the science officer reported, "Sir, one early nuclear blast, now another. I think a defender hit the first one, causing it to explode early. We may not get the results we were hoping for the group around the first blast."

"Very good. How long before the enemy missiles become active?"

"Soon, anytime between now and five minutes."

"Comm to fleet, prepare to defend against missile attack between now and five minutes."

Suddenly, both short-range missiles and laser fire could be felt in vibrations throughout the ship. This was the first time defensive fire has been needed in their fight against the Xones. There was a short delay and then they were fighting against the second salvo of the Xones.

"Comm to Fleet, report ship damage and casualties to Flag."

"Sir, two Cruisers were damaged. Both are able to maneuver. Casualties are two dead, nine injured."

"Comm to ships with casualties. Bring them to the Beast for treatment."

"Comm to hospital, expect nine injured to arrive within the hour."

"Comm to fleet. We will reverse last maneuver plus 50,000 miles as soon as shuttles with casualties arrive at the Beast."

"Comm to Flag. Casualties are aboard and shuttles are secured."

"Comm to fleet. Execute plan XRAY Two plus 150,000 miles on my command. Execute!"

"Comm to hospital, casualties are aboard and heading your way."

* * *

Lucy was fitted with a surgical gown as she had the most recent training, while Dr. Yutesler did the triage of the injured. They both checked for bleeders and the ones at the most risk. Lucy took the one needing immediate surgery, while Joyce worked on the others.

Three hours later the two doctors compared the variety of injuries they encountered. Two only needed cuts sewn up, one lost a hand, four suffered third degree burns, and two had deep puncture wounds. However, they lost no one and the two with cuts were released. The burn cases were taking turns under the burn recovery machine and should be released in three days.

The two doctors were enjoying a stress relief break of a cup of tea when there was a loud, "Captain on Deck!"

Captain Hanna Bloodworth said, "As you were!"

Seeing that the two doctors were taking a break, she took a seat herself and asked, "You got any more of that?"

The question was no more said than she had a cup in her hand. "Aah. I needed this. So how bad was it?"

Doctor Yutesler answered. "Whose idea was it to send all the casualties here?"

"Mine. I thought a single doctor would be overwhelmed."

"Well, you were right. If I had been alone I might have lost one of the bleeders. As it was, Doctor Lundberg carried the biggest part of the surgery load. She's quite good, by the way. I think we need an intern in all our heavies."

"Yes, it appears the Xones have changed their battle tactics significantly. We dodged their last salvo and are now approaching what remains of one of their fleets. We are being careful, but they may have another surprise for us."

Lucy said, "We have two patients ready to return to duty, and four burn patients that should be cleared in a few days. The one who lost his hand probably won't come back until rehab back on Earth. The remaining two should be ready for duty within a week."

Captain Hanna Bloodworth shook her head in wonder. "I was expecting much worse news when I heard we had two ships hit by missiles. Only two dead, one maimed, and eight eventually returned to duty. I hope we can continue to keep our losses low. I'll talk to Admiral Bloodworth about recruiting graduates from the medical schools to do their internship on board a Heavy Battle Cruiser. Lucy you may be the first of many in your position."

Doctor Yutesler asked, "Sir, I would like to share with the other three doctors aboard the heavies about what we experienced here? Maybe it will be useful later."

"That's a good idea. Copy me your comm and I'll include that in my correspondence to the Commander of the Medical Corp. Well, I better get back to the Bridge before they miss me."

* * *

Captain Bloodworth relieved her XO, so that she could get some rest before her next shift. They were no longer at Battle Stations, but instead were at Battle Ready. Checking the fleet's position she noted they were still four hours from reaching the enemy's debris field. She commed the admiral, "Admiral, if you are free I would appreciate you're joining me for dinner in our stateroom."

His response was, "The admiral will join you in twenty minutes."

Fifteen minutes later she said to her science officer, "Lt. Commander Namio, you have the Bridge."

"Yes Ma'am, I have the Bridge."

She made her way to her stateroom where she told her steward what dinner she wanted to order for her and the admiral. Yue He bowed and then left to fulfill her wishes. Hanna quickly removed her clothing, showered, and then donned a silk robe that clung to her body like a second skin. She looked into a mirror and smiled at herself. Satisfied, she then fluffed her hair and laid out what she wanted her husband to wear, hoping he had the time to fulfill her desires.

Yue He returned and set the dining table, while Hanna selected the recorded music they both liked. Just then, Eric arrived and took in what his wife had begun and smiled his appreciation. He quickly showered and donned the robe she had laid out for him.

After making adjustments to the robe he turned toward his wife who smiled and struck a pose that seemed to elicit the response she desired. The smile that began as he gazed at her was a promising start.

Yue He cleared his throat. "Dinner is served," he said and then disappeared.

Eric took her hand and escorted her to the dining table where they sat facing each other. They could have been eating anything for all the attention they paid their meal. Each had only eyes for the other as they ate. Finally, Hanna rose from her seat and sat in his lap with her arms around his neck as they started kissing each other. After several minutes of this, Eric picked up his wife and carried her to their bed where they made love. Slowly at first, but then building until they each found their release.

They were in each other's arms when their comm's buzzed.

They had been asleep, but were now fully awake as they each answered their comm, dressed and made their way to their Bridges.

CHAPTER 26

Admiral Bloodworth asked, "Status?"

'Yes, sir, we are approaching the enemy debris field. We count eight intact Xones' ships, but none have active engines. We are still too far away for our sensors to detect anything else."

"Comm fleet. All ships stay at least 100,000 miles away from any intact enemy ships. Shuttles from the heavies will reconnoiter intact ships and report to the Flag before any attempt is made to board. Captains, make sure your marines understand. They've committed suicide in the past when defeated. Also, make sure they do not enter any radiation hot spots."

Reports started to come in from the shuttles. Of the eight ships they thought to be intact, only one appeared to have retained atmosphere and it exploded before they were within 1,000 miles. They noted two explosions from the other enemy fleet's debris field, which must be from delayed fuses being activated.

Admiral Bloodworth recalled all shuttles and when aboard, the fleet reversed course for return to Earth.

* * *

Three months later the First Fleet was back in Earth orbit and the two damaged Cruisers were placed in repair docks. Three quarters of their crews were placed on extended shore leave. All other First Fleet ships were given the standard one-quarter crew leave.

Both Fleet Admiral Bloodworth and Captain Hanna Bloodworth were ordered to report to Admiral Randall upon his arrival at the UES Beast at 10:00 hours today. Captain Hanna Bloodworth immediately arranged an honor guard for the Admiral's arrival and placed a hold on both of the doctors' leave.

Admiral Bloodworth ordered the captains of the two damaged ships to immediately report to him for a debriefing and to temporarily turn over their ships repairs to their XOs.

The captains of the Charger and Wasp arrived at the Beast three hours before the scheduled arrival of Admiral Randall. Admiral Bloodworth met them at the Shuttle Bay and escorted them to his Flag Office where he introduced them to his Chief of Staff Dana Williams. Captain Anthony Ellis of the UES Charger asked, "Admiral, are we in trouble?"

"No, Admiral Randall is due to arrive here at 10:00 hours and I want to be sure I'm fully aware of everything that happened during the Xones' attack. When the missiles attacked the Charger during the first and second salvo, how many directly targeted your ship and how many hits did you take?"

"Sir, during the first salvo no missiles directly attacked my ship, but according to our sensor data, we killed six missiles. During the second salvo three missiles directly targeted the Charger, which we killed, but the last one exploded within yards of the ship causing damage to the hull and the compartments beneath. We had three casualties which we transported to the Beast and were subsequently returned to duty."

"Captain Allison Collins, what happened on the Wasp?"

"Sir, our damage occurred during the first salvo when four missiles attacked my ship. They just came in too fast for our lasers and defensive missiles, and one hit us near the port missile tubes. We lost two men to space and had four other casualties that we transported to the Beast, three have been returned to duty. Do you know if Petty Officer Jacobs will be returned to duty?"

"PO Jacobs will be returned to Earth for rehab and possibly get a replacement hand. It will be up to him if he returns to the Wasp. I would like for you two to stand by in case Admiral Randall wishes to speak with you, otherwise you may have breakfast or visit the hospital where your crew were treated. The reason they were brought here was that we have an intern helping our doctor. We thought two doctors would be better than one with that many casualties."

Bloodworth gave them each a handheld. "These are similar to what you use, but do a lot more. Just ask your question and be amazed."

The two captains immediately asked directions to the hospital and were surprised when they passed by the Children Care Center. They stopped and looked inside at the small children playing inside, and asked the marine sentry, "How many children are being kept here?"

"Sir, currently there are six. It varies as parents going on/off shift pick them up or leave them here."

The captains continued on with Collins saying, "The heavies live a different life than the rest of us."

"Yeah, I want one of these as soon as I can."

They soon arrived at the hospital and asked the corpsman if they could see the doctor about the treatment their crewmen received. She replied, "Sir, which doctor, we have two?"

Captain Collins replied, "Either, whoever is available."

The Corpsman pressed a handheld, "Doctor Lundberg, please come to the desk."

Lucy soon appeared and asked, "Yes, sir, what can I do for you?"

Captain Collins introduced themselves and why they were here.

She smiled at them and said, "Follow me and I'll give you the tour. We only have one patient now. Do you want to speak to PO Jacobs before he leaves?"

Captain Collins quickly replied, "Yes, I wasn't sure if he was still here."

Their small group stopped before the bed of PO Jacobs, who stiffened when he saw who was approaching. Collins quickly said, "At ease PO. I just wanted to see how they were treating you here."

"As good as can be expected. All the others have been released – they do miracles here. He held up his arm, this will take longer."

"I want you back, maybe we'll get one of these heavies soon."

"Don't worry Ma'am, I'll be back if they let me."

Lucy continued the tour showing off the medical machines that speeded up the recovery of the burn victims. Captain Collins asked, "Your name is Lundberg, are you related to the Flag Captain?"

"Lucy smiled. "I'm her sister and I've just graduated from medical school. I'm doing my internship aboard the Beast."

Captain Ellis said, "You must be the first. I hope they make internships a permanent position for all the heavies. Who knows, I might need your services sometime in the future."

* * *

Admiral Randall arrived and was greeted with a formal arrival ceremony. First the pipes, then a walk between a double row of marines to the United Earth Flag, where the admiral saluted and formally asked permission to Board from the Flag Captain. Once permission was granted they walked inside with a small marine guard following close behind.

Fleet Admiral Bloodworth chose his Bridge Office to have their meeting. They stopped for a moment while Eric spoke with his chief of staff, and then continued into his office. There was a small round table that they sat around. Before starting, Eric asked Randall if he desired any refreshment, who shook his head.

Bloodworth asked, "Sir, how may we help you?"

Admiral Randall said, "Are they getting smarter or are they trying various things to see if they work against you?"

"Sir, I think it's the latter. The only thing new was to copy our trick with cutting their power early so that when the missiles approach their targets they can turn them back on to maneuver. I've been watching for this trick, so I moved the Fleet 100,000 miles. It wasn't far enough evidenced by two of our Cruisers getting hit. On the next salvoes I moved the Fleet 150,000 miles and it worked. The commander of those two fleets apparently didn't know about our nuke weapons because he used the old ball formations for his attack plan and he didn't try to move after we fired. None of his ships survived, but they may have had an observer waiting at the gate if things went bad for them."

"They didn't move even after watching your maneuvers. No one is that stupid. He must have thought your single missile shot at each formation was a conventional weapon."

Eric grimaced at the thought. "Even so, you would have thought they would have taken some kind of evasive action. Maybe their commanders are political rather than an earned rank?"

Randall shook his head at the thought. "Isn't that system at the third gate getting filled with their debris? You would think they would avoid it like a plague by now. Instead, they keep adding numbers to the fight."

Eric asked, "Have you talked to the Katz. I was wondering if their performance had improved using our tactics?"

"No. I'm beginning to think they're using us to fight because they have no stomach for it. I noticed that you had all the casualties brought to your ship, why was that?"

Captain Hanna Bloodworth said, "That was my idea. The other three heavies only had one doctor, while we had two with our Intern. They performed quite well working together as evidenced that all but one has been returned to duty."

"Why not that one as well?"

"He lost a hand and is being sent to Earth later today for treatment and rehab."

"So this first battle with permanent casualties was two deaths. Our crews in the ship yards have more losses than that."

Hanna struck while the iron was hot. "Sir, we should start a recruitment program with the medical schools for graduates to spend their Internship aboard a Heavy Battle Cruiser. Ours has worked out very well, and we may start having more casualties now that the Xones are starting to change their tactics."

Admiral Randall looked at Hanna with a raised eyebrow. "Captain, just how did you arrange getting a graduate to Intern on your ship?"

Eric smiled at Hanna's embarrassed smile. "Her kid sister was aboard when we first went to Aqua. She was getting ready to start medical school when we left Earth, so to get the best use of her on the voyage, Hanna made her an Ensign working with the doctor. When we returned to Earth, Lucy was given detached duty to attend medical school with the idea that she would do her Internship aboard the Beast. You know that would be a great idea to entice medical students to come aboard. Pay their way, then spend four or six years aboard ship to pay us back."

Randall looked at them for a moment, and then a slow smile started. "It is a good idea, maybe even a great idea. I'll put it before the board, but I want to meet this sister of yours."

When two admirals and the captain entered the hospital reception area the on-duty corpsman's mouth dropped open in surprise, but she quickly came to attention. Captain Hanna Bloodworth told her, "Stand Down. Please page Doctor Lundberg to meet me in Doctor Yutesler's office."

The office was currently empty and Lucy soon hurried into the office, but the smile on her face quickly disappeared as she stopped and came to attention, saying, "Sir, reporting as ordered."

"Stand at ease. Lieutenant, Admiral Randall would like to ask you some questions relating to your experience on extended duty from Space Fleet while attending medical school."

"Yes ma'am. I'd be happy to relate my experiences."

Admiral Randall gazed at the two sisters noting the family similarities before he began. "Let's not be so formal. Why don't we all take a seat and consider this a friendly chat. I'm interested in trying to get other doctors to Intern on our heavies like you are doing. What would you recommend?"

"Sir, how I started is probably unique. I think I would send recruiters to the major medical schools to gain their support. They turn away many good prospects because of the lack of funds. Make an offer to pay their way through medical school if they would join Space Fleet on detached duty while attending school, and then after graduation return to active duty as an Intern on a Heavy Battle Cruiser plus X number of years. Rank and uniform while attending school, after graduation, and later would have to be determined."

Randall sat and looked at her in surprise for a moment, before turning to the captain. "She is definitely your sister. Okay, let's use you for an example. When you left the Beast to start school, what was your rank?"

"Sir, I went from Ensign to Lieutenant (jg) when I left the ship and when I returned to start my Internship I was promoted to Lieutenant. I wore a uniform to all my classes."

"You received your military pay while attending school?"

"Sir, yes, sir. That would be a big perk for students as well."

"While wearing the uniform in school, how were you received by the other students?"

"Sir, at first I was an oddity, then respect as they realized where

I was going after graduation. Sir, you might consider using this action as a recruiting point for doctors."

"Good point. When is your leave scheduled?"

"Sir, after Doctor Yutesler returns from her leave in fifteen days."

"Lieutenant, I'm going to have a photographer come aboard and take pictures of you and the hospital for use in recruiting doctors. Do you have any objections?"

"Sir, no sir. However, I think it would sell better if we had patients in the picture. Why not take the hospital pictures ashore with me attending a patient? Our last casualty is being sent ashore later today."

Admiral Randall turned to the captain. "Comm my office to send a photographer to the Beast to take PR pictures of the hospital. We'll hold the patient here until the pictures are taken and he can return with the photographer."

After Captain Hanna Bloodworth sent the message, Admiral Randall wanted to talk to the PO who lost a hand. Lucy led the way to PO Jacobs. He was in uniform sitting in a chair beside the bed when he realized what was heading his way. Jacobs quickly rose and stood at attention.

Admiral Randall said, "Stand down PO."

PO Jacobs relaxed somewhat, but two admirals and the ship's captain tended to make a tense situation.

"Are you in any pain?"

"Sir, no sir. They gave me pain meds and I feel a little woozy."

"I've got a photographer coming to take a picture of you and Doctor Lundberg. It's a recruitment effort to try and get more medical school graduates to Intern aboard heavies. Is there anything we can get you while we wait?"

"Sir, no sir. Well, maybe a soft drink or coffee. They won't let me have a beer with the meds I'm taking."

Lucy asked, "PO, coke or coffee?"

"Oh, a coke will be fine. Thank you Doctor Lundberg."

Lucy quickly returned with a coke for the patient and found he was conversing with Admiral Randall, who had asked about whether the lost hand was his primary.

"Sir, no sir. But until I get a replacement it's going to be hard to tie my shoelaces."

"I'm afraid that's going to be the least of your problems until you adjust to your situation. Those new artificial hands are a miracle, but it's going to take time learning how to use them. When you come back, if you can't do your original job, I'm sure there will be others you can do."

An hour later the photographer arrived and numerous pictures were taken focusing on Lucy and the remaining injured crewman. Admiral Randall, PO Jacobs, and the photographer shared a shuttle for the return trip to Star Command Headquarters.

CHAPTER 27

Three weeks later, Lucy took a seven-day leave to visit her mother. She didn't have the authority to use a direct shuttle, so instead she found a space available flight from Space Headquarters to Berlin, where she used a fast train to Hamburg, Germany. She hadn't notified her Mother about her impending arrival because of the uncertainty of her transports.

When she rang the doorbell at 10 p.m., the house became alive again. Alice opened her front door, gasped in surprise and dragged her youngest daughter into the house, showering her with kisses. With tears in her eyes she asked Lucy, "How long are you going to be home?"

"A week Mom. You are going to be tired of me before its time for me to leave."

"Come sit down over here and tell me of your adventures since you graduated from medical school."

With a little gleam in her eyes she suddenly realized she was telling her adventures rather than listening to her oldest sister's tales of battles in faraway space. She had finally reached the place of her dreams.

The next morning Clare, her middle sister, came visiting after dropping Ian off in school. The family sat at the dining table drinking tea, when Clare suddenly remembered something and retrieved a pamphlet from her purse. "Lucy, when I saw this I was really surprised."

Lucy saw her own smiling face on its cover and immediately knew what it must be. It read, "Become a Doctor and follow me into Space."

"Clare, where did you get this?"

"Yesterday in Ian's Doctor's Office. When I saw your face on it while in the waiting room, I was flabbergasted! How did this happen?"

"Wait a moment, I want to check this out."

She opened the pamphlet, which showed a picture of her and PO Jacobs. It described how she was serving her Internship aboard the UES Beast, the Flagship of the First Star Fleet. Then it described how she attended Berlin Medical School while on detached duty from the Star Fleet and how others could attend medical school as she did.

Lucy smiled as she said, "That was really quick. I had these pictures taken just a few weeks ago and they've already gotten the word out. Clare, Star Fleet was so impressed with me Interning that they wanted to try getting one for each of Heavy Battle Cruisers."

"Well, maybe so. But it's going to make you a star in the medical community. Wait and see if I'm right."

Alice said, "Let me see that. Oh my, Lucy you look marvelous in this picture – a regular poster girl. I wish I had more of these so I could pass them around to my friends. Oh poo Clare, don't look so glum. Be happy for both of your sisters. It's a wonder that the News people haven't tried to get an interview with you about your famous sisters."

Clare and Lucy looked at each other and smiled. "Yeah Mom, I'm really looking forward to that," Clare said in jest.

The doorbell suddenly rang. Clare answered and after a few minutes she shut the door and hurried toward Lucy. "The TV News people didn't know you were here, but now they want to interview you. I told them to wait while I asked you."

"I better. The admiral has put a lot of effort into this, so I better help all I can."

She went to the door and talked to the reporter for a few minutes, and then shut the door. "They're setting up outside for a shoot while I change into my uniform. Clare please come with me and help."

When Lucy had undressed to her underwear, Clare said, "Stop! What's that around your neck?"

Lucy looked at her uncomprehending for a moment, and then picked up the little chip. "Oh, this is my ID and medical files."

She quickly donned her new black dress uniform and beret with her Ship Badge. She was very proud to wear the badge of the Beast, the Flagship of First Fleet. She looked in a full-length mirror before turning to her sister. "Well, do you see anything off?"

Clare was suddenly very proud to be a sister of this beautiful woman. She twirled the fingers of her hand to get her to turn her body around. "Lucy, I really like the new uniform, and that beret really looks good on you! Wait a moment, there's something white on your sleeve. There, I got it."

Clare looked at her sister a moment longer as a tear worked its way down her cheek. Lucy came over and used her finger to remove the moisture from her sister's face. "I know Clare, but remember you have something neither of us have – a child. Even if we decided to keep one with us, the child would face the same danger we experience."

Clare took a deep breath and smiled at her sister. "Go out there and kill them with your performance!"

* * *

Admiral Bloodworth called a meeting of all First Fleet Captains and/or their XO's for a lunch conference at 13:00 hours today. He, Captain Hanna Bloodworth, and his Chief of Staff were in the Admiral's Bridge Office going over the topics he was going to cover. Commander Williams said, "I agree with your choice for the captains of the two new heavies, but are you sure you want their old Cruisers to go to the Home Fleet?"

"Yes, I intend to eliminate from First Fleet all but a few Cruisers for scouting. The new lasers can't be retrofitted to the old Cruisers and without them they present a weak defense against a missile attack. These old Cruisers can be better used to defend Earth with Home Fleet."

Captain Hanna Bloodworth asked, "How are we going to

determine which heavies get the two new Interns?"

Commander Williams thought a few moments before replying. "We have five heavies that need an Intern. Let's do a lottery – put five pieces of paper numbered one through five in a bag. Those that draw numbers one and two get the Interns."

Later, after lunch, the ship captains and/or XOs gathered in the conference room. After everyone was seated, Fleet Admiral Bloodworth said, "I wish to make an announcement regarding the two new Heavy Battle Cruisers. Captains Allison Collins and Anthony Ellis will each get command responsibilities of one of them. You will transfer crews from the Wasp and Charger ASAP, and begin trials when you have sufficient crews aboard. Your old ships will probably be transferred to Home Fleet. I'm sure everyone has heard of the fleet's recruitment efforts regarding doctors and recent graduates from medical schools doing their internship aboard our heavies. I want the captains or XOs of each of our six heavies, other than the Beast, come up to the stage and draw for the two new interns that will soon be available."

After the drawing Bloodworth asked, "Who's got number one and two?"

Captain Christopher Eiberger of the Raptor and XO Derek Bischof from one of the new heavies held up their hands. Bloodworth said, "Congratulations gentlemen, your ships will be getting the Interns."

"You all have been given a copy of the battle damage suffered by the Wasp and Charger. I feel certain that this damage could have been avoided if our new lasers carried on the heavies had protected these ships. I intend to eventually phase out Cruisers in our Battle Fleet as heavies replace them. Any comment?"

Captain Brennon Foster of the Heavy Battle Cruiser UES Missouri held his hand up and was recognized. "Sir, what happens if our battle damage escalates?"

"Hopefully, our heavies will continue to remain functional if not undamaged. I expect most of our losses will come from the Cruisers. If Home Fleet has no use for them, then they will become part of a reserve fleet. Does that answer your question? Okay, any other questions? No more questions, so let's continue with new business."

After the conference ended, the two commanders of the new

heavies stayed behind to speak with the admiral. "Gentlemen, both heavies are ready for you. All you need to do is transfer your crews, provision them with consumables and missiles, and make your shakedown cruise. Commander Bischof how long is it going to take you to recover your captain and crew?"

"Sir, the captain will be aboard tonight, the majority of the crew will take at least six days. However, we will begin bringing the ship alive tomorrow. Captain Collins will let you know tomorrow when we expect to be ready for the shakedown cruise."

"Very well, I'll expect her comm sometime tomorrow. Good luck on your shakedowns and I know you'll love your new ships."

They both said their goodbyes and hurried off-ship to begin claiming their new Heavy Battle Cruisers. Bloodworth went to his wife's Bridge to confer on the best time for them to take their own shore leaves.

Three weeks later they were at Hanna's family home. Hanna and her sister, Clare, went shopping for maternity clothing. They found nothing in the new black color of their uniforms, so they bought what was near in the style they desired regardless of its color. Their mother, who was a competent seamstress, first dyed the material black. Using a picture of a Space Navy uniform with a skirt as a guide she set to work altering the maternity clothing.

The skirt had an expanding waistband that was covered by a uniform jacket that would also expand. Hanna thought she could stand watches well into her third trimester. However, time will tell the truth of that wish. When Eric and Hanna left Hamburg, she had three outfits ready.

After a visit with the Bloodworths they returned to the Beast. Hanna stowed the maternity clothing for later needs, before turning her attention to getting the Beast ready for another voyage.

Fleet Admiral Bloodworth checked on the status of the two new Heavy Battle Cruisers, the UES Lightning commanded by Captain Jock Adams Ellis, and the UES Joan of Arc commanded by Captain Allison Collins. Both ships had successfully completed their shakedown cruises, and were crewed sufficiently to begin another voyage if called upon.

First Fleet had sufficient time for one more voyage before Second Fleet returned to Earth. They were scheduled to leave orbit in two weeks with all crew scheduled to return from leave at least a week before sailing time.

CHAPTER 28

First Fleet broke Earth orbit with six heavies and twenty-nine Cruisers; their destination was the heavily contested third system. Upon arrival at the third systems warp gate the six Heavy Battle Cruisers assumed defensive positions 10,000 miles from the gate, with the smaller Cruisers holding back another 50,000 miles.

The probes answering message torpedo showed no active ship signatures, so two heavies cautiously transited the gate checking for a possible minefield on its far side. Finding nothing they sent a message torpedo back to the Fleet saying all was clear, as the two heavies moved further away from the gate making room for the First Fleet.

Admiral Bloodworth ordered the fleet from Battle Stations to Battle Ready as they assumed a defensive formation traveling toward the next gate. They would check for a minefield on both sides of the gate into the next system.

Caption Lundberg commed the Fleet Admiral. "Sir, what do you make of this change in tactics?"

"Ominous. I'm thinking we are probably going to encounter a much heavier Xones' force either in the fourth or fifth system. I don't intend to go any further than a peek into the fifth system."

Bloodworth had all ships replenish their reaction mass as they passed near a large gas giant planet on their way to the next gate. It had become SOP to enter any suspected battle with full reaction mass storage. The trip across the third system took almost four days with their detour to the gas giant, so they made sure everyone was rested and any minor repairs completed before they stopped before the gate into the fourth system.

They encountered no minefields on either side of the fourth system and no active ship sign within the system other than one ship at the gate into the fifth system. The Katz's early exploration of the fifth system showed it had three warp gates; a good way to hide several fleets waiting in ambush.

The fleet stopped before the fifth system gate and the Heavies again assumed a defensive posture while a probe was sent through the gate. They waited twenty minutes until a message torpedo returned. It seemed that two ball clusters of Xones' cruisers were waiting about 500,000 miles inside the fifth system.

Fleet Admiral Bloodworth thought through what he considered an obvious ambush in the making. He saw no advantage in springing the trap, so what else could he do?"

He commed Captain Hanna Bloodworth and told her what was waiting and expected on the other side of the gate and then asked, "What would you do?"

"I'm with you, it's an obvious ambush. We could fall back toward home and leave them a surprise here on this side of the gate."

"I knew we each thought alike. How long do you think they'll wait before checking up on us?"

Captain Hanna Bloodworth thought a few minutes before speaking. "I expect they'll send someone through the gate between four and six hours after our bait ship transits the gate and then retreats. We'll need to be sailing towards the third gate when they check."

"Okay, now where do you think they'll assemble their fleets to come after us and the time factor?"

"At least twelve hours and 10,000 miles from the gate and if they assemble two ball clusters, I think they will be initially about 10,000 miles apart. I'd recommend three nuclear missiles with nil motion 15,000 miles apart and 10,000 miles from the gate, timed to explode in thirteen hours."

Fleet Admiral Bloodworth thought through the captain's plan before making a slight adjustment. He then commed the fleet with his plan and instructed three of his heavies to leave a nuclear missile stationary in the planned positions. He then asked for a volunteer from the Cruisers to act as bait and make a quick transit through the gate and immediately return as quickly as possible. The risk exposure would be about two hours.

All the Cruiser Captains volunteered their ships and with a smile Admiral Bloodworth replied, "Captains, the UES Thunder has the honor and will transit when ready."

When the Thunder returned, the nuclear missiles were then positioned and the UES Beast led three heavies, the Cruisers, and finally the remaining three heavies back towards home at 2g's. They were a little over six hours from the gate they had just departed when sensors picked up a ship leaving the gate, then stopping and returning back through.

Admiral Bloodworth commed his Flag Captain, "Captain it appears that our plan is bearing fruit."

"Now, will they pursue or not? This is a big mouse trap we're trying to bait."

Four hours later ships started to appear coming through the gate about two minutes apart. When thirty ships had transited, they formed a ball formation about 10,000 miles from the gate, while another group started coming through the gate. Eventually, another thirty ships formed a similar ball formation about 25,000 miles from the first; however, ships were still transiting the gate and forming another ball formation between the first two.

Three powerful nuclear explosions erupted among the enemy formations at the set time while ships were still coming through the gate. Later, sensors did not show any ships under power where the explosions left nothing but debris that were scattering in all directions, maybe even back through the gate.

The First Fleet continued toward home, now secured from Battle Ready to All Clear. The crew could now wear another battle ribbon on their blouses and jackets.

Almost five months later they were back in Earth orbit; however, they were absent almost ten months Earth time. Second Fleet still had a few months before they were due to return to Earth, so Fleet Admiral Bloodworth authorized up to thirty days leave for crews on a rotating basis.

Both Fleet Admiral Bloodworth and his Flag Captain were summoned to Space Fleet Headquarters to meet with the Board at 09:00 hours tomorrow. Eric showed the comm message to Hanna, who frowned at him. "What do they want me for? I just followed your orders."

"I told Admiral Randall that it was your plan that we used at the last battle."

"Crap! I hope they don't try to split us up over this."

"No, I expect something different than that."

Hanna's eyes opened wide in shock. "Oh please. Not another medal. I hate making speeches in front of a bunch of people. It's kind of embarrassing. I was just doing my job."

"Yes dear, but you do it so spectacularly well."

She took a deep breath and let it out slowly before looking him in the eyes. "Dear, you set me up, didn't you?"

"Me, why would you come to that conclusion?"

"Because you had already come up with a similar plan and brought me in to share the wealth. I'm right, aren't I?"

"You're not mad are you?"

Hanna put her arms around Eric's neck and kissed him passionately before leaning back and looked into his blue eyes with her own laser-like eyes. "Don't do that again. If I want recognition I'll tell you."

"Yes dear. However, I wanted you to become aware of your own tactical talents. You may be called upon to exercise them sometime soon. I'll still ask you for you opinion, but I won't pass it on to Headquarters unless you give me permission."

She gave him a quick kiss on the lips. "That's a good idea. I agree with that. How do we dress for this? A normal Dress Uniform?"

Bloodworth smiled at his wife. "Yes. I bet this will be the first time a woman wearing a white beret will be getting an award."

The next morning a shuttle from the Beast arrived at the Space Headquarters Shuttle Port where they were met with a car that took them to the Headquarters building where an escort showed them into the Board Room.

This was Hanna's first experience meeting the full Board and she was a little nervous as she walked into the room with Eric. Admiral Randall introduced the Fleet Admiral and his Flag Captain of the UES Beast to the Board. Its Chairman, Jackson Bryson, stood and introduced the individual members to them.

The Chairman, a silver haired man in his late sixties, looked at the two with almost reverence before speaking. "It seems that at almost every voyage we hear you two have accomplished great feats of courage and accomplishments with little damage to your own Fleet. When we heard what you accomplished at your last voyage, the Board thought that the pair of you receive something everyone on Earth would applaud. We had a hard time trying to find a name to call it, so we settled on *The Beast*. Starting with you, the award will be given to anyone who has demonstrated outstanding performance and courage during a battle against an enemy Star Fleet. Both of you met that criteria at your last battle, especially recognizing a probable ambush and turning it into a great victory in destroying about ninety ships without any losses of your own."

He picked up the trophy that was topped with a replica of a Heavy Battle Cruiser. The trophy had an engraving showing their names and ranks and the battle for which it was earned. The Chairman handed the trophy to Bloodworth saying, "This is only your first of these awards you'll receive based upon past events."

Fleet Admiral Bloodworth held the award above his head and said, "Sir, this is really an award for the whole ship and will be displayed next to the Earth Flag in Shuttle Bay One for everyone to see and admire. Naming it *The Beast* is the highest acknowledgement our ship can receive."

When they arrived back on the Beast after saluting the flag and being granted permission to board, Admiral Bloodworth held the trophy up trying to judge where to display it. XO Commander Betty Conner asked, "What award is this?"

After explaining the award and why he wanted to display it for the crew, the XO suggested contacting Engineering and have them give their opinion.

Captain Hanna Bloodworth agreed. "XO, contact the Engineering DH and explain what we want and to get back with me by 10:00 hours tomorrow with several options. Here, take the trophy so they know its size."

Two days later *The Beast* Trophy was on prominent display. Feedback from the crew was overwhelmingly positive and seemed to instill greater morale within the ship.

Eric and Hanna decided to take three weeks shore leave to visit their parents and then a week on some beach alone to decompress.

When they next left Earth it would be over eighteen months before they returned.

After their visits with their families they were lying under a beach umbrella sipping a drink with a slice of pineapple sticking out of it. Eric set his drink down and took hers out of her hand and set it aside while scooting close enough to touch her nose with his. "Hon, is it time for us to make a baby?"

Her eyes widened in surprise for a moment, before she smiled. "I've been waiting for you to say the word."

"What word is that?"

"Let's have a baby! By the way I've been off the pill long enough now that I can conceive."

They kissed each other long and well until he helped her up from the beach. "Well, you lead off toward our room while I watch those beautiful hips move. That bikini swimsuit leaves little to my imagination, so don't dally."

Later, after their third attempt at procreation, Hanna made a note of the date. She was sure that today was the beginning of her pregnancy. However, they spent each night recreating their first attempt and the days recharging their bodies' deficiencies from not being exposed to their sun.

After returning to the Beast, they quickly readjusted to ship life and responsibilities. Her second week back Hanna stopped by the hospital to talk to her sister. After talking about each other's visit with family in Hamburg, Hanna said, "Lucy I want a pregnancy test. Eric and I are trying to make a child."

Lucy looked closely at her sister for a moment. "Hanna when you first walked in here you seemed to have a glow. Before, I thought it was too much sun, but now…we'll see."

She returned with small package. "Here, go pee on the stick in the Head over there and let's see."

Hanna soon returned with a smile. "It has a plus symbol on it. That does mean I'm pregnant?"

At Lucy's nod, "That means I'm due about nine months from two plus weeks ago. Lucy if you haven't ordered a supply of baby milk, food, and disposal diapers, you better because I'm guessing I'm not the only female who came back aboard pregnant."

"I'll tell Doctor Yutesler about you and possibly others that will need these supplies. Oh, you've got to tell mother that she's going to be a grandmother again. She'll be ecstatic." Later that night she told Eric that they were going to have a baby. Afterward, when they both came down from their high, she reminded him, "Eric we both need to inform our parents of their expected grandchild. How old will our child be when we return to Earth?"

"Nine or ten months old, but to our parents we will have been gone almost three years. They must think we age very slowly compared to them."

* * *

Three months later Second Fleet arrived with two fewer Cruisers than they left with. Commodore Vlad Pavlova commed the Fleet Admiral requesting a meeting ASAP after he dispatched his action report to his superiors, Admiral Randall and Fleet Admiral Bloodworth.

Bloodworth read the message with a frown and then commed him to report aboard the Beast in two hours. In the meantime Eric read the dispatch from Pavlova with great interest. The Fleet Admiral was present when Commodore Pavlova arrived by shuttle. After he was welcomed aboard, Bloodworth specifically showed Pavlova *The Beast* Trophy and how it was earned. Fleet Admiral Bloodworth then escorted the commodore to his Bridge Office and had him take a seat.

"Commodore, I'm having coffee. Do you want anything?" Vlad, still as glum faced as the moment he arrived aboard, nodded his head. "Yes, I'd like a cup of tea."

Bloodworth ordered the refreshments and after they were served and were alone again, he asked, "Vlad, what's your problem?"

"You read my dispatch. I lost two ships so damaged that we almost didn't get them back to Aqua. They decided to scrap them rather than try to effect repairs. In addition, ten of their crew died and another twenty were injured. I'm the first to suffer any casualties in this conflict."

"Vlad, the Xones' are becoming more aggressive. That Trophy I showed you was from my last voyage. In the fifth system they tried to ambush me with fleets hiding behind a third gate. I knew the extra gate was there from the Katz survey and I suspected a trap. The observed enemy was two ball formations of thirty ships each, an easy target for my six Heavies and twenty-nine Cruisers. However, something told me to be wary of that extra gate. Long story short, I mouse trapped them into thinking I was running away, while I actually left three nuclear devices behind in the area I thought they would reassemble their fleets after transiting the gate. I killed the two observed fleets and most or all of another fleet that was hiding behind the third gate."

Vlad replied, "That's how I was hit. They ambushed me and I had to fight my way out of a jam. I wasn't as smart as you in detecting my ambush."

Bloodworth replied, "Well, I had a little help. The previous voyage I detected a change in tactics from the Xones. They went back to the Ball formation, but they shut down their missiles early and turned them back on later to help attack our ships. I detected them shutting down early and moved the Fleet 100,000 miles away. It wasn't far enough and two of my Cruisers were hit, killing two and injuring nine others. For their second salvo I moved 150,000 miles where their missiles didn't find me. So, don't give me I was the first with casualties crap; at best we tied. The Xones are changing tactics and we need to change as well."

Vlad looked at Eric with surprise for a moment before he rolled his eyes in self-disgust. "I guess I was feeling sorry for myself because I thought I'd really screwed up. I should have realized that something had changed and I'd better analyze what I should do."

Commodore Pavlova's face reddened in embarrassment. "I actually came here expecting to get canned for incompetence. What you're saying is learn from your experiences."

"Vlad, what did your Flag Captain say to you before you came to see me?"

"She told me I was an ass and should ask for more heavies, since they are the fleets best defense against enemy missiles."

"Did you agree with her assessment about the heavies?"

"Yes, and about the ass part too."

"Well, Rear Admiral Pavlova you are out of uniform. Here are my old pips and sleeve strips. I talked to Admiral Reynolds after reading your dispatch and he agrees with me on your promotion. There have been other changes since you've been in Aqua. Childcare is offered on the heavies, and we are recruiting to have new medical school graduates do their internship on our heavies.

Check these changes out. My Flag Captain is expecting our child in about nine months and she wants to stay on duty except for one month before and after the birth. Like I said, many changes. I'm sure your Flag Captain will want to converse with Hanna."

Vlad looked at him in shock for a few moments. "Star Fleet is following Aqua's lead in this!"

He then smiled at Eric. "Sir, is that all?"

"Yes, except that if you want my two damaged Cruisers that are being repaired, they're yours. I was going to let Home Fleet have them. It's your choice."

"Sir, thank you. I'll get back with you on that."

CHAPTER 29

Flag Captain Hanna Lundberg received a comm from her opposite in the Second Fleet requesting a meeting with her this afternoon at 15:00 hours on board the Beast. Hanna sent her a confirmation of the appointment and then commed her husband's chief of staff.

"Commander Williams, this is Captain Hanna Bloodworth. My opposite from Second Fleet will meet with me today at 15:00 hours. Please make yourself available to help me answer any questions she may bring with her."

"Ma'am, yes ma'am. Where should I meet you?"

"Shuttle Bay One at 14:30 hours."

"Ma'am, I'll be there."

Later, when Captain Hanna Bloodworth arrived at Shuttle Bay One, Commander Williams was waiting for her. Williams stiffened to attention when she caught sight of Captain Hanna Bloodworth approaching, and then relaxed when the captain said, "Stand Easy."

The captain had always been a little unsettled when interacting with her husband's chief of staff and now she thought she knew why. "Commander, after this meeting with Captain Annalisa Hansen from the Growler, we need to have our long delayed personal meeting."

"Ma'am, yes ma'am."

Just then a shuttle from the Growler arrived and they welcomed aboard Captain Hansen. After saluting the Flag and requesting permission to Board, Captain Hansen paid close attention to *The*

Beast Trophy before greeting Captain Hanna Bloodworth and Commander Williams. As they walked together Captain Hansen remarked, "I now see why Vlad wanted me to look at that Trophy. Whenever another ship gets their own Trophy, they are reminded who was the first recipient of the award by its name. It's a name you don't forget, *Beast*."

Captain Hanna Bloodworth smiled at her comment. "Yes, when I first saw the ship from space, that name just jumped out at me. Enough of that, I thought you might want to see our Child Care Center first."

The first thing Captain Hansen noted as they approached the Center was a marine guard posted outside its door. She asked, "Why the guard?"

"The care givers requested a marine in case of battle damage. During Battle Stations the marine is stationed inside the room."

They walked inside to find four children playing that ranged in age from two to six. Two older children were in another room taking computer school classes. "I see no infants. Do you have provisions for them?"

"Currently, we have no children younger than two. However, I and three other women who are pregnant in the First Fleet will eventually need infant care as well. Baby nurses are being recruited as we speak. All heavies in Second Fleet will eventually have Child Care Centers. Those crewmembers in Cruisers who wish to bring their children aboard with them will receive transfers to a heavy. Now, I want to introduce you to someone very dear to me in the hospital."

The corpsman on duty was getting used to the captain visiting, but the three high ranking officers had him standing at attention when they entered. Captain Hanna Bloodworth's "At Ease" command didn't stop the moisture from forming on his forehead, but he appeared calm as he asked, "Ma'am, how may I help you?"

"I would like to talk to Doctor Lundberg, if she's available?"

In response to the corpsman's page she soon appeared, but quickly came to attention when she saw all the brass waiting. Captain Hanna Bloodworth quickly gave the command, "At ease."

"Captain Hansen this is my sister, Doctor Lundberg. She's doing her internship here after her graduation from medical school in Berlin. We now have three recent graduates doing their internships aboard First Fleet Heavies. I recommend you try for the next available graduate. Doctor Lundberg was very useful when First Fleet had its first casualties. One Doctor can be swamped if there are numerous casualties."

Captain Hansen asked, "Doctor Lundberg how long has it been since you graduated? I grew up in Berlin, but I haven't been back for many years."

"It's been almost a year since I graduated. I'm from Hamburg originally and I was too busy to do much in the way of sightseeing. If you have a specific question maybe I can help. How long have you been away?"

"It's been at least fifteen years since my parents died and I haven't been back."

"Well, traffic is much worse, but the major attractions are still there and you should be able to find your way around. There's a fast train between Berlin and Hamburg that I've used many times."

Captain Hansen gave Hanna a wistful look. "Captain, you are very lucky to have your sister with you on these long voyages."

Hanna asked Lucy, "Is Doctor Yutesler using her office?"

"No, she's at a meeting on Earth and won't be back until tomorrow."

"Can I use it then?"

Lucy asked the Corpsman. "PO Simms, anything happening that we might need the office?"

"No Ma'am. Should I get the officers any refreshments?"

Hanna replied. "Hot tea for three would be nice and find another chair."

Lucy said, "PO you get the tea and I'll find a chair."

When the senior officers were alone, Captain Hanna Bloodworth leaned back in her chair and asked, "Captain, is there anything you need to ask me?"

Captain Hansen looked at her in wonder. "I'm amazed at how much you've accomplished since becoming Flag Captain!"

"I can't do a thing without the support of Star Fleet Headquarters. I just see problems and take steps to remedy them. Child Care was a solution to a future problem because of the Fleet's longer voyages. I foresee a future need to build even larger ships where Battleships that are two or three times the size of BC's will service our current Heavy Battle Cruisers. In order to carry the fight to the enemy, these ships will have to be able to sustain themselves on their voyages for several years at a time."

Hansen's face went blank for a minute as she visualized what she was told. "In order for us to do this we will have to carry our families with us. That's why the changes are coming so quickly. First, the ability to fraternize, then childcare, better medical care, and finally allowing women to work while pregnant. Does everyone at Fleet Headquarters know of this plan?"

"It's not a formal plan, but everyone is aware of our future needs. I expect that we will have approval for our first Battleship within two years, about the time when we have a Third Fleet."

Captain Hansen contemplated this new knowledge before nodding her head. "Captain, would you send me the details on childcare, whose eligible and the details of transfers to the heavies. I assume that whichever fleet is in Earth orbit get's any available interns and new heavies?"

"You're correct. Before we trade positions again you should have gained another two or three heavies. Admiral Reynolds is no longer building Cruisers; we should now consider them as Light Cruisers or Destroyers because of their armaments. Plans are to build several small fast courier ships to transfer information and personnel. These ships will have minimal armament and will rely upon their speed to stay out of trouble."

Captain Hansen nodded her head in acceptance. "Hanna, thank you for the information. I can already see the work ahead of me getting Second Fleet up to speed."

"Do you want to join us for lunch before returning to the Growler?"

She quickly looked at the time and nodded her head. "Yes, thank you. I might think of something else before I leave."

Later, after lunch and after escorting Captain Hansen back to Shuttle Bay One, Captain Hanna Bloodworth and Commander Williams went to the captain's office for their long delayed meeting.

Before taking a seat they each prepared their own hot tea. They took a seat and warily studied each other while sipping their drink. Finally, Hanna decided to bite the bullet. "Dana, I now know you long enough that I think you wouldn't do anything that would harm Eric. However, I'm not so sure that you wouldn't hesitate to allow something bad come my way if it didn't affect the Fleet Admiral."

Dana thought hard on how she should answer this question. "Hanna, I'm not in love with the admiral; however, I'm jealous of you because you found such a man for yourself while the man I picked was such a failure as a man and a husband. I hope I find someone soon because I'm starting to get lonely."

Hanna looked at the woman before her and couldn't help but feel sorry for her. She was obviously a very beautiful woman and it would be to her own benefit to be a matchmaker. Now who on the Beast would be someone much like Eric in personality?

"Dana, would you take offense if I tried to be a matchmaker for you?"

"Lord no. I'll take any help you can give me."

"Well, I'm going to have a little dinner party tomorrow night in my quarters and I can think of someone who you might find attractive. You're so attractive that the only thing that might put him off is if you act like a bubblehead. Just be yourself and try to get him to talk about himself."

"Keep talking, this is starting to get interesting. What section is he with?"

"No, I think it's better if you don't know anything about him. You may not ask the right questions if you already know too much about him."

"Oh, this is really making me anxious to meet him. What time should I arrive and should I wear a uniform or civvies?"

"Do you have a revealing cocktail dress?"

"You better believe it."

"Then we'll make it civvies and be at my quarters at 19:00 hours."

"What will the admiral think about this?"

"Don't worry about him. He's been worried about you, so this should ease his mind."

"Thanks Hanna. Even if it doesn't pan out, I appreciate the effort."

The following evening Commander Williams arrived a few minutes early, and was welcomed into the stateroom by Steward Yue He. Hanna gave her a critical eye as she motioned for Dana to turn around slowly, and then smiled her approval. She said, "He commed that he may be a little late because of some problem in his section. Would you like a drink while we wait?"

They were just starting their drinks when the door chime sounded. The steward let inside a tall man dressed casually in shirt and slacks, who gave the others in the room a short bow as he clicked his heels together.

Hanna stepped forward and shook his hand. "Jerry, you know my husband Eric, and this lovely lady is Dana Williams. Dana, this tall gentleman is Jerry Sullins. Jerry, we already have a cocktail. What would you like?"

When they were all seated comfortably with their drinks in hand, Dana asked, "Jerry it's hard for me to believe I've never met you before. What do you do?"

Jerry had grown a mustache during the last six months and he had recently trimmed it to a narrow line. He now used a finger to rub one side of it as he contemplated his answer. "I'm an assistant Department Head in Weapons, specifically the supervisor of the Laser Section. Dana, I know of you but this is the first time we've met. Being the Chief of Staff to the Fleet Admiral must be a daunting task?"

"Maybe, but you actually perform a task that directly protects this ship during a missile attack. How long have you been on this ship?"

"Since the Beast was named. I'm part of the founding crew. I remember your arrival shortly after Admiral Bloodworth was promoted to Fleet Admiral. You probably don't know this, but the crew has a lottery going on who you pick from the crew as your boyfriend."

"What! Hanna, did you know this?"

"Yes, of course. After all, I'm the captain. Something this big I'd have to be privy too. Jerry how much money is in the pot?"

"Not very much, just $5,000 because Dana hasn't shown any interest in men until now. I bet there's side bets now on how long I last."

Dana appeared miffed as she asked, "When does the Lottery end?"

"When you officially decide on a boyfriend. The rules say that happens when you have three consecutive dates with the same person."

"Well, Jerry that puts a lot of pressure on you. What are you going to do to keep my interest? Did you know I'm recently divorced because he strayed?"

"Yes. He must have been a real yoyo to have done that to you."

"How about you? Any steady girlfriends?"

"No. I was seeing someone, but she moved on when she found someone better."

"That's tough. What was her complaint?"

"I thought the sex was good, but she was into kinky, so I wasn't that sad when she moved on."

Dana shuddered at the thought. "Jerry, if you're agreeable I think we should have a real date to determine if we have sufficient common interests to continue. How do you feel about that?"

"Well, since you're the most beautiful unattached woman aboard this ship, I'd feel privileged to escort you wherever you'd like."

"Wow! Most beautiful woman, no you had a qualifier when you said unattached. Well, that's still something to live up to. Okay, Jerry let me know when and where you want to take me on our next date."

A slow smile started on Jerry's face. "I already know where, the when will need to be decided by our schedules. I'm free the rest of the week after 18:00 hours, at least until we sail."

"Okay Jerry, let's try 18:00 hours tomorrow. You pick the place we meet."

"Forward Ten Officers Bar, military uniform dress code."

Dana's face showed a slight pink of embarrassment at her own aggressiveness. "Done and done. I can't believe I'm doing this."

Jerry gave her a slow smile. "Sure you can. It's something you've always wanted to do."

Hanna smiled in triumph as she said, "On that note, dinner is served."

CHAPTER 30

Captain Hanna Bloodworth smiled as she remembered the first meeting between Commander Williams and Lt. Commander Sullins. Three weeks have passed and they've done much better than three dates as both were now contemplating marriage. The Beast was getting ready to break orbit for its return to Aqua leading First Fleet with six Heavies and twenty-seven Cruisers.

A little over three months later they arrived back into the Aqua System to find its Battle Fleet of three Heavies and three Cruisers on in-system maneuvers. Upon mutual sighting both Fleets headed toward Aqua.

Three days later Commodore Becker and Captain Fieldspire met with Fleet Admiral Bloodworth and Flag Captain Hanna Bloodworth aboard the UES Beast. After their initial greetings, Captain Fieldspire said with some humor, "I see you have adopted my idea of black uniforms and a white beret for the ship's Captain."

Admiral Bloodworth laughed. "Not only that, but your idea of carrying our children with us aboard the heavies. Hanna is pregnant and due to deliver in about five months."

"What! That's wonderful Hanna. How are you feeling now? Still queasy?"

"No, I'm past that now. My doctor tells me everything is coming along nicely."

"You have a doctor aboard? Robert, I forgot your heavies all have a doctor aboard. We need to start that too, and if your children are aboard then you must have a Child Care facility?"

"Mae, how old is your child?" Hanna asked.

"Oh, Karrie's almost two now, but she's on Aqua."

Admiral Bloodworth laughed. "Simmer down Mae, when we finish here I'll take you on a tour of our hospital and Child Care Center. Now, what's been happening since the Second Fleet left Aqua?"

Becker shook his head sadly. "There's not much we can do with our small fleet, but we sent probes through the warp gates until our sensors found enemies in the third system from Aqua. We placed a minefield on our side of the gate and returned home hoping for your early arrival. Those extra heavies you brought with you really looked good."

"I noticed you have more heavies too." He then brought them up to date on their battles and the change in Xones tactics. "Commodore Pavlova is now a Rear Admiral of Second Fleet and after hearing about my own problems with the Xones he is going to be very cautious in his future encounters with the enemy. Star Headquarters has future plans to build an even larger Battleship to lead a fleet of heavies into action, maybe within two years."

Becker looked speculatively at the admiral. "Star Headquarters wants to take the war well into Xones' territory and this is how they are going to do it."

"Yes, in the past we were limited on how far we could advance by the supplies we could carry with us. With the Battleship we have a superior weapon and if we use supply ships to carry extra missiles and other consumable supplies we can go at least double our previous voyages."

Mae said, "If we're done here I want to see your Child Care Center and how you went about finding people to crew it?"

Both parents were fascinated by the CCC and asked many questions. However, upon leaving Mae nodded her head at the marine guard. "He's there to help in case of battle damage?"

Hanna replied, "Yes, after all we are a war ship and occasionally we are damaged. That's another reason our Centers are only on heavies. Now let's look at our hospital, I wonder if you remember our new addition."

When they entered the office area, the Corpsman said in a normal voice, "Admiral on Deck!"

Bloodworth quickly said, "As you were."

Both doctors quickly came out of their office. "How may we help you?" Doctor Yutesler said.

Captain Hanna Bloodworth replied, "Doctors I would like you to meet the lead officers of the Aqua Navy, Commodore Becker and Captain Fieldspire. Captain I believe you know Doctor Lundberg who is serving her internship aboard our ship?"

Mae's face looked blank for a moment and then quickly turned into a smile of recognition. "You're the captain's sister who wanted to go to medical school. Wow! You did it and you made it back aboard the Beast. Congratulations Lucy. It is Lucy, isn't it?"

Lucy nodded her head and smiled. "I bet neither of us thought we'd ever see each other again. Is the Commodore your husband?"

Mae's face immediately turned crimson in embarrassment. "Yes, and we now have a child. I should explain. When I first came aboard I was extremely attracted to Robert and I quizzed Lucy as best I could about him. She almost immediately realized my attraction for him and basically told me to go slow as we were not of the same gene pool and may not be compatible. As it turned out, apparently we were."

Hanna quirked her face as she replied, "Our scientists back home think we're related to you Aquas because of our similar DNA. Perhaps many thousands of years ago someone seeded planets with people like us. I wonder if we'll find others like us out here?"

"Perhaps, but I'm more interested in the here and now. I'm going to have to recruit doctors for my three heavies, and people and equipment for a hospital."

Doctor Yutesler interrupted. "The hospital equipment came with the ship designs. You need your people to use the learning machine on how to use the equipment and some other advanced medical procedures. Lucy and I didn't have any problems after we used the learning machine."

Admiral Bloodworth told the Aqua Officers, "First Fleet will need at least a week to load provisions before they could leave on another patrol against the Xones."

Captain Fieldspire nodded her head. "Maybe I can get some

doctors recruited for my heavies before we leave."

Eight days later the two combined fleets left Aqua orbit heading for the warp gate that led to Xones' territory. It took a little more than sixty days to reach the gate into the third system. Captain Fieldspire led the way through their minefield until they were stationary before the gate awaiting the return information from their probe.

After twenty-one minutes a message torpedo returned showing that the next system had heavy traffic. There were two ball formations of thirty ships each located about 400,000 miles from the gate. Another two ball formations the same size were located 600,000 miles beyond the first group. Finally, there was an apparent observer located near the next gate.

Admiral Bloodworth called for Fleet wide Battle Ready, before asking his science officer, "Can we fire two missiles at the furthest group through the gate with any accuracy?"

Lt. Commander June McBride answered, "I assume you want to turn them off after 50,000 miles and back on when they reach 40,000 miles from target. That would give the missiles time to maneuver to the center mass of each target. We need to maneuver the ships that fire the missiles to 8,650 miles from the gate so that they have correct speed when entering the gate."

"How long from firing the missiles to arrival at targets?"

"Sir, that's a million miles. Average speed at time of cutoff/turn on times one million would make it approximately twenty-six point six hours."

"Very good, now compute what time we need to launch against the near group to have the explosions occur at the same time."

"Sir, you need to fire at the first group in seventeen point seven hours to match the arrival time at the furthest groups. It helps that the furthest groups are not directly behind the first group, so we don't have to fire through the first group to get at them."

"Thank you Lt. Commander."

"Comm to Raptor and Missouri. Move your ships to 8,650 miles from gate and each fire a nuclear missile at the furthest group. Raptor will target the left group, Missouri the right group. Program your missiles to turn off after 50,000 miles and back on when 40,000 miles from target. Comm me when in position."

Twenty minutes later both ships were in position to fire.

"Comm to Raptor and Missouri. Make ready to fire on my command. FIRE, FIRE, FIRE."

Science Office McBride said, "Clocks started to next firing time and to first target."

"Comm to California and Lightning. As soon as the Raptor and Missouri move from their positions you take their positions 8,650 miles from the gate. You will each fire a nuclear missile at the closest group. California will target the left group, Lightning the right group. Program your missiles to turn off after 50,000 miles and back on when 40,000 miles from target. You will fire in approximately seventeen point five hours. Comm me when you are in position.

Thirty minutes later both ships were in position to fire.

At the appropriate time he commed them to fire their missiles and then return to defensive positions.

Now they had to wait almost ten hours before they would see the results of their plan. Admiral Bloodworth, after consideration, commed his wife. "Captain, are you available for a meal?"

"Yes, sir, in about ten minutes."

"Very good. I'll call ahead and meet you in our stateroom."

When Hanna arrived at their stateroom, Eric kissed her at the door and escorted her to the table he and Yue He had set. Holding her chair he helped her move it forward to the proper distance and gave her a kiss on her neck before taking his place at the table. She gave him an appreciative smile before asking, "What are we having?"

"Your tastes are changing, but I think you'll enjoy the last of the spare ribs from Earth, and for dessert, peach ice cream."

"Oh Eric you spoil me rotten. Do you want to make a wager on whether or not any of the targeted ships moved after we fired our missiles?"

"I think it's about 50/50 odds that at least one of the groups has moved. I'm anxious to see how well we've done, especially since we fired through the gate."

"Yes, that was genius. The missiles weren't in space very long before they shut down. It's possible they weren't even detected."

They both took a nap before returning to duty and watched the clock count down to zero. When an extra twenty minutes passed, he commed the Trojan Horse and asked if they would join the

Beast in transiting the gate to view the results of their actions. When both ships were inside the third system they found four new debris areas and the observer ship in the process of leaving through the far gate. After taking thorough scans of the system they returned to the gate and headed back to Aqua.

When the combined fleet arrived back in Aqua orbit, Captain Hanna Bloodworth decided to step down for two months and have her XO assume command until she was able to resume her duties after having her baby.

Commander Betty Conner assumed the duties of captain until relieved. Science Officer Lt. Commander Bruce Namio would assume the duties of XO. When Captain Hanna Bloodworth stood and turned the ship over to Conner, all the Bridge personnel gave her applause as she left the Bridge.

Before going to her Stateroom, Hanna stopped at the hospital for her weekly checkup. In this instance her sister, Doctor Lundberg, examined Hanna. "Hanna, how are you feeling today?"

"Well, I waddled down here without too much effort, but I have to pee every half hour. Otherwise I'm just peachy."

"So you recommend this for every woman to go through?"

"Hell no! I wish I could take the fetus out of me and let it grow elsewhere while I go about my business."

"You know they're testing the feasibility of doing just that."

"Good! Maybe it will be ready by the time I do this again."

"Well, the baby appears to be doing fine. Have you thought of a name for him yet?"

"Eric wants to name him Adam, after his father. I don't have any preferences, so it will probably be that."

"Yeah, I wouldn't want to name him after our father, the bastard. Well, you check out okay too. Continue your exercises that I gave you and look forward to having this child in about three weeks."

CHAPTER 31

Hanna was lying in bed holding her first born, Adam Lundberg Bloodworth that weighed in at seven pounds, one ounce. Apparently the ship adequately shielded him from space radiation, as he had no deformities. He was also the first born on a United Earth Ship, although there were two more pregnancies close behind Hanna's."

It seemed all the Bridge crew wanted to see Adam as they visited during their down times. Betty Conner looked wishfully at the baby as she was approaching the age where having her own was fast disappearing.

Hanna, the ever matchmaker, asked, "Betty, do you have a steady boyfriend?"

"None that I would want to have a baby with."

"How about a wish list?"

From the look on Betty's face, Hanna knew there was a secret crush out there, when she softly said, "I'd like to know Lt. Commander James Downs better. He's in the Environment Section."

Hanna grabbed Betty's hand and squeezed it. "Who knows, sometime soon you and he might receive an invitation for dinner with the admiral and captain. Do you have a sexy civilian dress?"

"Yes. One just like you mean," she said with a smile.

"In that case I will specify that the dress code for dinner will be civvies."

Two weeks later invitations to a Dinner went out to the two

parties after checking their work schedules. Hanna had just put down a sleeping Adam when the doorbell softly sounded. Yue He answered the door and let Betty Conner inside. When she had Hanna's eye, Betty turned in place showing off her dress.

Hanna nodded her approval and quickly showed her the sleeping baby before turning and shooing away Betty before she could wake him from his slumber. The doorbell sounded again and after James Downs entered and was introduced to Betty, they sat together in the dining area and quietly talked. James declined to see the baby because he claimed they were afraid of him for some reason.

The two guests seemed to get along fine and conversed before and through the meal. During dessert Adam woke and wanted the bottle, so Hanna fed him while they all talked. James kept taking quick looks at the baby and when the baby was fed and burped, Adam started looking around at the new people in his life. Eventually, the two locked eyes and Adam smiled at James, which melted whatever resolve he had.

James stood and approached Adam, who smiled at James. Hanna showed him how to hold the baby and the two looked at each other with goofy smiles. Betty watched this interaction for a few minutes before approaching them and joining in on the fun. Eventually, Adam became fussy and wanted his mother, who took him back.

Before they broke up for the evening, James and Betty had agreed upon another date. Later, as Hanna and Eric were preparing for bed and Adam was again asleep. Hanna said, "I was beginning to worry about James' aversion to babies, but Adam took care of that."

"James was married before. His wife and baby son were killed in a car wreck about ten years ago." Eric said as he was climbing under the covers.

Hanna sadly looked at Eric. "No wonder. He was trying to avoid painful memories. But he seemed to get over it before he and Betty left."

Two weeks later Hanna was back on the Bridge as the ship's Captain. Adam was cared for by the nursery part of the hospital while she was on duty. Two new mothers were currently caring for their babies, but they too would soon be cared for by the hospital after the mothers returned to duty.

Hanna felt like she had been on a long vacation and her return to the Command Chair was a welcome relief. She had been receiving updates from Captain Fieldspire on her efforts to acquire a doctor and to start a Child Care Center for each of her heavies. So far starting a CCC was easier than attracting doctors. The parents of seven children took the offer to bring their children with them and attracting caregivers for them was easy. However, only one doctor has agreed to enlist as a Navy Doctor. Captain Fieldspire placed the CCC and the doctor on Aqua's Flagship, the Trojan Horse.

The First and Aqua combined fleets left Aqua orbit and started their second voyage against the Xones this tour. They didn't encounter any sightings of the Xones until they reached the disputed Third gate from Aqua. They were in their standard defensive formation in front of the gate awaiting the message torpedo from their probe.

When the message torpedo arrived their sensors detected only one lone Cruiser stationary 300,000 miles from the gate. After thinking what this could mean he formulated a contingency plan.

"Comm to all combined Fleet Ships. I believe this lone ship is an attempt to parley. I request the Trojan Horse follow the Beast through the gate, but remain close to the gate so that it can return to the fleet and report if something happens to the Beast. I will attempt to parley with the Xones, if that is their purpose for being here. Wish us luck."

"Comm to captain. Ease the Beast through the gate and stop 100,000 miles from the Xones' ship."

"Aye, aye, sir. Stop 100,000 miles from the enemy ship."

Forty minutes later they were stopped broadside to the Xones ship, which had not moved from its head-on position. "Comm to Xones' ship. What is your purpose?"

Bloodworth said to Williams, "Now we see if they came prepared to parley."

"But, how will they know Universe to answer our request?"

"I'm guessing they've captured Katz ships in the past and used their learning machine."

"How long do we wait before trying again?"

"Let's give them a chance to figure out what they want to say," he replied.

"Sir, I'm getting a reply. "Comm to warship, why do you attack our ships?"

"You know why. You attacked me personally without provocation. You have a history of destroying everything you don't need and other life forms."

"The Katz lie. They are an old race without the will to wage war against us, so they have found you to fight us."

"Yes. We suspected that was their primary goal; however, we cannot allow you to come any closer to our home worlds."

"There are more of you? Why is it that we haven't encountered you before?"

"Yes, our arm of the galaxy has many of our worlds. We have not had the ability to travel in space before the Katz arrived. We are explorers and will now follow your ships to your home world. Do you wish to surrender to us or wait for us to annihilate your species?"

They waited two hours before the Xones replied to Bloodworth's ultimatum. "Comm to warship. What do you call yourselves?"

"We call ourselves by many names. My particular race is called Humans."

"Your Human race ships are noted on two fronts and are very aggressive. But, we are many more than you can imagine and we will overwhelm you eventually. We will offer you a truce to expand no further if you will do the same?"

"As you noted, we Humans are very aggressive. The Katz were at first reluctant to give us space because they feared us almost as much as you. You notice we have improved the design of the Katz ships and are even now building better weapons in which to fight you. We are a tenacious race who will destroy you if you continue to fight us."

"What is your warrior name? Mine is Admiral Sissas."

"You have the honor of addressing Fleet Admiral Bloodworth. What is your answer to my ultimatum?"

"I will consult with my superiors and will return here with an answer in sixty units of time."

The Xones' ship maneuvered until it was pointed toward the next warp gate, then accelerated away from them at 3g's. When the ship was 150,000 miles from them it fired two salvoes of missiles at them.

Captain Hanna Bloodworth ordered, "Comm to weapons, fire four salvoes of missiles at the departing Xones' ship and then prepare for missile defense."

"Sir, yes, sir. Firing four salvoes now."

The Beast shuddered as the first two salvoes left the ship, and then the ship spun to bring the starboard tubes to bear, and shuddered again as the last two salvoes left the tubes. "Science Officer, how long before incoming missiles arrive?"

"Sir, fifteen minutes. Short range missile defense will fire in five minutes."

"Comm to CCC, prepare for missile engagement. Take shelter."

"Short range missiles firing."

"Lasers firing."

"Sir, incoming missiles all eliminated, no ship damage reported."

"Sir, a message torpedo has departed the Xones' ship."

"Sir, the Xones' ship is being engaged by our missiles. One hit...two hits."

"Sir, the Xones' ship has exploded."

"Any chance the remaining missiles will reach the message torpedo?"

"Sir, a million to one odds."

"Comm to Fleet Admiral. The Xones' ship has exploded and the message torpedo will likely reach its destination."

"Thank you captain. Please set a return course to the fleets. You may discontinue Battle Stations."

When the combined fleets reached Aqua orbit, Fleet Admiral Bloodworth informed them, "When my consumables are replenished I will continue on to Earth to inform Star Headquarters of recent developments. I will take five Cruisers as my escort when I depart and Commodore Becker will be in command during my absence. I recommend increasing Aqua's Home Fleet if the Battle Fleet leaves the system during my absence."

Three days later the Beast and its five escorts departed the Aqua system for the Earth system. During the return trip to Earth, Admiral Bloodworth wondered many times if he had overplayed his hand with the Xones Admiral. Captain Hanna Bloodworth just shook her head at his doubts. "Honey, they showed their lack of trustworthiness when they attacked you while leaving the system. These people would never honor any kind of treaty."

When they entered Earth orbit Bloodworth sent a comm to Star Headquarters, "I request an urgent meeting with the board regarding a top secret matter and place a hold on Second Fleet until the matter is resolved."

Admiral Randall returned the comm three hours later. "Your request has been granted. Bring your Flag Captain with you to arrive here at 10:00 hours today."

Bloodworth looked at the time. "Hanna that gives us two hours to stew. Besides our sensor data and recordings of our conversation with the Xones, have I forgotten something else we need to take with us?"

"Maybe Admiral Pavlova should be there as well?"

"Crap, you're right. I'll comm Randall and ask for him to join us."

When the Beast's shuttle left for Earth it made a detour to the Growler to pick up Admiral Pavlova. Bloodworth told Pavlova in general terms that he had talked with a Xones' envoy and didn't want to get into the specifics until his meeting with the board that they were going to attend.

"Crap-o-la. This is our first interaction with the Xones."

Two hours later they were sitting before the board awaiting the setup to replay the conversations with the Xones. Fleet Admiral Bloodworth watched the expressions on the faces of the board members as they heard what had transpired.

They all sat white-faced when the recording ended. The Chairman looked at the other members for a moment before standing. "Fleet Admiral Bloodworth you just did something that I'm not sure many military men would take upon themselves. You bluffed your way into maybe giving us some time to prepare for an all-out war with the Xones. They proved themselves untrustworthy in regards to any kind of treaty and we know now that we must not only defeat them, but crush them completely. Admiral Randall what's our timeline on starting construction of the first Battleship?"

"Sir, thirteen months."

"Advance that to ASAP and give the first to Fleet Admiral

Bloodworth, followed by Second Fleet's Admiral Pavlova. Are those new Lasers for the Battleships as good as promised?"

"Yes, sir. Their range is 50,000 miles, up from 10,000 for the Heavy Cruisers. I don't think the Battleships need short-range missiles with that kind of protection."

"Well, that means they can carry more long-range missiles. There's been some improvement in that too. What can they do that the old one can't?"

"They're larger, which means the Cruisers can't use them; however the Heavies can be modified to use them. They have a range of 150,000 miles, rather than 100,000 miles for the older model. They are faster with that added range and are easier to adjust their turn off/back on feature. That feature has also been added to the old version missile as well."

"Getting back to the present. Admirals, be very careful in selecting your battles. Before we have creamed them in every instance. They seemed to think increasing their force size is the way to go. Admiral Bloodworth seems to say the bigger they are the easier to kill with our nuke weapons. I can't see them continuing this logic for much longer; their losses are too great. We may have to use hit and run tactics when they change their tactics, at least until we get our Battleships. Then we can take the battle to them."

Admiral Randall said, "Fleet Admiral Bloodworth wants to get back to Aqua ASAP, but he and Admiral Pavlova need to discuss their strategies until First Fleet returns to Earth. We now know they are aware we are hurting them on two fronts. We need to explore other warp gates to see where they lead and if we are threatened elsewhere by the Xones. Admiral Bloodworth, when First Fleet returns to Earth give consideration to sending Cruisers out to explore at least three gates in every direction."

"Yes, sir. But, I want them to be strong enough to defend themselves from any small group of Xones' ships."

"That's for you to decide. Good hunting to the both of you."

In the shuttle taking Admiral Pavlova back to his Flagship, he said, "Admiral Bloodworth, that was one of the biggest military bluffs I've ever read about."

"Well, the Xones' Admiral was blowing wind up my sails about how many ships he had. I just replied in kind. They needed to think we weren't going to be an easy target. I think that's the main reason he tried to take me out as he left."

"Well, I just hope we find more people like the Aquas to help us in this fight. Two fronts are fine, but three would be better. I've noticed that the Xones are changing their tactics a little at a time. They really seem adverse to change how they do things."

"Vlad, that's really going to help us when we start to go after them with our Battleships led fleets. We're going to eat their fleets up and watch where they flee."

CHAPTER 32

Thirteen months later Fleet Admiral Bloodworth's Flagship was the Battleship, UES Hulk. She was twice the size of a Heavy Battle Cruiser and carried four salvoes of forty missiles each for each side of the ship. In addition, she had eight laser batteries covering each side of the ship and two covering its top and bottom. Each laser could reach out 50,000 miles and could be devastating to any incoming enemy missiles.

The Battleship carried a crew of 3,400, only 550 more than a Heavy Battle Cruiser. In addition, it carried 1,000 marines. A concerted effort was made to keep an even ratio of men to woman because of the expected long voyages of a year or more. The same officers from the Beast staffed the hospital and Child Care Center.

The Flag Captain continued to be Hanna Lundberg Bloodworth, the wife of Fleet Admiral Bloodworth. Adam Lundberg Bloodworth was now over two years old and when both parents were on duty, he spent much of his time in CCC. Most of the crew and DH's were transferred from the Beast when the Flag was moved.

The First Fleet, consisting of one Battleship, seven heavies, and twenty-two Cruisers were approaching the contested third system from Earth. Before leaving the Earth system, Bloodworth had dispatched a five Cruiser flotilla to explore all entries into their system to at least three gates outward.

Bloodworth was surprised to find the third system empty of any active ships. He sent three BC's ahead to clear any possible minefields before having the rest of First Fleet transit the gate.

The Battleship could easily generate 3g's acceleration, but they traveled a sedate 2g's toward the next gate, stopping along the way to refill their reaction mass from a Gas Giant. They stopped again at the warp gate leading into the fourth system and waited for their probe to return a message torpedo with its sensor findings.

This next system appeared to be quite active with three ball formations of ships of forty ships each about 800,000 miles from gate. Before Bloodworth could digest this information his science office reported, "Sir, enemy ships becoming active 800,000 miles behind us."

"Do you have a reading on their numbers?"

"Sir, there are two groups forming up. I think its going to be a thirty or forty ship ball formation."

"Comm to Joan of Ark and Lightning. When ready launch a nuclear missile at targets to our rear. Joan of Ark will take the left formation, while Lightning takes the right. Use standard cut off/turn on procedure. Comm me when ready."

Both ships quickly reported they were ready. "Launch missiles now!"

"Start clock on missiles."

"Yes, sir, clock set at forty-one minutes."

Twenty-three minutes later the science officer reported, "Sir, staggered missile launch noted from the two enemy formations."

"Start clock on the first launch."

"Yes, sir, clock set to arrive here in forty-six minutes."

"Sir, staggered launch continues as they come on-line."

Bloodworth grimaced. "We're stuck between two forces. I'm going to stay on this side until we decide this battle. Comm to fleet we are going to move 200,000 miles to our right in twenty minutes."

Twenty minutes later he said, "Comm to fleet, execute move 200,000 miles to our right. Execute now!"

The fleet moved as commanded and later watched as the majority of the missiles previously aimed at the fleet transited through the gate. "Sir, the nuclear weapons have exploded!"

Twenty minutes later, Fleet Admiral Bloodworth asked, "What

readings, if any, from the Xones' fleets?"

"Sir, there is nothing but debris from the sites of the two enemy fleets."

"Very well, Comm to fleet. The Missouri and California heavies will transit the gate first to clear any suspected minefields, followed by the Flagship thirty minutes later. Then the heavies first, followed by the Cruisers. Good luck to us all."

When the Hulk transited through the gate, its sensors verified the three enemy ball formations had not moved, but showed that all formations had fired a salvo of missiles toward the gate. Fleet Admiral Bloodworth immediately ordered that the Missouri and California fire a nuclear missile at the left and right side of the three formations, while the Hulk fired at the center formation. Clock to enemy formations was forty-six minutes. Estimate of enemy missiles to gate was thirty-eight minutes.

"Comm to captain. Move ship forward 10,000 miles to intercept enemy missiles."

"Aye sir. Moving ship forward 10,000 miles. Lasers are free to engage when enemy missiles are in range."

Time seemed to stand still as the Hulk's sensors showed the incoming missiles. Then the Hulk's lasers opened fire and it seemed space became hell as the missiles exploded when touched by the lasers. The exploding missiles destroyed even more of their kin as the fire from hell consumed all the enemy missiles.

"Comm to admiral. Sir, all the enemy missiles have been destroyed. No reported damage to ship."

Fifteen minutes later the nuclear missiles exploded among the three enemy formations. Later, after the disruption in space had cleared there was nothing but three debris fields were 120 enemy ships had been before.

After the fleet reassembled in the fourth system they headed toward the next gate in their first voyage of bringing the fight to the Xones.

THE BEGINNING

ABOUT THE AUTHOR

Hugh A. Flowers retired after almost thirty years with the Federal Deposit Insurance Corporation as a bank examiner. He now spends his time reading and writing novels and short stories and traveling the world.

OTHER PUBLICATIONS BY FLOWERS

The Salvation Trilogy
Salvation
Angel's Triumph
In Perpetuity

Other
The Adam Project
Emergence
Reclamation
Oklahoma Tomboy